DARK OBSESSION

A novel of erotic domination

by
Argus

From Bondage Books

DARK OBSESSION by Argus

The moral right of Argus to be identified as the author of this work has been asserted in accordance with the Copyright, Designs and Patents Act 1988

All rights reserved. No part of this publication may be reproduced, stored in a retrieval system, or transmitted in any form or by any means, electronic, mechanical, photocopying, recording, or otherwise, without the prior permission of both the copyright owner and the publisher.

Published by Bondage Books
PO BOX 110
Leeds LS13 9AF
England

An imprint of
The Electronic Businesses Organisation Ltd

First e-book edition, 2006

Bondage Books e-book editions are taken from:-
http://www.bdsmbooks.com
where there are over 130 e-books by Argus as well as many others by top authors – free site, free chapters, instant downloads. Those of our titles that are unsuitable for bookshops can only be found there.

Chapter One

It was another scorcher. The patrol car's tinny radio was playing an old country tune as Dara slumped low in the front seat, weakly fanning herself with an open comic book. A fly alighted on her bare arm where it lay along the top of the door. She glanced at it idly, watching as it crawled slowly and unevenly up the length of her arm, stopped, then flew off.

Dara's uniform shirt was open to the waist, revealing a tanned belly and chest and the moist, tanned upper half of her breasts showing above a lacy black bra. She rubbed perspiration off her forehead, further matting her short blonde bangs back against the top of her head.

She wanted nothing more at that moment than to abandon her post watching Highway One-Five and head for the Okanawi River, where she could spend the rest of her afternoon shift immersed in its cool, clear water. But that would have left her broke that evening, and stuck in her overheated house with nothing to do. She needed to make a little money to go out, to ease herself in the air conditioning of Joey's Bar, or the Fontana Roadhouse, to dance and drink and party and forget she was stuck in a backwater town in a backwater county in backwater Mississippi.

And the only way that was going to happen was if she could catch some tourist going by on Highway Fifteen and convince them they were speeding, or at least that it'd be worth their while to hand her a ten or even a twenty dollar bill so she'd let them go on about their way. She had parked the old Chevy in behind the Coke billboard in the only shade available, and had been waiting for an hour now without profit.

She shifted in the seat, grunting with the effort as she sat up a little. Her thin khaki uniform trousers were plastered against her body all the way down past the knees, and she sighed, scratching her thigh idly and wondering again how people could spend their lives in Kainlen County when they had the slightest choice.

The poor people she could understand, but there were plenty of rich people in the county, even if rich, to Dara, meant people who could afford to live somewhere else. It confounded her that they didn't.

She opened the comic again and examined the lurid and colourful drawings no schoolboy's eyes were meant to see. For the comic was not the kind meant for children. It was a translated Japanese comic featuring lusciously naked young women with enormous eyes who, when not beating up criminals, were being bound and sexually abused.

The page she was examining with considerable interest had the heroine in chains bound to a complicated and fantastical piece of sexual machinery which was violating all three of her orifices simultaneously while she writhed in both outrage and sexual abandon.

Dara couldn't help imagine herself on the device, and felt no little excitement stirring in her loins as she stared at suction cups affixed to the character's enormous nipples, and the ridiculously large sexual probes driving in and out of her writhing body.

She rubbed a hand over her face, wiping off more perspiration, then ran her damp fingers down along her chest to the well-exposed cleavage between the half-cups of her bra. She stroked the soft, glistening flesh of her upper breasts and felt an almost instant thrum of mild excitement between her thighs.

The heat of the day argued against it, but her arousal won over. Her fingers eased beneath the black lace of her left cup, slipping in across her soft nipple and stroking gently. She let the edge of her rough thumbnail scratch softly along the sensitive pink button, then plucked it and twisted it enough to cause a sharp sting as it began to heat and stiffen.

There were very few safe outlets for sexual hunger for a girl in Kainlen County. Everyone pretty much knew everyone else and gossip was their favourite pastime. It was a rural county and very conservative, in the heart of Baptist country. Dara had been as discrete as a virgin in all but her attitude and dress, and no one could say with any degree of reliability that she was anything other than a virgin.

That didn't stop the rumours, and her forthright attitude and revealing clothes had gotten her marked as a tramp from a very young age. The suspicious eyes of the churchgoers followed her wherever she went, suspecting her of all manner of nefarious activities and impious thoughts.

But they didn't have a thing on her. Dara grinned softly and a trifle smugly at that thought. She was six feet tall, athletic and blonde, with a trim waist, rounded hips and a generous bustline to go with her cocky attitude. Because of that she'd been pursued by every male she'd come across for almost ten years, including a lot of those pious churchgoers, and not a one had gotten a sniff - so far as anyone could tell.

No, Dara had been discreet. She'd been careful to leave the county on those occasions when she was feeling too wild and alive and seductive to keep control of herself. And then there was the truck stop on Old Highway Nine. Truckers could gossip all they liked so long as they did it far from her.

Her hand was firmly inside the cup now, her knuckles straining the material as she kneaded her breast gently and stroked her thumb back and forth across the erect nipple. She was feeling wild and hot, sighing and spreading her legs as she ran both hands up to squeeze her breasts. She was going to have to find someone discrete, maybe a married man who couldn't afford gossip any more than she could.

She tugged the cups of her bra down to bare her breasts, feeling a little crackle of sexual electricity run through them as she looked lazily around. Her nipples were firmly erect and she rolled them lightly between her thumb and forefingers as she felt the thrum in her loins grow stronger. She ran a hand down between her thighs and across the thin material of her trousers which covered her mons, squeezing lightly.

She looked around again, feeling cocky and daring, and undid the belt buckle holding her gun belt around her hips, then opened the buckle of her trouser belt and finally the trousers themselves, pulling the zip down and raising her bottom to peel the sticky fabric down her thighs, and, after a breathless moment of indecision, kicked off her shoes and pulled them entirely off.

She fingered herself within the dark lace of her thong, her breathing coming faster with each passing moment. She had an exhibitionistic nature she had been fighting since puberty, and being nearly nude out of doors by the side of the road was adding heavily to her inner heat.

She slipped the thong down her long legs, then unclipped her bra and shrugged off her uniform shirt. She wanted to be completely nude, and a little wicked shock of sexual electricity made her shudder when she was.

Fifty feet ahead of her a car drove past, just beneath the speed limit, the driver gazing at the patrol car as he passed, but seeing only her head as she slumped lower.

Dara drew her knees back and spread them wide as she slumped down. Her finger began to stroke up and down between the tight lips of her labia, and she gasped and involuntarily rolled her hips as it passed across her clitoris.

She propped the comic book on the steering wheel and stared at the pictures as the comic book girl was "tortured", placing herself into the same position, gasping as she thrust first one, then two fingers deep within the tight, elastic folds of her sex.

She pulled back her hand, fumbling for the contents of the gun belt, and drew out the long, thick nightstick. Sweat was beading across the surface of her body now as inner heat met the searing humidity of the day, but she didn't care. She positioned the end of the club at her entrance and slowly pushed it into her body.

It was thicker than any male organ she'd ever had, but her heat and wetness allowed it easy entrance, despite the sharp, tight ache of her pussy lips as they were forced in and back.

The machine chugged softly and she moaned as the straps dug into her thighs and ankles and wrists. She was bound bent over a machine, her bottom high, legs spread. She groaned as the two enormous probes thrust back and forth inside her abdomen, feeling the heat pouring through her body as she was remorselessly pounded.

Her nipples sparkled with excitement and heat as the two sucking devices pulled and twisted, and the nimble, rubber tipped metallic fingers kneaded and squeezed them. Ahead of her the long, thick rubber probe pushed forward into her mouth, driving deep into her throat.

Dara groaned as she pushed the nightstick in. It had to hurt, at least a little, and she forced it in against her cervix so that she ached, imagining it was the machine abusing her. She stroked her finger against her clitoris as she pulled the nightstick back, then thrust it painfully deep once again.

Her hand jerked away momentarily as she flipped the page, and her eyes lit as she saw the menacing character come up behind the bound heroine and bring down a many thonged flog on her bottom.

Her bottom burned with pain as the two probes continued to thrust in and out. Both were immense things, covered with studs and ticklers, pounding in and out so that her insides twisted and shook. And now the thongs of the flog lashed her sex and thighs as she moaned into the probe pumping inside her mouth.

Dara's head rolled from side to side, and her breathing became more and more ragged as she pumped the nightstick inside her sex. It hurt, but the pain was only an added excitement as sweat trickled down her body and her arousal deepened into a feverish desire.

Her legs were spread wide, the tendons in her thighs straining, aching, as her head rolled from side to side.

And then a car horn popped her eyes open and brought her head whipping aside and she saw another patrol car coming up the road. Shock hit her system, and she froze for a long instant, then her hands clawed at her uniform top, yanking it over her shoulders and jamming her arms down the sleeves, her fingers fumbling desperately with the buttons.

The car parked on the road, and Jerome Walker got lazily out of the door, yawning and scratching his enormous belly.

Dara shoved her feet into the trousers and yanked them up her legs as Jerome ambled over, gasping as she sat up a little straighter and realized she still had her nightstick deep inside her abdomen. There was no time to do anything about that as Jerome walked closer, so she simply slid the trousers up over the thing and pulled them around her hips, buttoning and doing the belt.

"Hey Dara."

She wiped her arm across her dripping forehead before turning to offer a feeble, tremulous grin at Jerome, gasping a little as the nightstick twisted painfully in her belly.

"Jerome. This's my spot," she said, her voice a little too high and fast.

"I know it. Hell, the whole office knows it," he said. "No luck fishin' yet, huh?"

'Nothing rich has come by," she said, wincing again as she tried to sit up straighter and the nightstick twisted deeper in her vitals. The club was two feet long and she had half of that inside her. The other half made a fairly noticeable outline down the side of her right trouser leg if Jerome got too close and looked in.

"Nah, I think it's too hot and the tourists have all stayed home."

"Heat don't affect the rich ones on account of they got air conditioning," he said wisely.

"Well, yeah."

Go away, asshole!

He was easing closer, looking over the edge of her door. She wondered if he'd noticed her braless state yet. Probably. They all tended to stare at her chest whenever they could.

"What are you doin' here then?"

"Bored. Thought I'd see if you'd found anything. If you had I was gonna park here and see what else was around."

"Well, nothing, but uh, you can have it anyways," she said.

If she didn't leave Jerome would stick around for half an hour, and the nightstick was aching her insides something fierce.

"I'm gonna try a new spot I found over on I-34," she lied.

"Yeah? Where's that?" he asked with interest.

"Never you mind," she said, starting the car. "I can't let everyone know where the best fishing is, now can I?"

He made a face. "If it was so good what were you doin' here?"

"I'll see you later," she said, stepping on the gas and backing away.

She gasped as the car jounced on the rough ground and she twisted herself even harder against the club. Her belly was on fire now, and she imagined the thing jamming all the way up into her chest and how she'd explain *that* to the doctors.

She groaned as the cars finally hit the pavement and quickly sped up, slumping and twisting her body to one side, gritting her teeth against the pain as she tried to ease the pressure on the thick club.

As soon as she was out of sight of Jerome she pulled over, slumping down low and yanking down her trousers. She grasped the club and slowly, gently tugged it out of her pussy, groaning in an almost sensual relief as the pain faded and she felt her pussy sleeve closing behind the withdrawing club.

She drew it out completely, closing her eyes and shaking her head as she brought it upright and stared at it. The part which had been driven inside her was marked fairly cleanly by the darkness of the moistened wood and she stared at it in no small satisfaction. With the pain gone her arousal returned almost full force, and she tried to mentally measure how much of the thing she had succeeded in taking, then gave it up and dropped it on the seat.

She debated going on to the new spot she had found to feed on tourists, which was not, of course, on I-34, but decided against it.

The hell with the tourists, she thought. She needed to find someplace more private, some place to quench the fires inside herself.

She pulled up her trousers and leaned forward, starting the car, then slowly pulled out onto the road and headed up the highway. A mile along she turned down an old dirt road that led to the abandoned Breckenridge mine. She expected it to be empty and was both surprised and irritated to see a figure walking some distance ahead.

She slowed, scowling. The figure was walking away from her, but towards the pond she'd wanted to turn off at. As she drew closer she recognized the figure. It was Emery.

Emery, she remembered, had a tiny farm out this way. She hadn't known it was on this road, though.

Troublemaker, the Sheriff had called him. Big and mean and violent. He'd killed a man once, and served ten years on a state work farm.

The car rolled up behind him and she slowed to a walking pace that matched his. Emery was stripped to the waist. He had no shoes either, and his pants were ragged.

Tight, and ragged.

He was a mountain of a man, a former blacksmith with enormous shoulders and a shaved head. He was about twice her twenty two years, and aside from his time in prison he'd spent all his life in Kainlen County, working his little farm out on the edge of the woods, alone. He had no wife, no kids, and as far as she knew, no friends.

He didn't look around as she drove along behind him, not

even once. The sun beat down on him as he walked. His nearly naked body glistened with sweat.

Dara licked her lips as she followed, then stopped, appalled and shocked at her reaction to him. She was about as liberal and daring as Kainlen County had, but she was still a girl born and bred in rural Mississippi.

And Emery was Black, Black as the ace of spades.

Kainlen's Blacks and Whites lived in an uneasy peace, caused mainly by their separation. Aside from those Blacks who worked in White businesses or on White farms or in White houses, the races just didn't mix. That was the way it'd always been in Kainlen, and as far as anyone could tell that was the way it would always be. Every little village and town had its White areas and its Black areas, its White stores and its Black stores. Segregation was illegal, of course, but you couldn't force people to live together and so they didn't.

She'd only seen Emery once before, when the Sheriff - her uncle - had pointed him out to her as a troublemaker. He was a sullen, dour faced man with suspicious eyes and a mean streak. He didn't mix with Blacks, never mind Whites, and kept pretty much to himself. Any woman who even considered involving herself with him was insane.

Yet Dara had felt an instant heat at the sight of his big glistening body, captured by the raw animal maleness of him as he walked along in front of her.

She pulled her uniform blouse up and quickly buttoned it, then roughly shoved the hair back from her face and wiped her moist face.

Emery just kept on walking.

Dara watched, heart pounding, then stepped on the gas again and started the car forward. Once again she rolled up behind him and maintained the same steady pace as he did, fighting to control her breathing as the Chevy rolled slowly along.

Finally he turned to look, giving her a sullen glare. Then he turned his head forward once more and ignored her. She waited for him to look back again, nervously, angrily, or at least curiously, but he never did.

Dara was sweating even more heavily now, her mind filled with turmoil. Doing it with a Black man at all was - shocking - to a Kainlen County girl, but with Emery?

Had Emery even had a woman since he'd gotten out of prison? What woman would dare be alone with him? Or did he even want women? What would he do with a woman? Rape her? Beat her? Kill her?

And yet as he walked along, that tight bottom swaying, those muscular shoulders glistening in the sunlight, she thought about being beneath him and her legs turned to jelly, her stomach fluttered and her chest tightened so she could hardly breath.

Rough sex? She'd had rough sex many times. She liked her sex rough and wild and passionate. But what would sex be like with a man like Emery?

Her foot pressed a little harder on the gas pedal, and she turned the wheel over, curving the Chevy in alongside him as he walked. She stopped just ahead of him, and put her head out the window.

"Hey there," she said, her voice almost steady.

He didn't speak, didn't even turn to look at her. But he did stop.

"Hot day."

Emery looked down the road, jaw set.

"Wouldn't like a ride, would yah?" she asked, her voice quavering slightly.

At that Emery slowly turned to face her. He was right next to the door and she found herself facing his crotch. His ragged pants were tight across his groin and she saw the thickness of what lay within with an almost dreamy state of awe. Surely he couldn't be that big. He must have something else in there.

She suddenly found herself breathless, her heart pounding, her mind whirling at the ridiculousness of the emotions rolling through her body. Emery was not any kind of a man to be lusting after, any kind of man to even be alone with, not for any kind of woman and particularly not for a white woman who was the Sheriff's niece wearing a county deputy's uniform.

It seemed like an eternity before she was able to raise her eyes from his bulging groin to the dark angry eyes in the midst of that sullen face. And even as she did he reached down with a massive hand and caught at the back of her head. She didn't have time to struggle or even react before his other hand was at the front of his pants, yanking down the zipper.

Shock rolled over her, shock, an almost desperate arousal, and a fear that had her insides turning liquid.

And then he had his erection out, and despite the fear she stared with awe. It was enormous, thick as her wrist, long, and purple veined.

Oh my God!

She stared wide-eyed and slack jawed, and he pulled her head forward and thrust his hips against her. In an instant his manhood rammed forward into her open mouth. Dara felt her jaw forced wider and wider, painfully wide, as his steel-hard cock drove forward and filled her oral cavity

Dara was a tough girl. She'd put big men down with a single

punch, and everyone in the County knew to stay well out of the long range of her knee if they were going to say anything impolite in her company. Dara was not a girl to be bullied or mocked or forced into doing anything she didn't have a mind to do.

And yet as that massive organ slowly forced her lips achingly wider and crushed her tongue against the bottom of her mouth all she could do was slap against his belly and stare in shock as inch after inch was forced through her straining lips.

It filled her mouth from top to bottom and side to side, and she could feel the thick veins sliding across her tongue and the roof of her mouth at the same time as his big hand pulled her head and shoulders out the window.

She looked up frantically to see those dark, angry eyes on her, and moaned helplessly as his lips had curled into a cruel smile. She felt like a rag doll in the hands of a giant, and strangely, a roaring heat gripped her at that helplessness, and she almost instinctively began to suck on the big cock filling her mouth. His smile grew, and he thrust deeper so that she gagged.

He drew back slowly, then pushed forward once again, fucking her with a slow, deliberate, almost casual pace as she gurgled and gagged and moaned around the sweating male meat filling her mouth. She struggled but she didn't even try to fight, didn't even think to. All she could think was how enormous his cock was, how thick and long and gorgeous and wickedly black it was.

And her body seemed to go limp, leaning out the window, sucking on him as pumped slowly in and out. She tried to work her tongue against the underside of the head but he was too thick. She could hardly move, and he was too deep inside her.

Her jaw ached as that monster cock of his pushed in and out, in and out, in and out. His big hand held her head in place with casual contempt as he used her and her own hands weren't even trying to fight him now, but gripping him to hold herself steady, pulled halfway out the window as she was.

Each time he pushed forward he forced the fat helmeted head deep enough to cause her to gag, as if taunting her, only to pull back.

And then, suddenly, he didn't.

Her body jerked violently and she slapped against his belly again as he thrust forward while pulling on her head. That big mushroom had made her gag, but this time kept moving forward, and Dara could feel the narrow passage of her throat invaded by Emery's monster cock.

It forced the tube wider, strained the elastic flesh as it pushed deeper and deeper. And the world seemed to take on a foggy tone as she watched his abdomen get closer and closer, until her face was jammed up against it and his cock was buried in her throat.

It ached.

But again she found she couldn't fight him, couldn't even try to fight him, and went oddly limp in his grasp as he ground his pelvis against her. Her throat burned, and her head throbbed for lack of air. Her chest pounded and her heart raced. But then slowly he drew back, pulling that thick, slick male erection backwards, letting light into her eyes again, light enough to watch that glistening cock sliding out, inch after inch.

The head came out of her throat with an almost audible pop, and she coughed and choked and gasped for breath as he held her in place. Saliva gushed out as he pulled his gleaming cockhead free and rubbed it across her face, and she coughed and gasped and gulped in air as he waited patiently.

Then he forced it into her gaping mouth again, and when her eyes looked upwards, beseeching him not to go further, she saw his sneer of contempt again, and his cock pushed deep.

Again she felt that monstrous prick forcing its way down her throat, scraping firmly along the bulging airway of her neck as it pushed deeper. Again she found her face pressed up against his abdomen, his cock deep in her aching throat, down into her very chest. He held her there a long minute, then pulled back. Only this time he began to use her, pumping in and out, using her throat for his pleasure as she choked and gurgled and fought nausea.

She could feel every movement of his thick, heavily veined cock as it slid up and down inside her throat, and found all her focus narrowing to that painful, uncomfortable sensation.

And yet, as it continued she felt oddly exhilarated. She had often wanted to deep throat men but never been able to force herself. Now she knew she had done it, could do it.

Or maybe it was the dazed state of her mind, growing dizzy and cloudy from lack of oxygen.

She found she could tell the difference in thickness between the helmeted head and the shaft that followed, could sense the head as a thicker lump in her throat and follow its movement up and down and up and down.

She was becoming light headed.

Just as she'd thought she would pass out for lack of air he pulled free - and came. He came a gallon, pouring his silvery white semen into her mouth so it overflowed and dribbled down her chin and then drawing back to spit wad after wad over her face.

Then he let her go and she half hung out of the door of the car, gasping and choking and gripping her aching throat in both hands as he turned and walked away. She stared dazedly at the dirt beneath her, then managed to pull herself back up and fall back into the patrol car. She lay on the seat, drawing in deep, quivering breaths of air as she rubbed at her throat, her chest heaving.

When she cleared her mind and vision enough to sit up he was well out in front of her, walking along in the same deliberate pace he had been when she'd first seen him.

And he didn't bother to look back.

She gaped at him, still coughing, rubbing her sore throat, swallowing again and again as she gulped in deep, shaky breaths and watched him walk away.

She stared at him until he disappeared in the distance, too shaken and frightened to go after him. She was indignant, as well, and angry, and sore, and embarrassed. And yet she still had a deep and burning lust in her gut. Her breasts were still swollen with heat and need, her nipples exquisitely sensitive. Her pussy was warm and moist so she knew her thong would be clinging to the furrow between her legs.

"Bastard," she whispered, her throat sore, voice gravelly.

She should go after him, should run him down, or handcuff him at gun point, or make him strip, make him - .

But she quivered in anxiety at the thought of confronting him. What if he thought so little of her he just ignored her? What if, satisfied, sated, he just sneered at her in contempt and went right on walking?

Worse. What if he didn't? What if he did take her, strip her naked, use her like an animal, pummel her with his - enormous - powerful - masculine body?

She shook her head dazedly. She was crazy. She turned and spat into the dirt outside the patrol car then. She reached up and felt the wads of semen across her face, and searched around for tissues, yanking them up and wiping at her skin. Then, hands shaking, she turned the wheel and the car around and drove unsteadily back to the highway. She stopped there, her forehead on the steering wheel, eyes closed as she tried to regain control.

She steadied herself after a minute, and drove back onto the highway, then turned and headed for the river. Ten miles along she found another dirt road, a fire road, this time, one she knew well, then drove through some brush and into a small clearing where the river curved.

She stripped off her top, then kicked off her shoes and unbuckled her gun belt, dropping it inside the car. She peeled her uniform trousers down and stepped out of them, then started for the river. She paused, still gripped by a dark heat and hunger, and pushed her panties down and off, then opened her bra and dropped it on the ground.

Naked, she moved towards the river and knelt beside it beside a small bush. She watched it roll slowly past, then slipped a hand between her legs and let two fingers drive smoothly up into her tight pussy. She moaned to herself, imagining Emery taking her, imagining him using her, rutting against her. Two fingers became three, then four, and she began to stroke her clitoris with rough, fast movements.

She grunted softly, frantically, panting for breath as she began to buck her hips forward against her fingers. She squeezed one of her breasts, roughly and repeatedly, the heat overwhelming, sweat dripping off her forehead as the sexual need grew and swelled and surrounded her in a hot, steaming haze of desperate desire.

She felt the orgasm roar up around her and then swamp her senses, crying out in helpless pleasure, jamming her fingers into her pussy with painful, desperate need, thrusting them up to the knuckles in her burning, spasming pussy as the orgasm rolled over her and ground her beneath its weight.

She collapsed, falling forward, grunting heavily as her breasts hit the ground and turning her head aside to keep from breaking her nose. She lay panting and moaning in the dirt, fingers still buried in her pussy as the soft afterglow melted her muscles and left her lethargic and drained.

She eased her fingers out and then slowly unfurled her body, groaning as she rolled onto her back and lay in the dirt and grass, her chest heaving.

Chapter Two

"Long day, Darling'?"

Dara slammed the door of the patrol car, gave Rogers a scowl and moved past him into the station.

"Sheriff wants ta see you, Dara."

She sighed and nodded at Becky, the receptionist, then turned and headed up the narrow hall to her uncle's office. The door was open and he was sitting behind his desk, the chair creaking as he rocked back and forth, reading a report.

"You wanted me for something, Uncle Bert?"

He looked up and scowled.

"Where in hell you been, girl?"

"Out and about. Patrolling." She shrugged.

"Bullshit. You were loafing somewhere, weren't you."

"Nu uh."

He got up and moved around the desk, then leaned in against her, sniffing. He reached out and touched her hair and then drew back, scowling.

"You were off swimming again, weren't you," he snapped.

"Only a little," she said defensively. "It was hot."

"It's Mississippi in the July. Of course it's hot! You want a cool job go get work at the grocery store or the library!"

"You could get air conditioning for the cars, y'know."

"I could do a lot of things. Don't mean I'm gonna. I could also fire your ass no matter what my sister says. And if you don't stay in your goddam car I will."

"It's so hot I can hardly breath! I can hardly keep awake!"

"Maybe if you weren't out drinking and dancing until three o'clock in the morning ever single night you'd be able to cope better."

"At least they have air conditioning," she said sullenly.

"Save your money and buy one."

"Oh right. That's gonna happen."

"You got a route you're supposed to patrol. You stick to it and do the patrol or find another job. You clear on that, girl?"

She nodded sullenly.

"Then get out of my office."

Dara kicked the side of a chair then stomped heavily out of the office, muttering to herself beneath her breath.

"I hate this place!"

Without any money she was going to have to spend the evening at home, being bored by the summer reruns on television and sweating all the while.

She wandered up the hall and paused by the dispatch desk where Norma Jane sat.

"Hey, Norma."

"Hey Dara. How you doin'?"

"It's hot as hell outside," Dara complained, leaning forward on the counter.

"Ain't it though?" The redheaded woman shook her head and reached up unconsciously to adjust her heavily frosted hairdo.

"I swear I near melted on the way in this mornin'. I'm so glad this place is air conditioned."

Dara made a face and Norma shrugged apologetically. "Not that that helps you, a course."

Dara heard movement behind her and turned her head slightly to see Billy Zane and Bobbie Chambers coming in from a patrol. She turned her head away, aware they had a very good view of her behind as she bent over, but too irritated to really care this afternoon.

"I wish the Sheriff would get air conditioned cars," she groaned.

"Well, his car is air conditioned," Norma said with a grin.

Dara made a face again then felt a hand on her behind as Bobbie came over to stand beside her. "Hey, Dara, nice thong," he said, grinning down at her.

"Get yer paws offa me, Bobbie Chambers," she said, indignantly slapping his hand away.

She remembered belatedly that her black thong would probably show up very clearly through the thin, pale beige pants she wore, especially given how tight they were.

"You keep yer mind offa my undies," she said with a glare.

"Hard ta do with your pushin' em out at me like that."

"Maybe the Sheriff could help you focus yer minds on other things, Bobbie Chambers," Norma said primly.

Bobbie rolled his eyes and moved on down the hall.

"You really wear them thongs?" Norma asked, her voice lower. "I tried one and it really felt uncomfortable."

"Yeah, well, I like them," Dara said. "They make me feel, I dunno, sexy."

"Well this ain't the place for that kinda feeling."

"I suppose." She sighed and straightened up, then reached back to pull her pants away from her moist bottom. "I'll just be glad when this heat wave is over."

She got back into the old Chevy and backed out of the lot,

then turned onto Main Street and drove north to Highway One Nine. She stopped there and bought herself a milkshake to ease her sore throat. It took the last of her money and she wasn't in a very good mood when she finished it.

That arrogant bastard Emery. She ought to put a bullet up his ass. That'd show him.

She glared sulkily at the cars passing her, thinking of how he'd used her so roughly and violently.

Now that's a man.

She shook her head. For him to use her and then just dump her like that bespoke an incredible gall. She might've run him over right then and there, or gunned him down and dumped him in the woods.

Did he think she couldn't do anything? Did he think she was some lilly livered little girl who couldn't look after herself? She'd beaten bigger men unconscious.

Bigger than her anyway, not as big as Emery.

Every time she thought about his enormous cock she felt a little tingle in her loins. What would it be like to feel that monster inside her?

Jesus!

She continued her patrol, sweating heavily in the late afternoon sun. She took a call on the radio to check out a report of boys throwing stones at the high school, but that turned out to be nothing.

That bastard. Must think he's really something else.

She signed off at the end of his shift, then drove towards her place. Somehow, and she wasn't sure quite how, she wound up on Highway One Five headed towards the old Breckenridge mining road.

She pulled over to the side of the road and sat in her car, her body pins and needles all over, staring sightlessly down the road at nothing. Her chest was tight and her heart was in her throat as she thought about Emery.

Ten years he'd spent in prison. He was a rough, mean, cruel man, and she'd be out of her head to go near him even if he were White.

The car started rolling forward, then stopped as she came into sight of a pair of shacks and a small field. She could hardly breath as she got shakily out of the car and wiped the sweat from her brow.

She'd just look in on him, maybe flirt a little. She had her gun. He wasn't going to do anything this time. She was going to just show him that she wasn't anyone to mess with.

A voice kept telling her she was insane, that approaching Emery's farm alone this close to nightfall was dangerous. Emery had used her cruelly and violently that day. Her throat still ached from it.

His eyes had been dark and mean, and she could sense in them an appalling capacity for violence.

So what was she doing here, her pussy throbbing, her heart pounding, her chest tight, fingers almost trembling as she eased along the wall to the roughly made door. She looked down at her uniform anxiously, wondering if it would provoke the man, but could not bear the thought of going now.

She drew her gun from its holster and tested the knob. The door was not locked.

She licked her lips and looked around in the darkening wood, then threw the door back and raised the gun.

It was a small shack of a place, with bare, unpolished wood floors. At the back sat a huge, ancient wood burning oven. To the left sat a roughly hewn wooden table which Emery had probably carved himself. To the right, a stone fireplace took up most of the wall. A tall, ancient pine cabinet sat next to it, most of the shelves empty.

Emery looked up from a dirty, patched armchair in front of the fireplace where he'd been sitting reading. There was no expression on his face.

Dara swallowed repeatedly, then eased into the room, keeping the gun on him.

"So. Guess you didn't think I'd show up, did yah?" she asked, her voice unsteady.

Emery did not reply.

"Yuh think yuh could j-just use me like that today and walk away?" she demanded.

He put down his book, then slowly stood up.

"Get back!"

He ignored her, moving forward as she backed against a wall. He walked past her and closed the door, and Dara felt like crying out.

He turned and walked to her and she raised the gun again.

"Don't," she gulped.

He placed his hand over the gun and pulled it away from her, then flung it across the room.

Dara stared at him, chest heaving, and he smiled grimly. Then in an instant he spun her around, gripped her by collar and belt, and slammed her belly down across the rough table. She felt his hands at her groin, and the tearing rip of fabric as he tore the crotch wide from her uniform trousers.

She cried out in shock and alarm, hands scrabbling at the rough wood of the table, but made no effort to turn or escape. She felt him grip the thin thong protecting her sex, and cried out again as it was torn away.

Her sex was bare now, her uniform pants peeled back from the crotch, exposing her inner thighs and buttocks. She shuddered as Emery's big, work-roughened hand cupped her sex and his big fingers began to knead the oozing flesh.

"P-Please," she moaned.

A heavy, sausage like finger stroked along her sex, then pushed slowly into her overheated body.

Dara shuddered again, her thighs un-consciously shifting apart as the big rough finger drove deep into her sex, pressing one way, then the other. Another finger joined it, and she groaned at the tension of her opening. A third finger, and she was clenching her teeth against the ache as they began to pump in and out of her pussy. She gripped the opposite side of the table, her knuckles white, her eyes closed as Emery pumped his fingers into her faster and harder.

She felt the heat pouring through her veins, felt the sexual need burning along her spine. Her bottom was up and open, and she grunted and panted for breath as she began to rock and jerk against the table. Fire ran through her nervous system and she spasmed involuntarily, then again. She felt as though she were sweltering in the heat. And then the orgasm hit her and she cried out helplessly, bucking back against his fingers.

She heard a throaty chuckle, and knew a terrible shame as he thrust his fingers in even harder, stabbing them cruelly into the soft moist flesh of her sex, driving them deep inside her as her hips ground against the rough edge of the table.

She was on the balls of her feet, her bottom jerking up and down repeatedly as those big fingers were driven into her aching, burning sex, and she could not repress the gasps and moans of passionate pleasure as the orgasm flowed over her mind and body.

And then he halted, his fingers withdrawing. She lay groaning across the table, eyes narrowed into slits, jaw slack, body limp, as he moved away. He opened the door, then sat back in his chair and picked up his book again.

Dara lay across the table for a long minute, gulping in breaths and trying to fit the shattered pieces of her mind together. When she finally succeeded she pushed herself erect, her legs rubbery, and turned, still breathing heavily, to see him ignoring her.

The door was open, he was reading his book. The message of contempt was obvious, and she flushed hotly as she understood. She stared in disbelief as he read, and a rage swelled inside her. She half staggered to where her gun lay and turned it on him.

"You fucking bastard!" she cried, half sobbing. "You think you're too good for me, you nigger!"

He seemed to flow up from the chair and she backed away as he towered over her. He snatched the gun from her hand as though she were a child, then turned it around and thrust the thick steel barrel into her mouth.

She moaned, eyes wide, as he backed her against the big cabinet. Her hands gripped his wrist frantically as she fought to keep from gagging on the barrel.

His dark eyes bored into her as he held the gun immoveable, and after long seconds of struggling Dara felt a strange feeling of resignation, a dazed sense of submissiveness, and her hands fell to her sides.

He nodded minutely, then drew the barrel out slowly. He halted with the tip laying on her lower lip, then pushed it back in once more. His other hand came up beneath her chin and he squeezed her mouth closed as he pumped the barrel slowly in and out.

She moaned as she stared at him over the gun, her eyes flicking down to the gleaming steel barrel. He nodded at her as if in answer to an unasked question. And though she had not asked it she knew what he required.

Her lips closed, pursed around the barrel, and she began to suck.

He removed his other hand, holding the gun steadily, pumping it slowly in and out, the eight inch barrel threatening to choke her each time he forced it deep. Dara stared at him, her eyes not leaving his, sucking and licking at the oiled steel as he moved it in and out. The sound of her wet sucking mouth was loud in the small, cramped shack, but she barely heard it over her pounding heart.

He drew the gun out at last, pulling it free from her sucking mouth, and then let it slide slowly down her body.

Her chest heaved as she felt the sweat trickling down her forehead, but her eyes remained locked against his as the barrel slid bellow her belt and then ground over her sweating sex.

She grunted as it penetrated her, gasped as it was slowly driven up into her pussy. She moaned as it drove deep, forcing her up onto her toes, and whimpered as the trigger guard ground against her soft, padded sex and the barrel twisted within her.

He twisted the barrel down, and the hard steel barrel jammed downwards within her. He twisted the barrel up, and again she felt the steel twist inside her body, felt it grind against her internal organs. He twisted it to one side, then the other, then began to pump it slowly in and out.

Fear gripped Dara's body, but it didn't seem to matter. Her pores oozed sexual wanting and need, and she felt her insides gripping the smooth steel barrel with hot hungry delight. He pumped faster, and faster still, and she began to grunt at the pain as the trigger guard struck her sex with bruising force.

She thought about it going off. Thought about dying. But it didn't matter. She was too hot, too feverish with the sexual heat to do anything but stand there and gasp and moan as she looked into those dark, hypnotic eyes.

Then he pulled the gun back and out, and again it was at her mouth. He slid it inside, letting the barrel stroke across her tongue. She moaned and licked at it, tasting her own hot juices as his eyes bored into hers.

He pulled the gun out and tossed it behind him. She was half sitting back against the cabinet now, gripping the edges as she trembled weakly. His hands moved slowly down to the front of her uniform, and he fingered her badge for a moment before plucking it free.

He set it aside, then gripped the front of her uniform top and ripped it open. Dara gasped, yanked forward briefly before the material tore, then fell back against the cabinet. Emery gripped her bra and tore it open as well, so that once again her body jerked forward, then fell back. He loomed over her like a giant, and pushed forward, forcing her back against the cabinet.

The cabinet was a foot and a half wide at its base, with three roughly made drawers in its bottom. The shelves atop were perhaps six or eight inches deep. Dara's bottom was riding up across the top of the lower section as Emery pressed his body forward, her head and back grinding against the narrower shelves above.

Her legs spread for balance, and she grasped one of the shelves just above her head as utensils and cans tumbled off onto the floor to either side.

Emery reached down to his trousers and slowly, tauntingly unfastened them, then lowered the zipper and pushed them down. He was naked beneath, and his cock was fully erect, a monster, just like him, just as Dara remembered it. She stared down at it, whimpering softly as Emery stepped out of his pants, then pulled his T-shirt up and off.

She felt a surge of heat between her legs. He was so incredibly powerful! He was so masculine! So strong in mind and body! He was a beast! A wild, savage animal!

He reached down and took her hands, then pulled them in around his manhood. His eyes sent a clear message, and despite the fear in her heart she guided him towards her exposed sex.

She felt the soft, blunt, spongy head against her weeping opening and a shockwave seemed to run through her. Emery pushed forward, and she groaned as her pubic lips strained. She was forced up harder against the shelf, her legs spreading further as he jammed relentlessly forward.

She moaned and then tried to ease his cock back. But he

would have none of it. He slapped her face lightly, his giant hand throwing her head against the back of the cabinet. Her hands released his mighty prong, and he thrust forward.

Dara cried out in pain, her body trembling now as her sex was torn wider, as the soft moist lips were forced back farther than they had ever gone before.

"No! Wait! Wait!" she gasped desperately, wriggling and twisting.

She felt the head pushing forward, her pubic lips spreading even wider, the tight, burning ache of stretching flesh rippling through her body.

"I-It's t-too big!" she gasped.

Her pubic lips spread even wider, and the thick girth of his head slid slowly between them and into her body. Dara cried out breathlessly, hands pushing feebly against his chest as the thick rounded head forced aside the taut, elastic walls of her sex and ground slowly deeper.

"Oh God! Oh Jesus God!" she panted.

She could feel the head bloating out the narrow tube of her sex, stretching and straining the silken flesh. She could feel the thick shaft grinding over her pubic lips, the hard, swollen veins and hairs clawing at her tender flesh as it pushed forward.

Her head jerked from side to side, falling back, jaw wide, gasping as she stared up at him. She grasped the shelves to either side of her body, whimpering as she felt more and more of the man's enormous cock passing through her opening and driving up into her soft belly.

"E-Emery," she panted. "Emery!"

Inch after inch slid through the aching flesh of her pubic lips, while the head pushed aside her constricted tube to drive ever higher. She felt cramps in her belly, and groaned as they worsened. The spongy head jammed against her cervix, and still he was not fully inside.

She moaned, her eyes beseeching him.

His eyes were cold and dark.

His hands moved down against her thighs, fingers sweeping around them, and he forced them wider. They were like bands of steel, bruising her soft flesh as his cock pushed even higher, and Dara sobbed aloud, slapping against his chest and belly again, trying to push him back.

She cried out, her head jerking back and striking the back of the cabinet.

His cockhead had forced up past her cervix, and her groin ached and burned as he shifted his grip upwards onto her buttocks and buried the last inch of his mighty staff in her trembling, shaking body.

She was crushed back against the cabinet, her face against his chest now, the breath leaving her in desperate little gasps and pants. He pinned her against the cabinet, his body like a wall, shutting out the light.

"Ungh!"

His hands shifted further, higher on her thighs, and he yanked her legs wider still and thrust forward, grinding his pelvis against her aching groin. Her body was like a rag doll to him as he jerked her up and forward, then back.

He eased his body back, grinning darkly, and pulled his thick cock backwards as well.

Dara felt it sliding slowly down her aching sex, the head popping past her cervix. She was half sitting on the narrow shelf now, slumped against it, her legs up and apart in Emery's hands. He drew his cock back further, and she could see it now, glistening with her juices. She marvelled at its thickness.

And then he pushed forward, slowly but firmly, and her fingers dug into the palms of her hands as she braced herself and moaned.

The cock drove up higher into her, forcing its way past her cervix, grinding against the very back wall of her pussy. Then retreated.

Slowly, the pain began to dull, to ease. Somehow her pussy began to adjust to the monstrous girth and length of his manhood.

Dara sat slumped back against the cabinet shelf, staring dully up at him, drained, soaking with sweat, hair matted against her scalp, legs spread wide as his thick black cock pushed in and out of her aching sex.

The sensation was like nothing she had ever imagined. She was utterly impaled on the mighty lance, and could feel its movements within her with a sense of shock and awe.

Then Emery began to thrust faster. The pain rose again and she moaned, pushing against his chest. Emery glared, then reached down to the belt around her waist. He unbuckled it and in an instant yanked it free of its loops. An instant later he had both her slim wrists in one mighty hand and was looping the belt around them.

"Emery!" she whimpered.

He cinched the belt tight and raised it over her head, then wrapped the end tightly around a support rod. His powerful hands tore at her pants, ripping them completely off her, and his hands forced her knees up and back against the rear of the cabinet behind her.

He thrust harder, faster, and Dara gasped and moaned and whimpered in pain as each powerful thrust sent the thick prong slicing up through her belly, pummelling her from the inside.

Again the pain eased, and as she stared up at him her aching, exhausted body began to respond, that dark hungry longing coming forth. She had never been so brutally used, so totally impaled. The big Black man was as remorseless as he was powerful, the scent of him filling her nose, the pure masculine odour of him curling around her mind.

The pain did not entirely leave her, but her grunts as he buried himself in her abdomen changed, altered. A shimmering haze seemed to hang before her eyes, and Dara felt her body beginning to burn with an almost feverish lust.

He was really giving it to her! He was giving it to her so hard!
So big! Like a bull! Like a wild animal!

The leather of her belt dug into her wrists as her body jerked back and forth, and the hard wood of the shelf bruised the small of her back. Her knees jammed repeatedly back against the rear of the cabinet behind her as Emery thrust himself into her body. Dara could feel the flesh of her insides sucking at his enormous cock each time it withdrew, then giving way before it as it was thrust forward once again.

Her head lolled back as the power of her sexual heat overcame her, and her mind began to tumble and roll like a cork in a flood. The cabinet itself was slamming back against the wall now, rocking back and forth as Emery's big body pounded forward against her. His cock was hissing in and out through her aching pubic lips, bruising her inside, thumping painfully and wonderfully against the back of her pussy.

She was still wearing her shoes and socks, oddly, and as he rutted against her his big hands slammed her legs back against the back wall of the cabinet again and again. First one shoe, then the other tumbled and flew free, while she stared up at him dazedly and grunted under the ferocious attack.

Dara came. It was a climax like none she had experienced before as a kind of wildfire sexual electricity tore though her nervous system. Convulsions wracked her body, her muscles spasming and jerking as repeated shockwaves of intense pleasure rolled up and down her spine.

Her sex was a furnace, consuming her, the pleasure intoxicating, overpowering.

His enormous cock was spearing up into her belly with hard, savage, brutal movements, her body jerking violently under its own internal storm even as Emery continued to hammer his hips against her. The climax rolled on and on, rising and falling, soaring and tumbling, and her mind with it. She couldn't think, couldn't breath, and existed alone in a universe of mindless animal pleasure punctuated solely by the hard, aching thrusts of his mighty cock.

The orgasm slowly faded, and she found herself dazed and

light-headed, having forgotten how to breath. She drew in a great, shaking gasp of breath and her lungs groaned in relief.

Emery continued to pound his hips against her as she gulped air into her starving lungs again and again, head rolling back against the rear of the cabinet.

And then he finished, coming, pouring out his hot seed, sending it gushing deep into her womb as he buried himself to the last inch in her aching, overheated body and emptied himself.

He stood unmoving for a long moment, then slowly eased back. His cock was softening already, and he drew it back from her and half staggered backwards to fall into his chair.

Without his hand supporting her Dara's legs fell, and she cried out in dazed pain as her feet hit the floor - barely.

The tight leather dug into her wrists to support her, holding her aloft, and only her toes reached the dirty wooden floor underneath as the edge of the shelf dug into her buttocks, thrusting her pelvis forward.

Still, neither of them spoke. Dara gulped in air and moaned weakly, while Emery looked sullenly at the door, then at her, as if angry he had given in and made use of her.

He got up suddenly, and Dara's eyes rose from the floor as he moved back towards her. She moaned weakly, then grunted as he roughly flipped her around so that she faced the cabinet. Now the edge of the narrow shelf dug into her hips, forcing her bottom out, and she felt his fingers moving slowly across her rounded buttocks, stroking the soft pale flesh, then squeezing tightly.

Only the balls of her feet reached the floor, and she whimpered softly, feeling another little gush of liquid heat, knowing how perfectly her bottom was presented to him.

She heard a soft hiss and her weary head turned to see him standing up from where his pants lay, his own thin belt in his hand. She stared dull-eyed, for a moment as he moved back behind her, then belated understanding came just as the belt cut through the air and slashed down across her out thrust bottom.

Pain ripped through her languid, exhausted body and she cried out, wrists jerking against the leather binding them above her.

"Stop it! Emery! No! What are you doing!"

"Slut," he said, uttering his first word. The belt slashed across her buttocks again, throwing her hips against the edge of the shelf, and she cried out.

Crack!

"Stop it!" she cried

"Whore," he said, his voice low and sullen, raising goose bumps on her flesh.

And she was a whore, Dara thought dazedly. Who else but a whore would have done what she had done, would have let this beast of a man use her, and come - come so powerfully?

Even now she was awed at the force of the climax which had ripped through her.

Crack!

She cried out again, twisting and writhing, her hips grinding against the edge of the shelf.

"Whore."

Crack!

The belt sliced into her buttocks, into her thighs. Pain burned into her as he brought the belt down with slow, deliberate strokes.

"A whore to tempt men," he said between his teeth, his voice a low rumble.

Crack!

And she deserved it, she thought dizzily. She was a whore by any measure she had been raised with. All through her fantasies about him, and all through his rough use of her she had felt that dark, excited shame at what she'd been doing. Her own uncle probably would have taken his belt to her if he'd known for a minute what she had done.

Crack!

She groaned, tears filling her eyes. She did not try to twist aside or fight him now. Something inside her accepted the beating as right, as proper, as earned. Her head hung as the belt slashed across her bottom again, and again, and again, tears trickling down her cheeks as the pain mounted.

He stopped, and then his big hands came around her sides, sliding up beneath her sweating breasts and squeezing them painfully. Rough thumbs flicked across nipples which were stiffly erect, and she felt a kind of static charge of sexual electricity pass through them.

She felt his groin pressing against her hot, aching, out thrust bottom, and with shock and awe realized he was erect once again. His thick manhood pressed against her thigh, then up against her buttocks.

She closed her eyes and groaned as his hands moved downwards and spread her thighs. Her feet rose onto her toes, then the tips of her toes, then just her big toes, and her bottom pushed out even further. She felt the hard spongy head of his cock pressing up against her still sore pussy lips and moaned in denial.

The pressure grew and he forced himself inside her. Then, as before, Dara could only moan and whimper as his thick cock pushed up higher and deeper into her belly.

No! She couldn't take another fucking like that! She couldn't!

Her mind fought in desperate denial, but Emery continued to force himself up into her, his fingers like iron steel around her thighs holding them open. His big thumbs were jammed up against the underside of her sweating buttocks just next to her pussy, stretching the soft flesh even further as they dug into her bruised flesh.

His cockhead jammed past her cervix and she let her head drop back, gurgling slowly in dazed pain and a suddenly rising heat.

He was faster now, her pussy muscles already bruised and relaxed. Soon he was able to rut in unrestrained force, his hips pounding against her buttocks, his cock impaling her, stabbing up with a terrible, wonderful force.

Dara half hung from her wrists, slack jawed, gurgling and sobbing and moaning as a steam bath of sexual heat caught her in its embrace and led her back into animalistic madness.

His thick cock was making a wet sucking sound as it thrust in and out of her, the lewd sound a counterpoint to her desperate gasps, the slap of his hips against her bottom, and the thump of the top of the cabinet against the wall.

The cabinet rocked back and forth as his body hammered into her, his spear of flesh slicing up and into her body with a cruel force that soon brought another shocking orgasm howling down around her. It was the twin of the one she had just survived, and she wondered dazedly if she would live through its terrible pleasure.

A fever gripped her, and the world spun and fragmented as the mad pleasure rolled and circled, dipped and rose, twisted and plunged. Her mind rode its back with ever decreasing energy, until suddenly she let go and her mind tumbled off into blackness.

Dara's eyes opened slowly.

She could see nothing. She felt a terrible ache in her head, and darkness surrounded her. Her body felt bruised and battered, nowhere worse than between her legs. She brought a weak, shaky hand up, or tried to, and found it weighed far more than it ever should have.

Her head was upside down. She realized it with a kind of strange satisfaction, as if this accounted for her confusion. She lay upon something hard and as she moved she felt its coldness against her bare flesh. Now she could see faint stars through the branches of the trees, and groaned as she wriggled weakly backwards.

She was on the hood of her patrol car, her head and shoulders hanging over one end.

It took considerable effort to slide her naked flesh back along the hood so that her head was raised. She rested for several minutes, the ache in her head slowly receding, but not leaving entirely.

Then she sat up, not easily, gasping as she fell back against the windshield. The night had turned chill, or at least felt that way against her damp, naked flesh. She wore nothing but her socks. She had no idea where her clothes were, but then remembered that Emery had shredded them.

He had apparently carried her out to the road as well and dropped her onto her car.

She marvelled at having lost consciousness, feeling awed at the power of the orgasm Emery had given her. Nothing else she had ever felt came close. She hadn't known such intensity was even possible.

The crickets were singing in the tall grass alongside the road. Dara rolled slowly and weakly aside, then grunted, almost falling, as her legs swung over the edge of the car. She clutched the cold steel to support herself, then made her way to the drivers door and eased it open, all but falling inside.

"Oh my God, Dara, you have been done," she whispered to herself. "You have been done like nobody ever got done before."

Her bottom stung as she sat back, but it was her groin that ached, and she spread her legs, slumping as she winced. She reached down and gently cupped her sex, feeling the hot, swollen flesh throb beneath her fingers.

"Oh Lord I have been done good," she groaned weakly.

Chapter Three

Dara called in sick the next day, and spent the day in her small home on the edge of town.

She rented the place from Old Mrs. Matthews who'd moved into town to live her last days with her daughter Mary Sue. It was tiny, with just the one long front room and a tiny kitchen and bath. Upstairs was the one bedroom where she had spent the night on her belly, nude, body slick with sweat as she had gazed out at the silent highway running past.

Dara found herself caught in the grip of a strange mental cloud all day, her bruised body recovering from the beating it had taken while she tried to understand why it had happened.

Every time the mere echo of her orgasms flashed through her memory she trembled. Who could have imagined that pleasure could be so intense it was almost painful? Was that what ecstasy was like? She'd read the word often enough in romance novels, but never thought to experience it.

Ecstasy.

She mouthed the word as she lay slumped in her big chair in front of the TV. Her legs were spread and draped across the armrests as she idly watched a soap opera on TV.

She thought about what her friends would say if they knew she had done that with a Black man, what her family would say, what the whole town would say. She felt a little smug at that, a little cocky.

Ha. They'd never guess. And Emery sure wouldn't tell them. The man barely spoke a word to her the whole time she was there.

Whore.

He had called her that, and she supposed he was right. That troubled her a little. She didn't like to think of herself as a whore, or even promiscuous. But what other kind of a girl would seek out a violent Black man out in the woods and let him use her so violently?

She could have stopped him. She could have shot him. For that matter, she could have just stayed away.

God, what a cock he had!

She cupped her sex gently, wincing slightly, yet feeling a slow thrum of arousal as she remembered how Emery had forced that monster of a cock up into her body. Oh how full she'd felt!

Ecstasy.

Her bottom was still striped from the strapping he'd given her, and she drew her legs back further, slumping a little lower to raise it up off the seat.

Emery wasn't a man to be messed with, not a man to take for granted. She was lucky she'd come through that incredible sexual assault unscathed.

Aside from the bruises and welts, of course.

Oh he'd done her good, all right. He'd done her like no man ever had. And like no man likely ever would again.

There were other big men, big men with broad shoulders and muscles. But there was something about Emery, something darkly arousing, dangerous and hot. A man like Emery was capable of anything. Being near him was living on the raw edge of a razor blade.

She fingered her nipples and closed her eyes, remembering how it had felt with him inside her, how overwhelmed she had been, how completely and thoroughly he had used her.

She would have to go back.

The thought alarmed her, and she felt a trembling fear and denial. But the memory of those incredible orgasms came to the front of her mind again and she felt her nipples stiffen. People got addicted to drugs, sacrificing everything for the momentary high the drugs gave them. Had those massive orgasms addicted her?

What would she risk to feel such pleasure again?

She rose and padded naked across the room to the kitchen. The curtains were wide, the windows open, but she was not worried about being seen. She had always felt a little excited at the way people lusted after her, and today, awash in sexual satisfaction, she felt immensely proud of herself, of her body, of her wanton ways.

She paused at the thick post which held up the ceiling, then hesitantly reached up high, pressing her body against it. Her breasts pillowed out against the wood as she stared up at her bruised wrists, imagining herself bound there, being beaten, being whipped. By Emery.

She let her head roll back, and turned, staring down, her insides growing warm as she thought of him staring at her with those big dark, cold eyes, a belt in his fist.

Crack! The belt would slice across her bottom.

She let her body grind against the wood and moaned aloud, rolling her head. She pushed in harder, thighs spreading around the post as she ground her pelvis against it.

Slut!

She turned away, trotting upstairs, then pulled the plastic dildo out from beneath her bed and trotted back down the stairs. Again she placed herself against the pillar, reaching back behind her and rubbing the rounded nose of the dildo against her moist sex.

She ached, but that only added to the fantasy as she slowly forced the sex toy up into her body. Her insides felt bruised, and she hissed as she worked the thing in deeper.

"Fuck me, Emery!" she panted.

It hurt now as she jammed it in higher still. Her hand slapped at the bottom, forcing in the final inch and she ground and rubbed her slick body against the post, reaching up to grip it with one hand, her right leg rising and curling around it.

A sharp knock to the door had her stumbling back, gasping and looking around with wide eyes.

"Dara. Open up."

She recognized the voice. It was Paul Hunter, from the County Attorney's office.

She discovered her hands had automatically gone to her breasts and groin, and that her heart was pounding with the sudden fear of discovery.

"Sheriff sent me," he called.

She cursed to herself, then grabbed at her robe and pulled it on. The robe was short and thin, made of blue silk with twining white flowers. She pulled it together and tightened the belt, then, swallowing a little nervously, her sexual heat rising again, she moved slowly towards the door.

She still had the dildo inside her, and reached down to tap at the base, pushing it up harder so that she gasped a little.

She combed the hair back from her forehead and then opened the door a crack.

"What'd you want?" she demanded.

"Sheriff said you was here," he replied. "He says since you ain't doing nothing else now's a good time for you to go over your testimony in next week's trial."

"Oh shit," she said, disgusted.

The trial was that of Morgan Fitzhue, who had damaged a Coke machine because it had robbed him of a dollar. Normally something like that would have been handled less formally, but the man had mouthed off to the Sheriff, and had been an irritation for some time, so the Sheriff was coming down hard on him.

"Who cares about stupid Fitzhue?" she demanded, opening the door wider.

Hunter's eyes widened, as well, when he saw her, and he licked his lips, looking behind him nervously.

"Ah, well, you're welcome to tell the Sheriff that," he said.

Hunter was a tall, thick bodied man. He was no Emery, but not bad on the eyes, she thought. She smiled inwardly and backed up, motioning him inside.

He looked around again, like a man afraid of being sighted entering a house of ill repute, then moved forward as she closed the door behind.

"I hope this won't take long," Dara said. "It's... hot, you know, and I'm not really in the mood for this kind of thing."

"No, no, no. The Sheriff just wants to make sure your testimony is uh, forceful, so the judge realizes the need to punish the man accordingly."

"Forceful," she snorted.

Hunter pulled out one of the two chairs at her small kitchen table and sat, placing his briefcase on the table. Dara looked down a moment, then pulled out the other and slowly, carefully sat down. She repressed a gasp as the base of the dildo pressed against the hard chair and ground the nose up deep into her sex, but a wave of sexual excitement spread through her as she settled her bottom on the chair and looked across at him.

"Okay," she said, smiling, considering. "What would you like me to do, Paul?"

He swallowed nervously, noting the way her thin robe billowed out, seeing the creamy cleavage before him.

"Ahm, well, you can uh, start by describing what you saw. And uh, make sure you make it, well... uhm, dramatic."

"Dramatic? He busted a Coke machine, Paul," she said.

"It's the sheriff," he said half apologetically.

Dara let her legs slowly come apart beneath the table, spreading them wider and wider as the short robe rode up her thighs. She smiled in apparent thought, her hand dropping below the table and lifting the robe higher, baring her groin entirely.

"Well, let me see," she said, fingering her clitoris.

"I was walking along Main street. It was hot out, and the sun was beating down. I was sweating bad. I mean, I could feel the sweat trickling down my chest," she said in a soft, husky voice.

Hunter swallowed and licked his lips.

"And there he was in front of me, bent over, his bottom sticking up in the air. That caught my attention, you know. He's got a right pretty bottom."

Hunter looked away briefly, and Dara shifted her hand. Beneath the table, she tugged at the robe, loosening it so that the top eased a little further apart.

"I guess that old machine wouldn't give him what he wanted," she said. "He's a... a forceful man, you know, and he wasn't going to take no for an answer. He reached his hand into the opening where the coke was supposed to come down, trying to reach up all the way inside there and get what he wanted."

Her finger was stroking her clitoris steadily now, and she leaned forward to let the top of the robe gape a little wider.

She was aroused, excited, her heart pounding. She wasn't sure if she wanted or dared to take Hunter or not. He was married and twice her age, but good looking. And the fact he was married argued he'd keep quiet about whatever happened.

"It was too small for him," she said. "He was big, you know, and he was thrusting up, pumping in and out, trying to work his way in deeper. I could see his bottom jerking up and down as he worked at it, and I could see the muscles moving along his bare arms and shoulders. It was really tight, but he was forcing his way deeper and deeper."

She leaned back, letting the thin fabric pull tautly across her breasts. "He was sweating, like I was sweating." She paused. "Like you're sweating now, Paul."

"I-it's hot," he gulped, pulling out a handkerchief and patting his forehead. "Would you have a cup of water?"

"Sure," she said.

She eased her legs back together, then tugged at the robe as best she could. She rose slowly, and his eyes stared hungrily. She was hot, and the thin silk was now plastered to her flesh where it touched her. The belt was loose, the top of the robe half open.

She turned and strolled to the nearby sink, turning on the water and filling a cup. She turned and pretended to hit the side wall. Water splashed over the rim of the cup against her chest.

"Oh," she said in mock annoyance. "I'm all wet."

She turned away from him and opened the robe completely, then picked up a clothe and patted it against her chest.

"I'm so clumsy," she said, looking back over her shoulder with an apologetic smile.

The raw, naked lust and desperation in her eyes momentarily surprised her, then she felt a sudden sense of smug satisfaction. But then it faded as she compared his eagerness to the cold, dark sexual beast who had taken her the previous night. Paul was no Emery. Comparing them was laughable. And she suddenly had no desire to have the man inside her.

She closed her robe and took him his glass, setting it down with a smile.

"That about it?" she asked.

He drank quickly and mopped his brow again.

"I think, maybe we ought to change the uh, tone of the testimony," he said.

"Okay."

"Strip."

There were no preliminaries with Emery, she thought, swallowing nervously.

Her hands went to her shirt and she unbuttoned it to her belt as he looked on. A slow flush crept up her neck and over her face as she pulled the shirt off and tossed it on the table. She gave him a confident look she didn't feel, then kicked off one shoe, then the other, before undoing her belt and easing her trousers down.

She slipped off her socks and stood straight in bra and panties. Strong men had trembled at the sight of her like this, but Emery just looked bored. Confidence shaken a little, she reached behind her and undid her bra, then slipped it down and off.

Emery's eyes continued to look on, his face showing no emotion. She sauntered slowly forward, letting a smile spread over her face. Her hands went to his bare chest and slid along the surface admiringly.

"Emery, you know you and me can -"

He thrust her back hard and she staggered against the wall.

His big hand cracked across her face, spinning her and throwing her against the wall a second time. She felt a sudden surge of fury and fear, and then felt both melt away under a torrent of sexual lust and desire. She straightened, gulping and wiping her sore face, meeting his scowl, and then dropping her eyes like a timid girl.

Then she licked her lips and slipped her thumbs into the waistband of her panties and eased them down. She stepped out of them and stood upright, nervously looking from side to side.

She could hardly see his eyes for the dark shadow. He stepped forward and then gripped her hands as she raised them protectively. Without speaking he forced them roughly up and back behind her head, pinning them there with one massive paw, then pulled back, forcing her to arch her back. His foot kicked her ankles apart and he slapped her bottom stingingly before he let go.

He padded slowly around her as she stood nervously, almost trembling with anxious excitement.

He leaned in over her shoulder, and she felt his hot breath on the nape of her neck.

"What you doin' here?" he hissed, his voice a low rumble.

"I-I came to see you because... because I thought..."

"You want my cock."

She flushed with shame and a dark excitement

"I-I want your cock," she whispered.

"You liked what I give you, didn't you."

"Yes," she said, her voice faint.

He moved in front of her and his dark eyes flicked up and

down.

He pushed his face up against hers. "Whore."

He drew back with a kind of snarl then ran a hand over her chest, casually and roughly fondling her breasts, then sliding it down between her legs.

She trembled, but held still as a fat finger sawed along her moist furrow and began to rub up and down.

"You like that... whore?" he rasped.

"Y-Yes," she gasped.

His finger curled inwards and pushed up inside her.

"You liked my snake, did you? All thirteen inches of him?" His teeth gleamed whitely.

Thirteen inches!?

He let his rough thumb stroke across Dara's clitoris and she gasped aloud.

He sneered in response.

He moved behind her and Dara felt his hand gliding down her spine and then cupping her bottom. A finger pressed against her anal opening and she gulped fearfully, eyes rolling sideways.

"Get down on all fours, whore."

Dara hesitated, then obeyed, kneeling before him.

He looked at her, then walked around her again, looking down scornfully.

"You look like a bitch in heat," he said. "Raise your ass and spread your legs. Show me you want it."

Dara obeyed, face scarlet, heart pounding as he circled her.

"Deputy dawg," he said, chuckling throatily.

He moved behind her, and she gasped as he dropped to his knees. Her head jerked around and he slapped her bottom hard.

"Turn around, whore!"

She obeyed, wincing at the sting in her flesh and he yanked her thighs further apart. His finger stroked along her slit and her back arched like a cat.

She heard him unzip, and closed her eyes, trembling as she waited for him to mount her. She felt his stiff erection against her thigh, then felt it sliding back and forth along her moist furrow.

Dara shifted her hands apart on the floor, bracing herself as he began to push against her pussy. She groaned as the pain rose, as her pubic lips began to spread and stretch. It was easier this time, but not much, and she bared her teeth as he dug his fingers into her hips and slowly drove his thick log deeper into her pussy.

What am I doing? What am I doing?! This is insane! Oh God he's so big! He can't really be thirteen inches? Can he!?

His hands moved along her flanks, along her ribs, then

beneath to cup her breasts as they hung below her. His fingers crushed up into them and mashed the soft, malleable flesh against her chest with painful force, and she winced, temporarily distracted from the deep, aching penetration.

"Unggghhh!" she groaned.

She felt herself forced still wider.

"Oh! Oh God!"

She ached with the fullness within her, her slick vaginal canal bloated and straining.

His hand cracked across her bottom and she cried out and jerked.

His hands clasped her waist, completely encircling it, and he began to pump.

Dara clenched her teeth against the pain and let the pleasure swallow her, grunting as he drove himself balls-deep into her aching sex.

Dara groaned with the fullness of his prick as it began to move back and forth inside her. Every deep penetration sent a ripple of cramps and a shudder of pain through her body. Yet the sensual heat of being so overpoweringly used overwhelmed it.

So big! So big!

His hands fastened on her shoulders, and he jerked her back. Dara squealed as his thrust came in harder. He pulled back, then thrust hard as he jerked her against him, and again his cock slammed up her pussy with brutal force. Again and again, and faster and harder, and Dara's head was rolling up and down, her breasts wobbling and shaking violently, Emery's hard, muscled hips slamming painfully into her bottom as he speared her.

Lord, Lord! Lord! Lord!

Her mind rolled and tossed on the floodtide of wanton sexual heat as Emery rode her with savage need, jerking her back to meet each brutal thrust. He shifted his grip suddenly, grabbing her wrists and yanking them out from under her. Dara started to fall only to have her upper torso jerked back by Emery's powerful grip.

Now her arms were forced back alongside her hips, and Emery gripped them like the handles of a wheelbarrow, yanking her to and fro as he pounded his cock down into her spasming sex. Dara's hair tumbled down around her face as her head shook violently up and down, her body hammered.

An orgasm twisted and twined around her mind, then cut in sharply, slashing at her senses. She cried out in mindless abandon, pleasure ripping through her body like a flashfire, burning away her mind and thoughts, turning her into a grunting savage as Emery continued to rut against her.

In the midst of it Emery pulled her wrists in together behind her back, then shoved them up along her spine until they were up behind her neck. She groaned dazedly, still dancing to the tune of her orgasm, her face jammed against the dirty floor now as Emery eased his big cock out of her sex and pushed it against her puckered anal opening.

Her shoulders ached, and she could feel the grit of dirt against her cheek, but her body still sizzled with overpowering lust and arousal, the orgasm only just beginning to fade as Emery pushed hard against her anus.

Her first recognition of what he intended came when the stinging heat was able to cut through the intoxicating pleasure and catch at her battered mind's attention.

Hurts.

She didn't recognize the source of pain, or the cause, or really care as long as the orgasm continued to clamour, but as it subsided the pain rose, and she realized what was happening.

"Oh no!" she groaned. "No! No! No! Emery no!"

Oh Lord! He can't!

But Emery's stiff cock gave a final thrust and the thick helmeted head forced its way through into her rectum.

Dara shuddered, her face twisting against the floor as Emery thrust into her harder, pulled back, then pushed forward again. She felt his thick prong ground forward into her bottom, lurching another inch, then another.

She felt as though she were being torn open, and she whimpered and moaned, the image of his massive cock filling her mind as she felt it forced deeper into her rectum.

Her wrists were jammed together up behind her neck, held there with one mighty hand, forcing her face down hard against the rough floor as he forced himself into her. She could not move an inch, could only kneel submissively, groaning, bottom raised, as Emery jammed himself in harder and deeper, growling with his impatience at her resistance.

He slapped her bottom hard, then again, then again, the pain distracting her, letting him force his prick higher into her belly. Dara felt cramps rippling through her gut, the cramps growing in strength and spreading as he forced his meaty cock up into her very bowels.

Thirteen inches. Oh Lord!

He chuckled as she squirmed, reaching down to squeeze and twist her breast painfully.

He eased back, then thrust hard forward, and his cock slammed another inch deeper. He pinched her nipple until she cried out in pain, then thrust hard again.

Her guts cramped and ached and twisted, and Dara moaned and gurgled in pain.

And then she felt his pubic hair brushing against her aching bottom. He pulled back, gave another hard thrust, and his testicles slapped against her pussy.

Thirteen inches! He's in me all the way!

He let out a low growl, grinding his hips against her, rolling his hips as he twisted his cock around inside her.

The train, as she had come to think of it, began again.

His cock jerked back then lurched forward, no more than an inch. Perhaps half that distance. Then again, then again, slowly at first, but building up speed. Now it was an inch, now two. Then it was four, and then six.

Oh Lord he's tearin' me up. It's so.. So goooood!

His hand cracked across her rump, and he laughed as he rode her, his hips rutting faster with each passing minute.

She was his prisoner, his toy. She felt a sense of wonder at his tremendous masculine strength. And a sense of shock at the primal lust it evoked in her.

His hips pummelled her upraised bottom as he sent his thick cock slamming deep into her bowels with every stroke. The pain tore at her vitals. And even so her pussy thrummed and burned and her mind rolled and pitched as the lewd dark heat gripped her.

Her mind suddenly flashed to the Sheriff's Office, the cool, calm, air conditioned hallways where deputies lounged and sipped coffee and chatted. That was what they were doing now, and not a one of them would have the slightest vaguest notion that deputy Dara Cooper was at that very moment naked on her knees in a Black man's shack, her arms twisted up behind her back being sodomised.

And glorying in it!

So good. So good. Oh! Oh no! Oh it hurts!

His free hand slid down over her hip and in between her legs, squeezing her pussy, and Dara gave a violent bucking heave as she came, twisting and moaning and gargling in mindless ecstasy as a kaleidoscope of lights flared and blinked before her dazed eyes.

So good! So good! So gooooood!

Her eyes closed and her jaw opened wide as she gurgled in feverish pleasure, her body still rocked by the hard, heavy blows of Emery's powerful rutting body. He rode her through the orgasm and out the other side, and still kept rutting, pounding, hammering himself against her, until another orgasm blossomed deep in her belly and she sobbed in agonized pleasure as she came again.

And then, somehow, she was laying alone on the floor,

moaning and fluttering her eyes, trying to remember where she was.

Emery knelt and rolled her onto her belly, holding a long length of thick, coarse rope. She groaned in confusion as he threw a loop around her chest, then another, pinning her arms to her sides as he wrapped it around her shoulders. One loop cinched tight just across the top of her breasts. The next jammed in hard against the underside. Emery led the rope down to her waist, and circled her hips, and Dara gasped as it dug into her flesh painfully tight.

Then he twisted the rope, fed a loop through the front of the one he'd just circled her waist with, and dropped it down her belly. He reached in between her legs, took the rope, and pulled it back through her legs, then yanked it up.

Dara's eyes bulged and she cried out in pain. The rough rope jammed up into her soft mound, crushing up into her sensitive, pink furrow as Emery pulled the rope up between her buttocks and tied it off tightly at the small of her back.

Then he lifted her up, and to her surprise, slammed her back against the wall. She felt him tugging at the ropes behind her chest, and then she dropped and cried out again as she lay hanging there against the wall.

She hung from a hook somehow, helpless as a newborn. The rope cut into her flesh as it took up her weight, and she groaned weakly.

Most of her weight was coming down on the thick strand between her legs, and her pussy ached as her legs trembled and shook. Her bare feet pushed feebly against the wall and she gasped as the loop beneath her breasts dug up harder.

Emery pulled on his ragged pants and walked across the room to the back, where there was an ancient wood burning oven and began to feed it cords of wood.

From time to time Dara kicked her heels against the wall, struggling to break free, but Emery continued to ignore her.

"Emery! Set me down!" she moaned.

The aroma of cooked meat began to waft through the room, and Dara realized it had been some time since she'd eaten. Her aching throat watered and she stared past him at the frying pan and the venison steak sizzling on the stove. He'd probably poached it somewhere, she thought weakly.

The pressure of the rope dug in harder and harder against her pussy, and no matter how much Dara twisted and jerked, no matter how she pulled and slapped her legs, she could do nothing to lesson the terrible growing ache, an ache that soon had her sobbing in misery and the frustration which came from unrelenting pain.

"Please," she moaned. "Please!"

Emery brought his steak across to the table and sat down, ignoring the whimpering blonde girl. He sliced a thick chunk of meat and popped it into his mouth, chewing hungrily.

Dara groaned and he looked up finally.

After a moment of visible indecision he stood up, pushing back his rough chair, moved over to her and then gripped her hips. He lifted her up with ease, and Dara almost sobbed with relief as the pressure came off her aching sex.

Emery dropped her to her feet and she immediately fell to her knees. He released her hips, gripping her hair instead, forcing her to crawl forward on her knees until she was beside the table.

He sat again, and resumed his meal, glancing down at her occasionally as he ate. Dara hung her head, panting, her body still aching from the tight clutch of the rope.

Emery cut off another piece of steak and then carefully placed it in the palm of his hand. He turned and lay the hand out in front of her.

Dara jerked her head up, staring up at him, then at his hand. Her mouth began to water and her stomach rumbled. Yet somehow, despite all he had already done to her, something inside her shrank from taking food from him like this.

He grinned, watching her fight for control, and the grin broadened as, with a moan, her head came forward and her tongue lapped at the meat and took it from the palm of his hand.

She felt shamed as he patted her head, but chewed ravenously on the meat, ignoring the ache in her sore throat as she swallowed.

He cut another piece and ate it, watching her with a smirk, and Dara looked up hopefully, ignoring the shame which clawed at her.

He let her take another piece from his fingers, then later another, and another, each time petting her as though she were an animal which had learned a trick.

He reached down for her, then and grasped her by one arm. His strength was enormous and he half lifted her upwards even as her legs scrabbled for purchase on the floor. He dragged her up across his lap so she sat across it, and curled an arm in around her shoulder.

He fed her another piece from his fingers, then pulled back on her hair, bent in, and chewed along the nape of her neck.

His free hand cupped her breast, squeezing painfully, mauling it with his big sausage fingers. He pinched the nipple until she moaned and squirmed, then chuckled as he released it.

He hesitated, as if a thought had struck him, and he looked down at the nipple again. His thumb and forefinger pinched in against her areola so the stiff nipple pushed out, and he grinned as he inspected it.

He reached a hand up to his earlobe and flicked at the skull earring dangling there.

"You like?" he asked in a throaty growl.

Dara nodded shakily.

"Used to do it in prison, tattoos and piercings. Cigarette for a piercing, a pack for a tattoo."

He looked down at her and his face twisted into an ugly smile. "You want a tattoo?"

Dara shook her head frantically and he chuckled darkly.

"Maybe you don't know what you want."

He stood with Dara in her arms, and carried her across the room, dropping her in the big armchair.

"Wh-what are you doing?" she asked anxiously as he fumbled through the lower drawers of the cabinet.

"Looking for my old needle."

"I-I don't need a tattoo please," she gulped.

He grinned and came out with a small, ugly looking needle. A moment later he found two thin bands of stainless steel and returned to her.

"Emery! I don't want a..."

"Shut up!" he snarled.

He gripped her hair and yanked her head up and back across the top of the chair back.

Dara cried out in pain as her scalp burned, arching her back across the chair. She felt his big hand roughly seize her right breast.

"Emery! Please! No!"

"No tattoo," he said agreeably.

Dara gulped down her protest as she stared at the upside down world behind the chair. Then felt him squeezing her breast, felt him pinching at the base of her nipple. Her eyes widened.

No!

An intense flash of pain stabbed through her as Emery forced the needle into her nipple, then through it. She screamed, but the pain fled almost at once, leaving a low, throbbing ache behind. She felt Emery fumbling at her nipple, then abandoning that breast for the other.

She clenched her jaw, waiting, and another terrible pain tore into her as her other nipple was pierced. As before the pain faded almost instantly, and when Emery jerked her forward to drop down heavily onto the seat again she saw that the two small rings hung neatly from her pierced nipples.

She stared with shock and fascination.

Pierced! My nipples are pierced! I have pierced nipples!

Emery chuckled and ruffled her hair, then moved back to the cabinet and put his needle away.

"You owe me two cigarettes," he said.

Chapter Four

What am I turning into?
Dara examined herself in her mirror, looking at the nipple rings dangling from her pink buttons. She'd bought them herself, though, of course, hadn't told Lilly, at the pharmacy, they were intended for somewhere other than her earlobes.
This looks so hot!
She put her arms up behind her head, arching her back, and gave herself a pouty look as she examined the nipple rings.
She cupped her breasts, then ran a hand down her smooth, concave belly and in between her thighs. She winced slightly. Her pussy still ached, and her backside hurt even more. She felt shamed, in a way. But there was a wild, heady elation at what she'd done, in the daring and forbidden acts she'd experienced.
She felt feral and alive. She wanted to strut through town and grab every man she passed, force them to acknowledge her beauty, and then let them use her just like Emery had used her.
But there were few men like Emery, few men with that raw edged, barely contained violence and powerful strength.
Whore!
Not that there ever *was* an emergency.
She parked in her usual place at the station then looked down at herself a tad nervously, hoping her nipple rings weren't visible through her uniform. She got out of the car, feeling more than usually smug as she walked through the rear doors. What all of them; Bobbie, Joey, Mike, John, Peter, Delmar and the rest would do if they only knew that she was wearing rings in her nipples!
She knew they'd been masturbating to mental images of her since they'd been in high school together, and not a one had gotten so much as a touch. Little turds. For all they were responsible, respectable men they weren't half the *man* Emery was.
She gave her breasts a little squeeze through the blouse before rounding the corner, feeling a hot little rush of heat.
"Hey, Mike," she said, nodding cordially as she passed him.
"Dara. How you doin'."
Wouldn't you like to know, she thought, with a small private smirk.
She sauntered through the hall and picked up the reports on what incidents there were the previous day. She paused inside the squad room to pick up new batteries for her flashlight. They were in a

top cupboard. She reached up for them, standing on the balls of her feet, and as she did so the sleeves of her blouse slid back to reveal the darker skin where the leather of her own belt had cut into her wrists that first time she'd gone to see Emery.

The leather cut into her wrists as her breasts pushed against the back wall of the cabinet. Her hips ground against the lower shelf and her pushed out bottom ached as Emery dug his steely fingers into the underside of her buttocks and thrust himself deep into her pussy.

She swallowed and jerked her hands down, blinking her eyes at the sudden flashback. She looked around but no one had been looking.

She smiled to herself and looked around again.

Wouldn't they all be shocked!

She felt a little tremor run down her spine and reached up unconsciously as her nipples quivered. She could tell they were fully erect. She looked down and saw them pressed against her blouse.

How bizarre it seemed, here in this clean, cool, dry, brightly lit office to be thinking about that dark, sweltering little shack with its peeling paint and dirt covered floor.

"Dara."

"Wally," she said, looking up as he passed her by.

Her hand dropped to her bottom, smoothing over the material, and she imagined she could feel the belt slashing in against her and the sharp pain as it hit.

Her pussy began to throb, and she ran her fingers through her hair, shaking her head to clear it of the darkly seductive images.

She got through her shift that day, somehow. She'd kept fondling and toying with her nipple rings, and had gotten so hot once she'd shucked her pants right there in the patrol car and used her nightstick to pleasure herself, driving it up so hard and deep it ached - just like when Emery did her.

She hurried home, changed into a pair of tight denim shorts and a halter, then drove out to the highway and parked out of sight of the truck stop. She licked her lips nervously, then got out of the car and walked around to the front of the building.

Truckers were not a sophisticated bunch, and the magazines which sought to catch their eyes were crude and graphic. Dara felt her nervousness rise the moment she entered the shop. It was busy, and there were two men at the back leafing through the pornographic magazines.

Everyone looked at her, and she swallowed as she turned her eyes away, pretending not to notice. She walked to the back, ostensibly examining the more mainstream magazines, hoping the two men there would hurry and leave. When they did she was able to move closer to the porno magazines, and examine the titles.

She winced as she saw the covers which went with them. They all had enormous breasted women, or women with their legs spread open. Most of the ones Emery wanted were Black.

Another man shuffled to the back, and she knew there was no point putting things off. She snatched the first one "Black Slut!" then the second "Spread wide". She moved over and picked up "Deep Cunt" and "Pink Gash", then "Splatter".

The man was looking at her with interest, eyes moving up and down her body as she pulled down another porn magazine, no doubt imagining her naked.

She turned away, and hurried up to the front of the store, blushing. There was a fat bellied middle aged man behind the counter. He raised his eyes at her as she dumped the magazines on the counter in front of him, then ostentatiously examined the magazines for prices.

"Lessie," he said. "Deep Cunt is three ninety five."

He punched the numbers into an antiquated machine as other men in the store turned at the words. Dara felt herself flushing.

"Black Slut... Hmm? Can you see how much Black Slut is, honey?" he asked, showing her the picture of a huge breasted Black woman with her legs spread.

"Three fifty," she gulped.

"Yeah, right. Black Slut is three fifty," he said, punching in the numbers.

Another man moved to stand behind her at the counter holding a carton of cigarettes. Then another man lined up behind him carrying several bags of chips and a coke.

"Pink Gash. That's four bucks," the man at the counter said, leering at her. "I like pink gash myself," he said.

Dara looked away, face burning.

"Screwed and Branded," he said, picking up the magazine and leafing through it. "Never saw this one afore. You got any interestin' tattoos, honey?"

"No," she growled.

He grinned, his eyes dropping to her chest, then he did a double take, and Dara realized her nipple rings would be prominently displayed through the thin halter.

"Always wanted to see a girl with pierced nipples," he said, punching in the numbers.

He set the magazine down and picked up the next, looking at her breasts. "That musta hurt some."

"Just punch in the fuckin' price, okay?" Dara snapped.

"Okay, okay. No need to take offense. We're a broad minded bunch here, ya know."

"Yeah, minded to fuck broads," one of the men in line said with a snicker.

"That'll be twenty four ninety eight," he said. "Sorry we don't have none with men in em. Well, cept for men fuckin' these ah, models here. Maybe next time."

"They ain't fer me, okay!" she snapped, slapping the money down.

"No? Ain't that strange. I had a gal like you I sure as hell wouldn't be wasting my time lookin' at dirty magazines."

Dara snatched the magazines and hurried out of the store, ears burning as she caught bits and pieces of obscene comments from behind.

Goddam Emery anyway! What'd he want these for with her there?

Bastard was probably just wanting to embarrass her.

But it was done. She tossed the magazines onto the floor of the car and quickly pulled around the building, heading back for Kainlen County - and Emery.

She rubbed her pussy as she drove, feeling a tingling spread over her body the nearer she got. She felt herself becoming breathless as the anticipation mounted. What would Emery do to her tonight? How bad would that thirteen inches of black cock feel as it was jammed up into her body?

And how good would it make her feel?

She pulled the car off the road and behind the bushes, then scooped up some brush and placed it over the hood. Heart pounding, she gathered up the magazines, and made her way up the weed filled path to the little shack of a house.

She took a deep breath, knocked, then pushed open the door.

There was no sign of Emery, but she heard sounds coming from the bedroom and moved forward, just reaching the doorway when a large figure came forward.

Dara stared, shocked.

"Who the fuck are you?"

It was a Black woman, a very tall, very powerful looking Black woman with broad shoulders and large breasts. She was wearing nothing but a G-string and glaring angrily at Dara as she gaped back at her.

"What the fuck is this?" she demanded, snatching the magazines out of Dara's hands and looking at them.

"You the bitch whore been fuckin' my man?" she demanded.

"I-I...Didn't...I-"

Dara was stunned as the angry woman pushed forward.

"You is, isn't you? Fuckin' bitch!"

"But I- ."

The woman's fist slammed into Dara's jaw and threw her up and back across the room. She staggered and fell back against the wall near the old buzzing refrigerator, then slid to the floor as the woman stalked forward. Before she could gain possession of her senses the woman slammed a foot in between Dara's spread legs and pain ripped through her.

"You like that big cock, bitch?!"

The woman grabbed at Dara's shorts and yanked them furiously down and off, then as the blonde girl tried to climb to her knees ripped off her halter. Dara screamed as the woman caught at her hair and yanked her head up and back, then punched her in the side.

Dara fell heavily to the floor.

"That cock is mine, bitch!"

Dara kicked up at her and the woman jumped back, then grabbed at her foot, lifting it upwards, pulling it high into the air. Then she slammed her foot down hard against Dara's sex, once, twice, three times, as the blonde girl screamed and sobbed in dazed pain.

The Black woman dropped Dara's leg, then knelt beside her. She gripped her slim right wrist and forced it up high behind her back, then did the same with her left. Utensils went flying as she yanked a drawer right out of the wall and it dropped on the floor. She plucked a roll of rough cord from it and wound it tightly around one arm just above the elbow, then used her knee to jam the two arms together, winding it around the second arm.

She bound the sobbing blond girl's wrists up high beneath her neck and forced her elbows back together, the cord whipping around her slender limbs faster and faster.

"I got some left over. What should I do with it. Bitch?"

She yanked up on Dara's hair, lifting her torso off the kitchen floor. Ignoring her scream of pain she wound the rough cord in around Dara's right breast, looping it and then yanking tight. Dara howled in pain as the cord cut into the soft flesh of her breast. The woman changed hands, brought the cord back across behind Dara, then wound it around her left breast, once more looping it and yanking the loop viciously tight.

"Fucking White whore! You want something big up your pussy I'll give it to you!"

She yanked open the old fridge and pulled out a cucumber, thick and long and green, then stabbed it against Dara's pussy as if it were a weapon.

Dara had been moist and ready, in anticipation of another hard riding, but even so the cold, hard vegetable jammed against her opening, refusing to enter as she sobbed and moaned and twisted in pain.

The Black woman cursed, pulled out a wad of butter, and shoved that against Dara's sex, rubbing the cucumber over it, then thrusting it against her pussy. The slick butter eased its path, and Dara felt her sex spreading, opening, wider and wider. She groaned and sobbed.

"Please! Don't! I didn't know!"

"You gonna know, bitch!"

The cucumber was even wider than Emery's cock, and Dara sobbed as her pussy lips strained tautly. The woman slapped at the bottom of the cucumber and it slid forward, deeper and deeper. Dara shuddered and trembled as it slid upwards into her pussy sleeve until no more than inch remained

"You like that bitch?" the woman sneered, squeezing her belly. "Maybe that's what you doin' here? Looking ta get yer pussy filled?"

"Please! Please! Please!" Dara sobbed through tear filled eyes.

The woman yanked her up onto her knees, rising as well, then glared down at her.

"Whas your name, bitch!?"

"D-D-Dara," she whimpered.

"You been fuckin' my man, bitch!"

"I'm sorry," Dara whimpered.

"I'd cut your bitch throat but Emery don't like it when I do things like that. So you can wait until Emery gets back and we have this out. But you ain't waitin' here."

She yanked her hair and forced the moaning girl to her feet, then kicked at her bottom as she threw her towards the door. "Outside, bitch!"

Dara staggered and then stumbled to her knees outside in the dirt. She felt bow legged, the thick cucumber aching as it filled her abdomen.

The woman gripped her by the hair and yanked her to her feet, pulling her into the small work shack, then glared around her. She spotted an old sawhorse in a corner and dragged her towards it.

"Get on, bitch. You like riding' so much, you can ride this."

Dara cried out as the woman forced her to straddle the rough sawhorse, and felt the wood jam up against her thighs.

"Sit down, bitch."

"Please, I didn't - ."

A slap rocked her head to the side and the woman forced her head back painfully, then kicked her foot out from under her. Dara screamed as her weight crushed down against the narrow top of the sawhorse, and the cucumber was forced deeper into her belly. Cramps rippled through her body as she stumbled frantically to lift herself up, but the woman stepped on her toes and she screamed again.

"You're goin for a ride, bitch."

The woman picked up a length of old rope and bent, snatching up Dara's left foot, then pulling it up and back behind her. She wrapped the rope around her ankle, yanked it tight, then pulled it up against the sawhorse behind her. She moved around to the other side as Dara blubbered and moaned and kicked her in the ankle, then yanked that one up and back, too.

Dara's eyes bulged and a violent tremor rocked her body. Her entire weight came down on the top of the sawhorse, which forced the cucumber fully into her body. She screamed helplessly, her insides exploding with agony, as the woman tied her ankle up back behind her.

"Now you can take your ride, slut," she sneered.

She stomped out of the shack and slammed the door behind her, leaving Dara alone.

Sweat beaded on Dara's forehead as pain ripped into her belly. Her insides were bloated, her guts aching as the fat, thick hard vegetable ground against her internal organs. For long minutes it was all she could do to cope with the pain inside her.

Then, slowly, it seemed to fade, or perhaps she merely grew numb to it. It became bearable, tolerable. It throbbed and throbbed, but she was able to almost ignore it. Almost.

Who was that horrible old bitch?!

Dara moaned to herself as she stared down at her bulging breasts. The cord cut into both breasts right next to her ribs, forcing the soft, malleable flesh out hard, like fat balls of flesh.

She hadn't put up much of a fight. She'd been taken completely by surprise, and so overpowered she felt shamed and miserable. She ran through "if only" scenes in her mind, all of which ended with her beating the hell out of the Black woman.

She felt the ache in her groin now that the pain in her belly had eased. Her soft mound was jammed hard against the narrow wood, with all her weight behind on top of it. She tried to ease the pressure by shifting her weight backwards, but could only go so far with her feet lifted up behind her and tied to the rear of the beam.

When she did manage to ease her weight back the pressure came down on her tail bone, and that soon began to ache too.

How had this happened? This hadn't been what she'd planned! It was all so unfair!

It was hot in the closed in little shack, and she moaned as the sweat began to drip down her face and run down between her breasts, to trickle slowly down her spine and between her buttocks. She moaned weakly, head dropping forward.

The pain against her sex was relentless. Her groin throbbed with a terrible ache she could not escape. Whenever she tried, easing her weight back onto her tail bone, she felt a lessening of the pressure, but then the pain on her tail bone would grow so terrible she had to lean forward again.

And every time she did that the pain seemed worse. And every time she leaned back the pain on her tail bone seemed worse.

The door opened and she moaned, raising her eyes to see Emery coming in, trailed by the Black woman. They walked up beside her and Emery looked down. With the light behind him she could not see his eyes in their deep-set sockets and shuddered as he towered over her. The woman had a sullen expression on her face and glared at her.

"Please Emery! Please let me down!" she moaned.

He looked down at her silently, then his hand came in behind her hair, gripped a loose fistful, and forced her head up and back.

"Ow! Ow! Emery, please!" she moaned, forced back onto her tail bone.

She felt his big fingers slide down onto her clitoris and rub lightly, then probe lower. His head turned towards the woman who shrugged.

"Cucumber," she spat. "I gave the bitch something big up her cunt, just like she wanted!"

Emery chuckled softly, deeply, his fingers rubbing against the top of her sex, then eased his grip on her hair and let her pussy crush down against the sawhorse again.

"Please, please, please, please, please!" Dara panted.

Emery moved deeper into the shack and rummaged around on a crowded work table. He returned and moved in front of her, turning his back as he worked on a post in front of the sawhorse. He turned, still not having spoken, and his hand moved silently towards her.

In the dim light she saw nothing until he plucked at one of her nipple rings, then the other, stretching them up and out towards the post and forcing her to lean forward and let her sex sink down onto the narrow board.

"Ow! Ow! Ow! Ow!" she gasped.

He stood back and she gasped as she realized he had slipped a wire through both nipple rings.

"E-Emery," she moaned, her voice shaking.

Emery chuckled again, his white teeth showing.

"You gotta be strong for me," he said with a wide grin. "You strong, baby?"

"I-I...y-yes," she whimpered.

"You strong enough? You stronger than Carla here?"

Dara blinked her eyes rapidly, sweat dripping into them.

"Yes," she gasped.

"You show me then," he said.

Then the two retreated, and Dara watched them go, filled with despair. She moaned as the door was slammed shut again, and the pain seemed to reach greedily and smugly up to engulf her again.

She sobbed piteously.

It hurts!

Her sex burned with the pain, and rocking back on her tailbone was no improvement at all. She couldn't go as far as she had before, and even rolling back a little stretched her nipples painfully.

Emery wanted her to feel pain. She could see the cruelty in his eyes when he came into the little shack, could sense the dark pleasure in him as he enjoyed her pain. She had always sensed it, she supposed, but paid it little heed. So it wasn't surprising he would test her like this. Strong? She would be strong.

Somehow.

Did he get off on her being in such pain, she wondered. Did it turn him on to see her naked and bound, tormented and broken?

Of course it did. The only revelation in that was the wonder she hadn't seen it before. Or perhaps she had but not cared. Or worse. Perhaps a part of her craved that cruelty and pain. She remembered the first time he had slashed the belt across her bare bottom, and the flash of heat and excitement which had accompanied the pain.

Oh it hurts! It hurts! It hurts! What a thing to do to a girl!

Outrageous. It was outrageous, shocking and wicked to hurt a girl like this, to torture her poor sex against a hard wooden board.

And something inside her flickered and then came alight at such outrage, at Emery's cruelty. It didn't matter that it was the woman, Carla, who had bound her and set her on the horse. It was Emery who kept her there. Emery who leered in pleasure at her pain. Emery who challenged her to bear up under it. Emery who was probably adding to the outrage by fucking his Black whore even then.

She felt a wave of self pity. And almost immediately afterwards the little fire of dark, masochistic hunger grew. She moaned and let her weight pull her back, only to sob at the burning in her nipples.

"Emery!" she cried. "Emery please!"

She moaned and hung her head, the pain beating at her.

"Emery!" she screamed.

It was not agony, but a deep, intense, throbbing ache which went on and on and on to the point of driving her insane. There was no relief, and as the sweat dripped down along her flanks, down from her straining breasts and down along her tightly bound arms she screamed in fury and outrage and frustration and misery, screamed until her lungs were out of air and she collapsed brokenly, sobbing.

Pain throbbed with every beat of her heart. Dara moaned and then gasped and whimpered as she tried to lean farther back. Her nipples burned like fire but surely that was better than that horrible pain in her sex. But then the pain in her tailbone grew more and more terrible and she broke and sobbed again, rocking forward, grinding her sex down against the board.

She threw her head back and shrieked but no one heard.

Her head fell forward again, whimpering, sweat dripping off her scalp

"Please," she whispered, her voice low and gravelly.

She was aware of the rising sexual heat inside her, aware of the flickering fires of her own dark masochistic nature basking in the pain. But the pain was such it could only briefly distract her.

As it rose, however, as it twined its tendrils around her mind, it strengthened and spread out, and almost unconsciously she began to rock back and forth on the sawhorse. Her eyes were dull slits as she moved, shifting her weight slowly forward, then back so the flare of shifting pain.

Slowly, the pain was being pushed into the background, the sensual heat rising to enfold her. She rocked faster, grunting softly, dully. She leaned forward, further and further, and let out a soft cry of agony as the top of the wooden beam drove up a little deeper between her aching pussy lips and ground against the end of the cucumber. That in turn ground the cucumber even harder into her belly. With that came a flare of pain and something else.

The pain was dulled, numbed, but the wicked burning pleasure was sharp and fiery. She leaned forward again, groaning with the pain and gasping at the pleasure.

Her mind suddenly flashed back to the station, the crisp, clean air, the bright florescent light, the neatly dressed people walking back and forth, their heels clicking on the polished linoleum tiles, sipping coffee and sodas, telling small jokes, leaving through reports. They were doing that now. Right that second. The Sheriff was sitting at his desk, grumbling at some report. Norma would be at her desk taking phone calls from old ladies who had nothing better to do with their time. Maybe Bobbie and Levon would be gossiping about the women they knew, maybe even about her.

She flashed back with a startled moan, blinking the seat out of her eyes, gasping in the moist, overheated, shut in air of the dark shack. She felt a little shudder of wicked satisfaction. Not a one of them knew. Not a one would even guess. And oh how their eyes would bug out if they could see her that second.

She rolled back again on her tailbone, which ground down on

the hard wood as her nipples screamed. A flash of fire ran up her spine and she let out an inarticulate cry of shocked pain.

But again the pleasure outpaced it, and the dazed girl began to rock on the sawhorse the pleasure grew from a storm into a maelstrom. Her head fell back, her back arching, she began to ride the horse in earnest. The muscles of her legs began to work, to lift her up, ever so slightly, and drop her down again. Again and again, despite the sweat dripping down her pale, feverish body, she rode the horse, grunting and gasping and whimpering with effort until the orgasm screamed down around her and caught her up in its embrace.

She screamed herself, her head thrown violently backwards. She began to bounce frantically atop the horse, grinding and jamming her aching sex down against the hard wood as the climax bubbled and boiled and burned through her nervous system.

They were in the room, she realized, watching her. She wasn't able to think in any kind of coherent fashion, wasn't able to form words or thoughts. But the awareness of their presence intruded upon her and she gloried in it. That they would see her at her sluttish worst, see her glorying in her own degradation and agony, was desperately exciting.

Her climax spiralled higher and higher as she bucked and jerked and rode the horse with maddened desperation, and then slowly collapsed, seeping away from her despite all attempts to cling to it.

She sank down exhaustedly and the pain began to rise once again.

Emery chuckled softly, his teeth white in the dark shack. He slid a hand down between her quivering thighs and a huge finger probed against her clitoris.

Despite the pain Dara hissed as it made contact, a lightning bolt of sexual electricity ripping through her. He gripped her hair again, forcing her head and body back, and began to rub carefully at her clitoris.

The pain tore at her nipples and burned at her tail bone, and Dara shuddered, tears filling her eyes again as her breath came in frantic little puffs and pants. But she made no protest. The sex heat had blossomed like sun between her legs and her body was already beginning to tremble with sexual fever.

"Ungh! Ungh! Ungh! Ungh!" she grunted, eyes rolling wildly.

He stopped suddenly, stepping away. She moaned, rocking forward onto her sex, as he folded his massive arms across his chest. Then he turned and walked away.

Dara hung her head, deep in shame and pain and misery as the Black woman leaned in. "Fucking whore!" she spat. She hurried after Emery, slamming the door, and Dara was alone once more.

She whimpered piteously, but her despair was delayed. The

sexual need was too great, and she began to slowly rock and jerk back and forward.

And then the door was flung open again. She turned her shaking head in hopes of seeing Emery, but it was her again, and she smirked cruelly, brandishing another cucumber.

"You got room, bitch," she said.

Dara stared uncomprehending, eyes slits, sweating face pale and dull, jaw slack. And then Dara saw Emery in the doorway and felt a wave of lust and excitement and... something more. There was a challenge in his eyes, and she turned to see the woman as she moved forward

The woman moved up beside her and Dara tried her best to glare, to show her that she wasn't at all frightened, not the least bit in pain, to show her what contempt she felt. And then the woman pushed on her head, forcing her to rock far forward,

Dara cried out as her sex rolled down onto the narrow edge of the board. The pain was terrible, and she was momentarily breathless. Her nipples were now being yanked upwards by the taut wires, stretched to the tearing point.

She felt the woman's fingers between her sweating buttocks, jamming against her aching anal opening. Then the cucumber was thrust against her.

"No," she whimpered, her voice hoarse. "You bitch!"

"Show us how strong you are, baby," Carla sneered. "Think you can take two of `em? Hmm? Gonna burst into tears again?"

Dara spat towards her weakly. "I can take anything," she said hoarsely.

The cucumber rammed forward hard through her sweating opening, riding a slippery coating of butter, and Dara choked as it pushed deeper, inch by inch cramming and grinding up into her already aching belly.

"Like that? Want me to stop?"

"More!" she croaked. "I want more of it! Deeper!"

Carla sneered and thrust hard then eased the pressure on her back, and Dara began to rock backwards. She gasped and halted as the base of the cucumber pressed against the edge of the board.

"Want more?" Carla asked in a silky voice.

And a hand shot out, gripped her hair, and yanked her back. Hard.

Several more inches of thick cucumber slid up into her anus and her eyes bugged out, her body shaking violently. She threw back her head to scream and - came.

The orgasm took her like a hurricane, and drops of sweat pattered to the floor around her as convulsions wracked her body. Jaw slack, head back, she gurgled in mindless, feverish ecstasy, twisting and grinding and shaking atop the sawhorse as the pleasure roared over her in waves and swept her away.

She felt them fumbling at her ankles, undoing the rope, and wept in relief as they lifted her off the horse. She moaned incomprehensibly as they carried her across to Emery's small house and into the bedroom then spread her arms and legs, binding them to the four corners of an old brass bed.

She was just alert enough then to see that it was the woman, Carla, who stripped and climbed into the bed with her. She stared dazedly at her, noting the woman's feral gaze as she straddled her body.

Then the woman was laying atop her, fingers digging into the soft flesh of Dara's breasts, lips caressing her nipples, teeth chewing at her areolas. Emery, she saw, sat back and watched, and she moaned, wanting him to join her.

The woman whispered into her ear, but Dara didn't hear. She lay her head back and groaned exhaustedly as the woman began to lick her way down her overheated body.

Her pussy flared with agony at the woman's first touch, and she arched her back, crying out.

She heard low chuckles, and the woman's fingers eased aside. Then something softer and warm gently caressed her throbbing sex.

She moaned as the woman's tongue began to glide through the soft, swollen, aching folds of her pussy. As soft as it was it still ached, but in a deliciously sensual way. Her wrists and ankles pulled feebly against the straps Emery had set around them and she groaned weakly, staring up at the ceiling.

The woman's tongue was insistent, dipping lightly in between the sore, burning slit, teasingly circling her sore clitoris, then coursing back down to the bottom of her sex.

Emery yanked the pillow out from under her head, then climbed in to squat just above her. He reached down and roughly yanked her head back hard, so it was almost upside down and staring back at him, then thrust his erection into her mouth.

Dara was too dazed and too weak in mind and body to even realize he was there before his cock was sliding down through her throat. Her hands jerked against the straps, but to no effect, and her back arched as he rolled her head backwards.

Emery slid himself into her until her face was jammed against his groin and his testicles sat on her eyes, then caressed her exposed throat as he chuckled cruelly.

"This throat feels a little dry," he said. "Guess I should have given you something to drink first."

"You wet it down, baby," Carla said.

Her tongue slid along Dara's slit and the blonde girl moaned, her legs jerking spastically as she rolled her hips.

"Does that hurt?" Carla cooed.

Dara's pussy sparkled with pain and the wonderful relief its absence brings. She had no idea how long she had been sitting straddling the sawhorse, but it had seemed like forever, and she had thought she might go insane with the constant pressure and pain against her poor mound.

What remained was painful enough, bruised tissue and muscle, but compared to what she'd been through it felt glorious. And the soft pink tongue skating along it was drawing pins and needles of pleasure and pain to her aching groin.

Emery was pumping his cock back and forth in her throat now, one hand in her hair, the other moving roughly over her breasts, squeezing and fondling, pinching and slapping them as he used her for his pleasure. He pulled out briefly to let her cough and gulp in air, then sheathed himself once again, forcing her head even further back with both hands as he thrust straight down her throat with hard, pitiless strokes.

"Swallow, bitch," he growled, reaching out to slap one of Dara's breasts.

He looked up at Carla, watching as she tongued the girl's slit, and glared with dark angry eyes.

"Don't play with your food, bitch. Eat!"

Carla licked more energetically, her fingers now joining in, and Dara's hips ground up harder as the pain rose inside her. But the pleasure rose as well, and she groaned wetly around Emery's plunging cock.

Dara whimpered and moaned, her hips bucking upwards now, twisting from side to side. Her belly groaned with the thick girth of the two cucumbers embedded within her pussy and anus and she felt the churning rush of heat and energy begin to overpower the pain and turn her insides to churned jelly.

She felt prying fingers digging into her sex, forcing her aching pussy lips aside, and the pain rushed around her. Then she felt movement deep in her belly, and her mind groaned in delight as the pressure against the deepest part of her pussy finally eased. A flood of relief swept through her as the cucumber gave another lurch and jerked back down along her straining tunnel.

As the thicker part of the cucumber pushed out her pussy lips spread wider, and the added tautness blew her over the edge.

It was a different kind of climax now. It was not shockingly overpowering as those she had felt earlier. Her body was too exhausted, too drained. Instead of the ripsawing crackling of lightning she felt a deep, soothing, glorious wall of rapturous bliss overcome her. Her limbs strained against the straps with a slow, continuous, trembling. Her back, already arched, twisted even further as her hips rolled gloriously from side to side.

She felt the cucumber pull back further, felt it as a distant thing, but somehow important. Then it thrust back into her and the orgasm, starting to soften, peaked once again. Her eyes rolled back in her head as the rapture continued.

Emery's cock was a constant, pumping steadily up and down in her throat, but this time it was no part of her orgasm, almost a distraction. The cucumber pulled back, then thrust back into her, almost all the way, filling her, and again she quivered, the orgasm rising.

She felt Carla's tongue on her clitoris, whipping firmly back and forth, and a small part of her knew a sense of outrage that a woman, particularly *that* woman was daring to touch her in so intimate a fashion.

Bitch.

But it was the merest whisper of a thought at the back of her mind.

Emery was thrusting faster, his testicles slapping against her face as he drove himself powerfully into her throat. She couldn't breath, and didn't care. And the light headed state only added to her sense of joy and bliss and glory as the orgasm rolled onward.

"You gettin' enough sleep, girl?"

Dara blinked sleepy eyes and then repressed a yawn. "Yeah, fine Uncle Bert."

"You're lookin' run down a lot lately. You gotta stop spending all night dancing."

"I'm not... really."

"How come your voice is off then?"

"I just got a bit of a cold, I guess," Dara said, flushing slightly.

Her throat felt raw and her voice was rough from the abuse Emery had given it.

"Take some cough drops or something."

She nodded, feeling bizarrely smug and nasty. He couldn't have the least idea why her throat was sore, not the least idea. And oh how shocked he'd be if he knew, if he imagined for even a moment that the reason was the enormous black cock which had been jammed down her gullet with such frenzied lust the day before.

"Your momma will roast me if she finds out you're out partying every night. And if she does you can be damn sure who I'll take out on."

"I'm fine," she said.

"Well good, there's a man comin' in this morning from the Drug Enforcement Agency."

"A fed? What for?"

"Dunno. Except it has to do with drugs, of course. And you."

"Me?"

"Well, your area, the Okinawi River area. You know it as well as anyone around here so I figured you oughto sit in."

"Great!"

"Don't get too excited. Either he's wasting our times or he figures there's something to do with a major drug ring in that area. Neither is any reason to be pleased."

"Major drug ring? Around Okinawi?" Dara scoffed. "They supposed to be selling to the squirrels and possums?"

The Sheriff grinned and shrugged, then sat back in his chair, which creaked at the weight.

"All I know is what I done told you. We're just gonna have to wait until this feller shows up and starts talking."

The DEA man, when he did arrive, was a tall, young Hispanic man with longish hair and an attitude which immediately began to grate on Dara's nerves. He seemed condescending towards them, towards their town, and even towards Mississippi. He came from New York, which she thought of as the home of the most arrogant Yankee northerners in America, and she looked on resentfully as he lectured her uncle about drugs and smuggling.

"You have to remember that the Terrigan river empties right into the Mississippi," he said, "and from there the drugs can float easily all the way up through the heart of the country."

"So why wouldn't they just run them up from the mouth of the Mississippi where it starts in the Gulf?" she demanded.

"Because we're paying a lot of attention there, both watching for boats offshore and searching barges moving north. If they come up through here they can bypass almost all our regular search activities."

"We'd notice if there were any strangers around," she said.

"Doesn't have to be strangers. We're not talking about a lot of people here."

"Why would they even need anyone?"

His brows lined in annoyance.

"They're careful people. They ship them a little at a time up the Okinawi, and then store them somewhere around. Then when they've got a sizeable amount it goes up the Okinawi to the Terrigan and on to the Mississippi and then north."

"Sounds pretty stupid to me."

"Nobody asked you your opinion," her uncle said in irritation.

"The most likely people to be taking care of the transhipment are those living in a rural area with ready access to both rivers, without nearby neighbours."

"That could be most anyone," she scoffed.

"All we're asking at the moment is for you to keep your eyes out for people acting suspiciously, people who suddenly have a lot more money than they should, who disappear for unexplained reasons, especially at night."

"People around here tend to mind their own business," her uncle said, rubbing his jaw. "Hard to pick one out who's gone off somewhere if it's only for a few hours."

The man, his name was Hernandez, nodded. "We realize that. But sooner or later these people invariably make it obvious they have an unexplained source of wealth."

Invariably? What sort of word was invariably, Dara thought in resentment. Big shot northern wetback thinks he can talk down to us with his big words. Thinks he's so good. Why, Emery would break him in half without working up a sweat.

As always when she thought of Emery a little flush came to her face, and a sensation of guilt and excitement filled her.

Dara was coming to feel more and more as though she were living a secret life, as if she were different from all the people who moved around her during the day. As if she were a stranger in the town where she'd spent her entire life.

At times she was filled with shame, at other times wicked glee. Sometimes she felt naked, even as she walked along the halls of the station, as if that were her natural state and wearing her uniform was nothing but a foolish lie. She had the urge to strip down and walk as a naked sluttish wild woman right down the hall so everyone could see what she was. What a sensation she would be! The whole county would be talking about her for years!

She wandered back into the hall as the Sheriff and Hernandez shook hands, feeling put upon. She wanted to go back and see Emery again, and her insides twisted every time she thought of it, but she knew that bitch was still there, and her face flamed whenever she thought of her. She thought she could still taste the woman's sex against her mouth, and made a vile face at the thought.

What a sick thing that was, licking a woman down there. You could tell she was a city girl. No country girl would ever think of such a wicked thing. What was her last name anyway? Maybe she was wanted by the police somewhere.

Dara smiled as she let herself imagine having Carla in handcuffs, maybe taking a billy club to her as she lay curled up in a cell. That would show the bitch. She looked around, then reached down to cup her pussy lightly. It was still sore and aching from that ride on the sawhorse.

Yet it wasn't the pain Carla had caused her which burned in her mind, but the pleasure she had forced upon her. Dara did not like to see herself as weak, and certainly not weaker than another woman. But coming like that, coming and coming as the bitch had sneered at her for it, that was almost too much to bear.

She pushed open the door to the street and wandered out into the hot midday sun, pulling her cowboy hat down a little lower to shade her eyes and reaching into her breast pocket to pull out her sunglasses.

There was a folded up piece of paper in the pocket her glasses had come from, and another in the second breast pocket. They were needful, she had decided, in case someone noticed the little bumps of her nipples where the rings were dangling. She didn't have to wear them to work, of course, but couldn't bear to part with them. Wearing nipple rings around regular people made her feel wild and wicked and smug. She was probably the only girl in town, maybe in the whole county who had her nipples pierced.

But people would start asking questions if they knew, start wondering why, and who'd done it. Then they'd be watching her more closely, and their minds would turn nasty if they suspected who she was spending her time with.

She saw herself in a shop window as she passed, kind of hunched over. She straightened. She was always doing that, kind of scrunching as if it could hide her height.

She sighed and pushed open the door to the drug store. Stephanie Jones was behind the counter, and greeted her as she took a Coke from the machine and wandered up. She'd been in her classes all through high school and was now married to Ed Rawlins, with two kids at home and expecting a third in three months..

"Hey, Dara."

"Hey, Steph. What you doing?"

"Nothing. Just trying to survive the heat."

"Yeah, it's a scorcher."

"Kids hate it. They can't sleep and are crying all the time.'

Dara made a face, thinking of the life she was supposed to be leading by then, pushing out babies and getting up several times every night to feed them, working at a dull job and dealing with a dull witted husband.

Stephanie looked tired and much older, and Dara couldn't help thinking how much she'd aged in the few years since school. Dara didn't feel as if she'd aged herself, not even a bit.

"What about you? Still partying every night?"

Dara shook her head. "Don't have the money for that."

"Ain't that the truth. Things are so expensive these days."

She moved across to serve a lady at the cosmetics counter, and Dara watched her with a jaundiced gaze, shaking her head. All the fun they used to have, and now Stephanie was an old lady mother, working all day and going home to whining brats at night. She wondered what Ed was like in bed but couldn't believe he was anything but one of those slam-bang-thank-you-ma'am types. Stephanie'd sure never been ridden by a great powerful, wild man like Emery, and now she never would. Stephanie'd experienced about all the excitement she was going to by the time she finished high school.

Dara took another drink, vowing to do things; nasty things, exciting things, wild and wicked things. She was going to see the world, too, maybe with Emery. He wouldn't want that bitch over her for much longer. She was sure of that. He was probably tired of her already and wishing she'd go back wherever she came from.

She thought about Hernandez and her resentment surfaced once again. What business did he have being a big shot federal agent and getting to travel all over the place like that while she was stuck in dumpy Kainlen County? She wondered how to apply to join the DEA, or maybe the FBI or someplace like that. They were trying to get women, or so the TV said. But then she didn't have the education. They wanted college girls.

Like college girls were good for anything, she snorted sulkily. They'd probably scream and run away on their fancy high heels the second anyone said boo to them.

"Like makeup is gonna help her ugly puss," Stephanie said, coming back as the customer left.

Dara nodded and grinned.

"So tell me about this Spanish guy."

"What Spanish guy?"

"You know, the federal guy."

"How'd you hear about him?"

"Hell, Dara, everyone in town knows by now. He's staying at the Gilmour motel. He's supposed to be gorgeous."

"I don't think so," Dara sniffed.

"So what's he look like?"

"Skinny. He's got long hair. Talks like a Yankee. Uses big words."

"Mmm, don't like him, huh?"

Dara shrugged.

"You don't like many men. I swear, Dara. Sometimes I wonder if you aren't one of those lesbian types."

Dara glared at her, thinking of Carla.

"I ain't no lezzie!" she snapped.

"Well when're you gonna get married? If you ain't no lezzie you're sure a damn site high with your standards. Already most of the good ones are taken. What do you think you're gonna be left with?"

"Maybe I'll move to Atlanta or Dallas or somewhere there's real men," Dara said defiantly.

Stephanie laughed. "With what money? What'd you even do there? Work in a shop? Without your uncle being sheriff I don't think you'll get to be a deputy, or whatever they call em there."

"There's lots to do in a big city. I'd find something."

"You been saying that for years."

Dara finished her Coke and banged it down heavily on the counter.

"Oh don't get mad," Stephanie said. "I was just teasing."

Dara was mad, but, she realized, not so much at Stephanie as at herself, and at not being able to go to see Emery that night.

"Never mind," she said. "I gotta go."

"You ain't mad at me are you?"

Dara shook her head, and pushed out into the bright sun again.

That night she lay awake on her bed, sweating in the heat, unable to sleep. Several times her hands moved over her body, and she masturbated to orgasm, always thinking of Emery, of him and his huge cock, using her.

She was tired the next day, hot and tired, quick tempered and surly. It was Friday, and she ought to have been looking forward to the weekend, to partying and enjoying herself. But she hadn't made much money that week, and all she could think of was having to wait another few days and hoping the bitch would leave so she could see Emery.

She drove past the road leading to his small farm a half dozen times, pausing each time to look down its length as far as she could see, hoping to spot him walking along alone. She was called away to a loud argument at a bar, but returned, sitting and watching. As the day neared its end and the sun began to lower she stared with growing desperation, feeling a mixture of anger and yearning.

The radio called her, and she replied. Lou, the dispatcher, told her to call it a day and head on home. She started the car and hesitated, then turned onto the old dirt road.

The tires crunched over the dry earth and stones as she moved slowly along, sweating more heavily than ever now, her heart pounding as she drew nearer to his little farm. She halted, and parked, hardly able to breath with the tension in her chest. After long minutes of watching she opened the door and stepped out onto the empty road. Her legs seemed to shake a little, and she wiped her forehead once again, looking both directions for a sign of him or Carla.

She made her way up the weed strewn path to his door and put her ear to it, listening for voices. Then, licking her lips, and ready to fight if Carla was there, she opened the door and stepped inside. It took a moment for her eyes to adjust to the dim light, but when they did she found the front room and kitchen empty.

She moved forward warily, looking at the door to the bedroom, then reached it and peered inside. The bed was unmade, the sheets half on the floor in a tangle. She sniffed to herself as she looked around, her eyes focussing on the bed again. They'd probably done it there, that bitch.

She thought of Emery riding the woman as he'd ridden her and burned with jealousy.

The door opened behind her and she whirled around to see Emery coming through. A moment later, however, two more men came in behind him, and she inhaled deeply, her face flushing. One of the men spotted her and jumped in alarm. His hand flashed behind him and he pulled out a long knife. Dara barely had time to blink before Emery slapped it out of his hand.

"I see you later," he said to the two, his eyes on Dara.

The two men looked at her suspiciously, but they obeyed, the first one snatching up his knife and putting it back in his belt before shutting the door behind him. Emery stared across the small, dim room at Dara for a long moment, then strode forward. He reminded her of a lion as he approached, and she felt her legs tremble as he moved up in front of her.

He gripped the front of her uniform blouse and tore it open, as Dara had known he would. A wave of excitement and raw carnal need swept through her as he bent his head and bit at the side of her throat, his hands pushing the tattered blouse back over her shoulder so it fell behind her to the floor.

Dara's hands moved up over his shoulders and she groaned as she pressed her body against him. She felt his hands sliding down to squeeze her buttocks, the big fingers digging painfully into the soft flesh before rising and undoing her bra. He yanked it away, tossing it on the floor behind him, then eased back, grinning down at her cooly as he undid her belt and pulled off her gun. He tossed it onto the chair, then undid her pants and pushed them down.

Dara kicked off her shoes and stepped eagerly out of her pants, breathless with excitement as she straightened to face him. She threw herself into his arms, groaning in hunger as his hands moved roughly over her naked flesh.

Abruptly, he pushed her back, and he grinned cruelly in a way which made her toes curl. "Get that," he said, his voice a low rumble.

She followed his pointing finger to the top of the shelf, and a coil of rope laying atop it. Her heart skipped a beat and her insides seemed to melt. She drew in a deep breath, heart pounding, and moved to obey him, reaching up high to catch the coiled rope and taking it down, then returning to him.

He took it from her and tied a loop in the end, then held it out in front of her. Dara stared at it for a long moment, quivering, then put her trembling hands together and slowly pushed them through the loop. Emery yanked it tight, then curled the rope in under the loop, in between her wrists, twining it twice before lifting it high above, forcing her arms up and raising her to her toes.

She gasped, feeling the rope cut into her wrists, and stared up at him, almost light headed now with excitement as she waited his next move. He glanced overhead, and she followed his gaze to where rough two by fours supported the little roof. He threw the rope up and watched it sail neatly across one, dropping back to him. He drew that across to the old wood stove and tied to a leg there, then returned to her.

He circled her slowly, his hands moving out to cup her buttocks and squeeze, then pulling in. He cupped her breasts, then gripped the small nipple rings and pulled up and out, stretching her nipples to the point they stung, to the point she could no longer keep quiet and cried out softly. "Please," she moaned.

He let them go and moved behind her again. She felt his hand sliding down the cleft of her buttocks, easing in beneath her to cup her sex and squeeze. He pulled back and circled her again. He gripped her hair, forcing her head back, then bit down on the nape of her neck, his other hand squeezing one breast and twisting the nipple. He bent and took the nipple into his mouth, chewing on the flesh around it as his hand slid down her body and over her sex.

A thick, powerful finger drove up between the lips of her pussy and she gasped in pain and pleasure. A second joined it, then a third, spreading her open as he chewed roughly on her breast and nipple.

"What the fuck are you doin' with that white slut!?"

Emery lifted his head casually and smiled as Carla stormed into the cabin.

Dara tugged against the rope holding her wrists high but only made them dig in deeper against the soft skin of her wrists. She looked up anxiously at Carla, face red as the Black woman glared angrily at her.

"Dirty little White slut!" Carla snarled, swinging a fist at her.

Emery caught her hand and twisted her around to face him, then clutched her bottom with his other hand, bringing his lips down onto hers. She struggled briefly against him, then relaxed, and a moment later her arms slid up across his shoulders as their kiss grew in passion.

Dara tugged again against the ropes, looking nervously from side to side, feeling a growing sense of humiliation and jealousy. She watched Emery's hands slide down Carla's back, then peel up her tank top. There was no bra beneath and his hands moved up and down the broad expanse of her smooth Black skin as their lips rolled together.

His hands moved down into her pants, squeezing her bottom, then pushing the pants downwards to bare her lower body. Carla turned and sneered at Dara, then tugged off her pants to stand up naked. She dropped to her knees in front of Emery and took him in her hands, then began to lick at his thighs. She licked her way up to his testicles and began kissing and massaging them, then one by one took them into her mouth, moaning softly as she rolled them about with her tongue.

Dara could do nothing but look on, burning with embarrassment and anger as the Black woman took Emery's big cock into her mouth and, with a sideways smirk at Dara, slid her lips down half its length before pulling back. Her hands massaged his balls as she bobbed up and down, then she tilted her head back and took him straight down her throat, again giving Dara a sideways look of triumph as she swallowed the last inch.

Emery stood over her, eyes slitted, hands stroking her head as she worked her lips slowly back along his gleaming shaft, then abruptly pushed her head forward again, taking him deep before withdrawing. She pulled free and stood up, pushing Emery backwards into a straight backed chair, then straddled him. She turned again to sneer at Dara, then positioned his long, thick shaft and sank down onto it with a groan of pleasure.

"Fuck me, baby," she panted. "Fuck your Carla, baby."

She leaned forward and Emery began sucking and chewing on her breasts as she began to slowly ride up and down on his thick cock.

Dara pulled again at the rope, feeling humiliated by Emery's preference for Carla over her, and a burning jealousy as she watched the Black woman riding his beautiful cock. Her hands clenched into fists as Carla groaned in pleasure and rolled her head back.

"Oh God that's so good!" she moaned.

Emery clutched her buttocks and then leaned forward. He stood, lifting her in his arms as if the big woman were weightless, then carried her past Dara and into the bedroom. Dara turned, following them with her eyes as they disappeared. She could see only the lower third of the bed, and a moment later she saw Carla's feet and legs as high as the knees. She saw them spread wide as Emery appeared, then his body moved out of her vision, beyond the frame of the door, and she saw his lower legs between Carla's.

"Oh yes!" Carla groaned loudly.

Dara snarled, pulling again at the rope, but it would not loose her and she could not bring herself to call out to them, especially as Carla began to grunt and moan, and she saw the mattress beginning to rise and fall on its springs. She heard the low, rhythmic creak, heard it growing faster and faster. Carla began to cry out in pleasure, groaning and gasping and begging him for more, her voice filled with passion and pleasure, much of it, Dara was sure, for her benefit.

Carla screamed suddenly, a long, drawn out wail of ecstasy, and Dara saw her feet drop onto the bed from wherever they had been. They lay there, spread wide, for some time as the bed continued to creak, then spread and rose again, disappearing from sight.

On and on it went, as her arms grew cool and her back began to ache and she tried to shut out the sound of them or at least work up the courage to demand her release.

They went quiet, and then she heard very low voices murmuring. After a time the sighs and groans arose again, and the mattress began to bounce up and down, up and down as Dara watched jealously. She was sure her pussy was tighter, that she could give Emery more pleasure than that slut. If she only had a chance.

And despite her anger the sound and sight, and the knowledge that Emery was pounding his long, beautiful cock down into a woman, even Carla, began to warm her insides again. She squeezed her thighs together, hearing the gasps and groans from the other woman, wishing she could see Emery as he used her. She heard the harsh slap of flesh and thought it must be his hips smashing down against her upraised buttocks.

"Fuck her," she whispered. "Fuck the filthy whore. Pound her cunt!"

Carla groaned and panted and cried out again, a long, guttural sound of animal passion as she climaxed. Dara cursed her and envied her.

There was quiet again, and Dara's head hung low. Her back was stiff and her legs ached. She lifted one, then the other, bending her foot up and back against her bottom, growing tired of standing there straight-backed on the hard wood floor. She almost called out several times, but didn't want to give Carla the pleasure.

After more than an hour Carla appeared, wearing a pair of shorts and a bra. She gave Dara a long, slow smirk, then sashayed past her as if she weren't there. There was a hand pump in the corner of the kitchen, and she worked it to fill a bucket with cold water. Dara looked away, unable to face her, but the Black woman only smiled more broadly and moved up behind her.

"Ungh!"

Dara cried out as the woman seized her hair, her feet scrambling for purchase on the floor as her head was forced far back.

"Are you enjoying yourself out here?" Carla enquired. "Maybe you wish you had never come, hmmm?"

She bent and licked along the side of Dara's cheek, then in beneath her ear. Dara cried out again as the woman bit into her earlobe hard, twisting violently to pull herself free as Carla laughed in amusement.

She let go of Dara's hair, and as the blonde woman twisted around to face her, took a deep drink from the pot of water, then spat it onto her face. Again she laughed, backing away as Dara tried to kick her, and disappearing into the bedroom to kick the door closed behind her.

Dara stood in the darkened room, shoulders aching, legs and back stiff, feeling low and ill used, alternating between rage and misery, between shame and jealousy. It was hot and close in the small, still room, as the hours passed. She did not even think to call out now, for something seemed to have broken within her and the futility she felt gave way to hazy acceptance that what would be done with her would be done.

And then there was a knock at the door.

At first she thought it merely more of the noises which had been coming, off and on, from the bedroom, but it repeated, and she raised her head, then turned about to stare at the narrow cabin doorway. It was poorly constructed, the wood warped, and she could see movement beneath. She held her breath, tugging weakly at the rope, hoping whoever it was went away, but they knocked again, louder.

There was a curse from the bedroom, and the door was pulled open, letting light spill out into the nearly dark front room. Emery appeared, naked, carrying a lantern in his hand, and went through the room to the front door. He pulled it open, and Dara tried to cringe back as she saw two men in the light before him, the two who had been there earlier.

The three spoke together in quiet voices, and after a moment Emery laughed throatily, turning his head to look at her, then turning back to speak again to the two black men. He nodded, then closed the door before coming back to stand before her. Carla appeared in the bedroom door and leaded against the frame, looking on sullenly as Emery smiled down at Dara.

"My friends," he said, his lips inches from her ear. "They want to use you."

Dara gasped as his big hand slipped between her legs and cupped her sex.

"They want to use you hard."

His fingers were thrust up into her pussy and Dara moaned in pain, forced to her toes. The fingers ached inside her, yet despite this she felt a suddenly blossoming arousal as his lips moved along her throat.

"You will do whatever they want."

"N-No!" Dara gasped.

His fingers pushed deeper.

"You do what they want because I say so," he growled. "And tomorrow, when Carla is gone, I will fuck you until you scream."

It was just about the longest he had spoken to her since they had met, and it was both a promise and a threat. Dara suddenly felt the sweltering room close about her as his fingers pushed deeply inside her and twisted, his thumb curling up to press against her clitoris and roll it from side to side.

"Don't!" she whimpered.

His lips curled up as he continued to stroke his thumb roughly back and forth across her clitoris.

Dara felt her legs going rubbery, forced onto her toes by the hard, almost painful thrusting up into the softness of her sex.

He pulled his fingers back down, then smeared the moisture they had absorbed across her face, his teeth white in the darkened room. He gripped her head suddenly and crushed his lips against hers, his tongue driving into her mouth. Dara felt herself melting against him, felt her body quivering with suddenly blazing arousal.

And he pulled back, strolled casually to the outer door and flung it open. Two eager pair of eyes stared in at Dara as he turned and walked calmly back towards the bedroom. Dara's eyes were wide as she stared after him, wanting to scream, to demand he release her, to order the strange men out. Yet she said nothing, and Carla smirked at her as Emery walked past her, backed in, and closed the door.

Dara's head whipped back as she saw the two men come forward, closing the door behind them. Shock and embarrassment flooded her as the men lifted the lantern and carried it forward, eyes ravishing her. She turned her head away, half turning her body as if to hide. She gasped as a hand cupped her bottom, and then the men were before her, grinning, leering, the front of their trousers bulging as they stared at her in a mixture of lust and awe.

"How ya doin', Deputy," one of them said with a sneer on his face.

The other man thrust his hand between her legs, squeezing her pussy painfully, and Dara's head jerked to him, then back as the first man cupped and squeezed her breasts. Both men seemed fascinated by the rings in her nipples, and each seized one, tugging and twisting it up and out until she gasped in pain.

"Ain't that somethin'," the second man said.

Their hands moved over her as Dara squirmed and twisted in pain and humiliation. Yet despite her anxiety and shame her body, already aching with need, responded to them, and she felt a thrum of electrical heat through her groin as fingers pushed up inside her, front and back, and hands squeezed and kneaded her breasts and buttocks. She was too ashamed to speak, to even look at them, and turned her head away.

One of them dropped his pants and drew out a thick erection.

"Ol Emery, we call him Horse," he said. "We's just little ponies, but I bet we give you a good ride anyways."

The other man snickered wildly as the first forced her legs apart on the floor, spreading them so that only the tips of her toes still held contact and she was almost hanging from her wrists. He held his cock in his hand and pressed the head up against her mons, rubbing it up and down along her moist, puffy opening. Then he grasped her buttocks, pulling her forward, and thrusting himself up inside her.

The penetration shocked her for but a moment, then she felt a sense of wonder and vast relief, as of a terrible itch finally scratched, a pain eased, a thirst quenched. She had felt so empty, so desperately yearning for Emery's hardness inside her. And though it was not Emery she groaned in satisfaction, savouring the sense of fullness as his erection lodged deep inside her belly.

He gripped her bottom with both hands, fingers digging into the soft, damp, pale flesh as he began to rock, to thrust up and forward into her, grunting at each thrust, smirking down at her as the other man looked on, smirking as well. She tried to turn her face away as he used her, even as the movement stoked the hunger and fire within her body. His shaft was sawing harshly against the very top of her slit, so that her clitoris buzzed and sparkled, and she began to gasp and moan, unable to repress the pleasure building within her.

She felt weak, and filthy, and degraded, but her body was almost glowing with the heat and pleasure and raw, desperate hunger, and she began to pant and moan as the man used her, as his fingers kneaded her buttocks and he yanked her against him to meet his hard thrusts.

The other man moved back, and a moment later she felt the rope go slack above her. Her arms fell, too weak to hold, and he leaned in so that they fell behind his head. His fingers dug in harder and he lifted her into his arms, carrying her to the rough table and setting her on its edge. Then the other man joined them, and he pulled back.

They turned her around, and she almost fell, legs too weak and stiff to support herself. She was bent over the edge of the table near the corner, and without conscious thought raised her bottom, shifting her feet apart. She groaned aloud as she was penetrated once again, and a hand gripped her hair, twisting her head to one side as the second man stepped up to the side of the table, his erection in his hand.

He thrust it into her open mouth and her lips snapped closed around it. Her hands, still bound before her, reached up to squeeze his balls as he grinned down at her and thrust himself deeper. At the same time the other man began to drive himself hard into her open sex, his hips slapping painfully against her raised bottom, grinding her thighs into the edge of the table.

Her nipple rings made small clicking sounds as her body was twisted and jerked on the table, and her soft breasts pillowed out against the hard, rough wood. She felt a heady sense of triumph as her inhibitions seemed to melt away and she became little but a voracious sexual animal.

The flickering light of the lantern threw huge shadows on the near wall as the two men used her. Dara sucked avidly on the cock in her mouth, feeling wild and electric with the lewdness of what she was doing. She raised her bottom higher, spreading her legs further as the man behind continued to thrust strongly into her body.

Her tongue stroked hungrily up and down the cock in her mouth and then, chest tight with excitement, she forced herself forward and took him down her throat.

If that bitch can do it so can I!

She fought the sense of gagging and the panic over her blocked throat, gulping and swallowing continuously as the men cursed in appreciation, their hands moving feverishly over her body.

Two men at once! She'd never taken two men at the same time. It was an incredibly wild feeling to have a big cock in her mouth and another slicing back and forth between her swollen pussy lips. Four hands roamed her flesh, four strong, rough male hands. Four black hands.

Their soft rough voices as they used her made her feel like their toy, their slave. They showed her little concern, treated her as their - .

Bitch!
I'm their bitch!
She groaned as she pulled her tight lips slowly back up the length of his slick cock and then gasped as it popped free of her throat. She pulled her mouth free, gulping in air, saliva trickling down onto the table below her as she shuddered from the effort of holding her breath.

A rough hand cupped her right breast. Another pulled at her hair. She didn't know which belonged to which in the dark, shadowy room, and it didn't matter anyway.

The steady slap, slap, slap of hard, strong hips hammering against her upraised bottom was counterpoint to the men's soft curses and her own ragged breaths.

"Suck that cock, bitch! Suck it!"

Her head was guided back to the glistening black flesh and she felt it slide across her tongue again. She closed her lips around it, sucking rhythmically, sliding her lips up and down its length as her bottom continued to be slapped and bruised by the hard pounding behind her. Her hips ground against the rough edge of the table and her breasts ached as several hands fought for possession.

The heat soared within her and she felt the steady stroking building up the sexual pressure. Her entire body seemed to tingle with sexual electricity, and her sex throbbed, alive and burning. Every time his hips slammed into her bottom she felt a jarring bolt of fiery delight as the intensity of her arousal deepened. Already she was in a sexual delirium, where nothing mattered but the raw, carnal physical sensations pouring through her body.

And then the orgasm howled up out of the deep recesses of her body, slashed across her mind and set her nervous system to screaming. She bucked back wildly, her muffled moans growing heavier and louder around the cock now thrusting down into her throat.

So good! So good!

The fire of ecstasy washed over her. Another fix lashed her mind. This was worth anything , everything. Her nervous system flared with overload and she felt as though she were drowning in pleasure, spinning helplessly around and around. Nothing existed but the pleasure.

Or almost nothing. Even through the shining curtain of bliss encompassing her mind she could feel the steady pumping of the hard erection inside her spasming pussy, the *slap, slap, slap* of hard hips against her bottom, the cock sliding back and forth in her throat, the hand tugging roughly on her hair, and the hand pinching and twisting her right breast.

So good!

Chapter Five

For hours they used her, turning and positioning her, slapping and groping and twisting her. They were not cruel, as Emery was. Yet even so there was something eager in the way in which they used her so roughly. It was the eagerness of being able to do what was long forbidden, the eagerness of those who had lived their lives with their eyes down being able to do anything they wanted to those set above them.

She was a deputy, a law officer, and in Mississippi men like these spoke respectfully to law officers, who had so much power over them. More than that, she was a white woman, and a blonde. And just as generations of middle class cultural myth whispered of the sexual prowess of the black man so too did poor Blacks like these eye those haughty blondes they did not dare approach and wonder at their reputation.

They were defying the rules even more than she. Half the White men in the county would have shot them both dead in an instant had they come across the scene, even if her wrists weren't bound. But there was no need to speak politely on this night, no need to keep their eyes respectfully downcast, no need to keep from giving the slightest hint of their lust for a white woman.

On this night they were free to ravage her to their hearts' content, to grope and paw and fondle and slap and use as roughly and powerfully as possible. On this night they could exercise their frustrated male desire to conquer, to rule. They were not Emery, but their hands would leave bruises all over her body that night as they seethed with the hunger within them and rode her into the ground.

At three in the morning, when Carla opened the door and looked out, they were still at it. The men had thrown the rope back up across the ceiling beam and Dara, grunting softly, was being sodomised by one as the other slouched on the chair and watched, the tip of a cigarette glowing orange in the dark room.

She closed the door with a smile.

When Dara heard the door opening next the sun was streaming through the front room's one small window and bathing her in golden light. The men had left and she was alone, body straining tautly down from where her wrists were bound so far above her. Her eyes were narrow slits and she was exhausted.

"Ungh!"

Emery pulled her head back by the hair and looked down at her, then he leaned in and bit lightly at her earlobe.

"You make my friends happy?" His voice was a low rumble.

"Y-yes," she panted.

His hand was between her legs, and his finger sawed slowly along her slit. She groaned again as he bent and took one erect nipple into his mouth, chewing and sucking strongly as his finger continued to move against her.

"Emery," she moaned, her bottom rolling.

"Hot little slut," he growled.

"I-I am," she panted.

Two thick fingers drove up into her as his thumb began to stroke against her clitoris. She bucked against him, twisting her head, trying to reach his lips with hers.

He pulled back and then, suddenly, Carla was there, naked, smirking, gripping Dara's hair where Emery had, pressing her heavy breasts against Dara's, sliding her hand down between her legs, finger stroking teasingingly against Dara's sex.

"S-Stop it," Dara gasped, her head trying to twist away.

"You make Carla happy now," Emery ordered, standing back.

"Emery!" she whined.

Carla sneered at her, then crushed her lips against Dara's and pushed her tongue forward. Dara moaned as the Black woman's fingers tightened in her hair and she pushed her tongue up defensively as the other woman's tongue slithered up and down within her oral cavity.

Carla drew back with a feral grin. "You gonna be my bitch, too, little girl," she said.

Dara groaned in denial, but her legs shifted helplessly as the woman's fingers sawed along her sex and sent white hot sexual energy burning through her groin.

"Do-don't," she moaned.

"Slut," the woman spat. "You do what you're told slut meat."

Dara's back arched involuntarily as a shudder of pleasure ran through her body.

Emery was behind her then, untying her wrists. But they never came free, as his big hands simply pulled them down and back behind her before binding them again.

"I got work to do," he said, moving away.

Carla's eyes gleamed cruelly, and she plucked one of Dara's rings, pulling her forward, forcing her towards the big chair as Emery left the room, left the cabin.

"Don't!' she moaned.

"Slut," Carla sneered.

She gripped her hair again, forcing her head back, then slapped her breast.

"Ow!"

"Emery, he say you do what I want. You got that, bitch?"

Another slap against her other breast.

"Got that, bitch?"

"Yes!"

Carla sat down heavily, then dragged Dara face down across her lap.

"Dirty little whore," she said, fingers sliding between her legs. "I seen your kind before."

Three fingers pushed up into her pussy, twisting and squirming as Dara groaned in pleasure and pain and embarrassment and anger.

"Think you're tough, don't you?" Carla demanded.

A hand slapped sharply against her bottom and Dara gasped in pain.

Then those fingers pushed back inside her and she felt her bottom buck up helplessly.

"Whore."

Her fingers twisted behind her back, her wrists burning as she pulled against the rope binding them in place.

"You my bitch too," Carla said.

Her middle finger began to stroke against Dara's clitoris and the blonde started to shake and gasp and push back in mindless, wanton need.

Abruptly, she found herself grunting in pain as she hit the floor, then crying out in pain as Carla drew her head up and forward by the hair.

"Now do what Emery said, bitch," Carla demanded, guiding her between her legs.

"N-no," Dara moaned, trying to twist away. "I don't know how!"

Carla laughed coldly. "I think you know how, bitch. I showed you the other day and you couldn't get enough. Now show me what you learned."

The pain in her scalp brought tears to her eyes, and Dara pushed her tongue out desperately, sliding it along the pink slit of the woman's sex.

"Come on, bitch. Do what Emery said and make me happy."

Carla slumped low, spreading her legs wide, and forced Dara's mouth in against her sex. Slowly, uncertainly, anger, disgust and embarrassment twisting inside her mind, Dara began to lap at the woman's sex. As Carla tightened her fingers in Dara's hair and jerked continuously, Dara gasped and moaned in pain, allowing herself to be guided upwards and downwards, her tongue darting and dipping, driving deep into the musky depths of the other woman's sex, then sliding upwards to circle her clitoris.

Her knees ground into the hard grit and dirt on the rough wooden floor, and her wrists pulled futilely against the ropes binding them tightly together behind her back. She became aware that her legs had shifted apart, and that her bottom was high and vulnerable, as if she unconsciously sought to be mounted. She could feel the heat of her own loins and the still steady thrumming of excitement within her groin. Her breasts hung heavily below her, and occasionally ached as Carla reached down to slap or squeeze one.

Again and again Carla jammed her face in against her now moist sex, grinding her up and down so that her entire face glistened with the other woman's juices. The musky scent of the other woman's heat filled her nostrils and the taste of her filled her mouth.

She remained angry and ashamed, filled with resentment against Carla even as she sucked carefully on her clitoris in order to raise her pleasure higher. Emery had promised to give her what she wanted, what she needed, and she resented having to pleasure the hateful Black woman instead. She was also unhappy at this further evidence that Emery valued Carla more, that he had set her above Dara.

"Oh yes! Yes! Right there! Lick hard! Faster! Ungh!"

Carla jerked her face into her groin as she began to buck her hips up. Her back arched and she jammed her thighs in against Dara's head, squeezing her painfully as she thrust herself up in sharp, quick motions.

Dara realized the woman was climaxing, and felt a strange twisting mixture of satisfaction and resentment.

And yet that was not, as she had hoped, the end, for Carla had no sooner relaxed then she insisted Dara continue to perform on her, to rouse her to further pleasure, and the painful pull at her hair brooked no resistance as Dara's face was once again plunged into the woman's groin and her tongue began to work.

A second climax, and then a third had the Black woman's body twisting and bucking, and still she held Dara between her outstretched thighs, taunting her and pulling on her hair, forcing her to continue licking. Yet Dara's jaw now ached fiercely, and every movement of her tongue made her wince and gasp.

"I can't!" she moaned.

"Lick, bitch," Carla ordered.

Tears filled Dara's eyes and she cried out as the woman twisted and pulled on her hair, and then she gasped as she was dragged upwards across Carla's lap and a hand cracked sharply against her upraised bottom.

"Ow!"

"Nasty little slut," Carla said.

She squeezed one of Dara's breasts and twisted painfully, then began to bring her other hand down hard and fast on her bottom. The stinging blows turned her pale flesh pink, then red, and the pain grew and spread until she was yelping and cursing and then sobbing as the spanking continued.

"Ain't so tough, is you?" Carla said with a sneer.

Her fingers slid roughly up and down along Dara's smooth sex. She pressed two fingers down against the soft, sweating flesh alongside her hooded clitoris, then began to gently brush her thumb across the hood. Despite herself Dara felt intense jolts of pleasure as her clitoris throbbed and swelled and pushed out from beneath its hood.

"Like that, don't ya?"

Dara ground her teeth together, moaning in shame, and the Black woman chuckled and continued to stroke against her.

Dara felt a finger stroke slowly over her wrinkled anal opening, then push into her rectum. Another slid through her moist pussy lips and twisted inside her.

"Nasty little white girl," Carla said tauntingly. "You want another cucumber, baby? You need a big cock inside you?"

A second finger pushed into her pussy, pumping in and out, then a third, driving in slowly but firmly so that the knuckles jammed against her opening. Four fingers wedged together thrust deep into her sex, and she shuddered as she felt her throbbing sex overheat, felt a sense of helpless sexual submission take hold of her where only the pleasure mattered.

The wedge of fingers grew thicker, and she groaned as her pubic lips strained, as the wedge tried to force them wider and wider. Carla continued to gently stroke her thumb against her clitoris, but then suddenly turned it and let the tip of her nail grind into the soft, throbbing button.

"Ahhh!" Dara bucked up wildly in pain and Carla chuckled, resuming her soft, gentle stroking.

The contrast gave frightening strength to the sensory power of her touch, and Dara's clitoris felt swollen into golf ball size, hot and burning, the woman's touch almost too intense to stand.

"Ungh!" she groaned as she felt the wedge of fingers twisting from side to side, still thrusting softly, firmly, trying to gain entrance to her body.

"Dirty girls need big cocks, don't they?" Carla taunted.

It hurt, yet pain was her constant companion around Emery and his monstrous cock, and so something inside her mind twisted and a savage sense of dark hunger gripped her as the pain grew, as her pubic lips strained wider and wider, and then she felt the wedge of fingers push forward and through her opening, growing wider still, and then abruptly narrowing.

And she realized, dazed, gasping and reeling from the heat and wildfire sexual fever gripping her, that Carla had forced her entire hand into her body. She felt a sense of shocked dismay and fear, but also a terrible lust and desperate desire.

She heard Carla chuckle as her hand twisted inside her belly. She could feel the fingers probing along the walls of her sex, pressing one side, then the other, twisting and wriggling in a way which was driving her insane. The sharp pain of her straining pubic lips now wrapped around the woman's wrist sent a sizzling wall of flames through her groin, and she abruptly climaxed.

Nor was it a climax she could hide, a soft, gasping sort of pleasure which could be missed by her tormenter. The pleasure hit like a freight train so that her head whipped back violently and her hips began to rut like a wanton bitch. Convulsions wracked her body and a wail of mindless ecstasy flew out of her lips.

And in the midst of a universe of blinding, sparkling lights, pleasure which howled like a hurricane, and spasming muscles she felt the woman's hand driven deeper, the fingers crawling up the sleeve of her sex until they pushed against her cervix.

Then, quickly, painfully, Carla's long fingers twisted back into her palm until she had formed a fist, a fist which allowed her to thrust her hand several inches deeper into the writhing, sobbing, bucking blonde girl's body. Her wrist slipped inside, and then her forearm began to follow, forcing Dara's aching pussy lips still wider.

Dara felt on the edge of insanity, the world spinning and twisting and bucking around her. The pleasure was too intense, too powerful, locked together with pain in a maelstrom of sensory overload as her orgasm grew and deepened, then like a string of firecrackers she began to climax again, and again, and again as the Black woman began to pump her fist in and out of Dara's aching sex.

She could feel it like a thick, hard lump inside her abdomen, moving up and down her too tight pussy sleeve even as the woman resumed her hard spanking, bringing her hand down sharply against Dara's hot, red bottom.

And then, as she opened her mouth to scream through still another climax Emery was there, his rough hand yanking back on her hair, and his thick cock pushed into her mouth and down through her throat to block her howl of crazed pleasure.

"That's four dollars and thirteen cents."

Dara handed the woman a five and thanked her as she walked back to the car. On her left wrist she wore a watch with a very wide band, on her right, a half dozen gaudy metal wristlets

Beneath them were the still visible rope burns which testified to her long night of debauchery at Emery's cabin, and which would be difficult to explain away to anyone who saw them.

She had needed most of the weekend to recover, and even now her body felt bruised and sore, especially her pussy. Every time she thought about Carla forcing her whole hand up inside her like that she blanched, her mind twisting with shame and disgust.

She had told herself a hundred times since that night that she would have nothing more to do with Emery, and despite the lewd fantasies and images which came over her seemingly every other minute she had managed - for five entire days now.

She had used most of her pay to get out of Kainlen for a few days, claiming sickness to her uncle as she had travelled to the nearby city (of sorts) of Jerna and stayed at a small motel. She had gone out partying every evening, taunting and teasing the men, acting slutty, looking for someone who was tough and cruel to satisfy her needs, yet not so tough and cruel as Emery.

Her first evening she had danced wildly at a disco with flashing lights, and taken two different men into the parking lot beside it to kneel at their feet and take their cocks deep into her throat. Yet it was so easy. They had been large, strong men, but staggered by her, their knees wobbling, gurgling in pleasure like little boys, and their cocks had been tiny in comparison to Emery's. How easily she reduced them to moaning weaklings.

The next evening she had let a big trucker take her into the sleeping cab of his truck and do what he would with her. He had been heavy and rough, but a dull, panting, grunting thing who had thrust his cock into her like a mindless machine until collapsing atop her.

There was nothing menacing about him, nothing exciting, nothing dramatic or wild. Sex with him had been boring, commonplace, hardly worth the effort.

She drove to a rough bar on the edge of the city and parked, then climbed out and sauntered inside. Her long legs seemed even longer in five inch stiletto heels. She was wearing a very short, pleated skirt and a button down blouse pulled up and tied together beneath her breasts. She wore no bra, and the rings which impaled her nipples were obvious through the thin fabric.

The bar was as wild as she had heard. A hand groped her bottom within seconds of her entering, then drew back as she turned to slap at it. The bar was jammed, the lights low, the music pounding so loudly it was hard to think straight.

She pushed her way through the crowd to the bar, and another hand slapped her bottom before she got to it. Two men parted before her, and each tried to buy her a drink, arguing with each other, pushing and shoving until one threw a punch and two enormous bouncers dragged them away.

Another offer was quickly made and she accepted as she looked up at the low stage at the end of the bar and butterflies moved through her belly.

She had felt dazed and lost after returning home, with no one she could turn to. She had had to get away, and had thrown caution to the winds. She would not be able to pay her rent this month, nor her electric bill, nor the insurance on her car. Now that she was less dazed she was feeling a growing sense of anguish over what she was to do about that.

"Where you from?"

She hardly noticed the man who had bought her a drink. He was twice her age, with a belly on him.

"Mako," she lied.

"I'm George Foster!" he yelled above the music.

"Sarah Miller," she yelled back, staring at the stage.

She had come here for something wild, something lewd, to experience that electrifying sense of dark excitement again. She had come for a wet T-shirt contest.

She looked around the crowd, searching anxiously for anyone who might know her, for anyone familiar to her from Kainlen County. If word got out she had been in a wet T-shirt contest in a grotty little bar in Jerna the whole town would be aghast. Kainlen was Baptist country, solid religious and deeply conservative. Even wearing the skirt she had on would have had tongues wagging all across town.

She finished the drink she'd ordered and let George, or whatever his name was, buy her another. He had a companionable arm around her waist by then and was trying to impress her with how much authority and power he wielded as foreman at a dress factory. His fingers were rubbing at her belly, inching slowly higher.

What was she doing? She tried to reassess her life, tried for the thousandth time to figure out what she wanted to do and how to do it. Acting the slut for an ignorant backwoods ex con had never been on her list of things to do, and the degree of wildfire excitement it gave her was confounding.

She had never let men treat her badly, never let them look down on her. She had often been described as prickly and proud. Why did she let Emery treat her like a whore? Why did it thrill her to the point of becoming a boneless, trembling puddle of flesh to have him demean and degrade her? To say nothing of his bitch girlfriend.

Oh, the Black White thing was certainly a part of it. She had always seen herself as a rebel against the rigid social conventions which wrapped Kainlen so tightly. Violating them so brazenly made her feel wild and wicked and free. And there was something about just giving herself to a man like that, to a brute of a man, just letting him do to her as he wanted, tying her up and even giving her to men - .

She shuddered anew as she recalled the two men, strangers, and her, there in the darkness. Two men she didn't even know, two men at once. And wasn't THAT a shocking thing for a girl from Kainlen County! Oh how the church types would scream if they knew!

She danced with George, or whatever his name was, and let him slide his hands over her backside before going off with another man and letting him buy her a drink, then another.

The music stopped and a man in a dirty white T-shirt stepped onto the stage to announce the wet T-shirt contest. A shock of anxious excitement ran up Dara's spine and she looked around for other girls to step up. One did, then two more, then another, and another. Her breathing was coming in short gulps and her chest was tight as she eased forward through the crowd.

She thanked the darkness for hiding her red face as she stepped up onto the stage behind a cheap looking, phoney redhead, and followed the other girls to the back behind a screen. There they were undressing, taking off whatever top they'd worn for a tissue thin half T-shirt with the bar's name across it.

She felt terribly self conscious at that moment and wanted to back out. She looked around her to see if she could discretely ease back into the crowd but she would have had to cross the brightly lit stage to do so and standing out like that seemed to her to be worse.

She felt a little light headed as she undid her top and then shrugged it off. Naked from the waist up, and exquisitely conscious of her nipple rings. She snatched up one of the little T-shirts and tugged it over her head and down across her breasts.

It was very tight, and very thin and very short. It strained across her breasts and pulled in tight against her chest just beneath, leaving her belly bare, more of a halter than a T-shirt. She was almost the last of the girls to change, and already the first was being announced as one of the gum chewing waitresses moved through the stragglers getting their names.

"What's yer name, hon?" she asked

"Sarah," she said, blushing.

The girl moved back and Dara turned her eyes to a buxom phony blonde who was sashaying back and forth at the edge of the stage, her little T-shirt already soaked and showing off large brown nipples to the yelling, hooting crowd.

A little brunette came next, bouncy and more than a little drunk, squealing as the announcer poured water over her chest, then prancing to the edge of the stage to flaunt herself a the audience. She was small breasted, but made up for it with enthusiasm, then, teasingly, she slid her T-shirt up to flash her bare breasts to great applause.

Dara looked nervously to the announcer, who laughed and clapped along with the crowd. Another girl took her place, shaking her hips so her breasts swung from side to side, then teasingly sliding the shirt up over top and squeezing her breasts from underneath as she yelled out to the whistling, cheering crowd.

Another girl strutted out, rolling her hips and sliding her hands up and down her wet torso, baring her breasts as the others had, arching her back with her hands behind her head.

Dara was growing more anxious and yet more excited as the feeling of sexual electricity grew around her. The next girl not only showed her breasts but tugged her shorts down to show her thong covered bottom, rolling it from side to side at the yelling audience.

The girls who had already pranced around were still up front, and were rolling hips, yelling at the audience, and in several cases, flashing their bare breasts or flipping up short skirts.

And then, shockingly, suddenly, it was Dara's turn, and the waitress gave a hard push which sent her stumbling up to the announcer. She didn't hear a word he said into his microphone, staring at the pitcher of water as it was placed over her chest and cold water poured over her.

She gasped, shocked, shuddering, and then, almost sleep walking at first, moved forward to the edge of the stage. The bar seemed all too bright to her now, for she could see the large crowd of eager men staring at her, could hear their yells and chants.

"Show us your tits! Show us your tits!" they chanted as she began to awkwardly roll her hips.

Her hands were on her belly, feeling the slick, wet flesh, and then suddenly she slid them up, and pushed her chest out. Hoots of appreciation greeted her, and a sense of sexual power filled her. She laughed self consciously, but danced to the music a little. She wasn't even aware of what she was doing until she had her see through shirt up over her breasts and the crowd were whistling in appreciation.

She rolled her hips, then tugged her skirt up to show the little V of black lace over her sex. More howls rose, and she beamed, swinging and rolling her hips, turning and flipping her skirt, grinding her bottom back at them.

"Nice ass!" she heard above the whistles and yells.

"Show us your tits!" several voices chanted.

She turned, flipping up the T-shirt again, rocking from side to side as she taunted them. A sense of wildness filled her and the announcer had to pull her back by the arm among the other girls so the last girl could go.

And then there was a vote, a vote of the audience conducted by how loud they yelled, and all the girls were eliminated except for four "finalists" - including Dara. She had known nothing about how things would work, and now watched, panting, as the first of them went out to parade anew.

There was little pretence of showing herself through a wet T-shirt. She slid the thing up to bare her breasts and rolled her hips, then tugged her jeans down beneath her bottom to show off her thong covered buttocks.

The second girl had lost her jeans completely, and danced wildly in thong and shirt, with the shirt up over her breasts. The third girl squeezed her breasts together as she bent forward, yelling and laughing at the crowd. They were huge breasts, and she lifted one up to lick at the nipple.

And then Dara was pushed forward, and rocked and swayed before them, breathing in the lust she felt coming from the audience, heady with excitement as she slid her shirt up to bare her beasts and then brought her hands up underneath, squeezing them up and together as she bent forward.

She turned, rolling her hips, lifting her skirt, and then, she undid it and let it fall around her ankles, stepping out of it to howls of cheers, dancing and showing off what seemed to them to be endlessly long legs, turning and spinning, even as the world spun around her.

She taunted them with her bottom, her head turned as a sense of near hysteria gripped her. Her fingers slid down along the narrow strip of silk, then back up and underneath, tugging the crotch up against her pussy, sliding her fingers back and forth beneath the strip as she bent forward and spread her legs.

She felt a powerful temptation to remove the last thing which stood between her and complete nudity, to strip off her thong and prance about the stage completely naked, and barely suppressed it as she straightened, turned, stumbled, and let her fingers toy with the small silver rings, showing them off.

And then the announcer was calling for a vote, and they cheered and shouted as, still wearing only her thong, the little white strip of cloth bunched up beneath her armpits, he pointed to Dara.

She won, and was given a small, ugly looking statue with a pair of big breasts on a pedestal, as well as two hundred and fifty dollars.

She stumbled back, heart pounding, to the screen, to step back into her skirt and tear off the dripping wet rag. She pulled the shirt on and tied it tightly, feeling the pressure of the fabric against her stiff nipples.

And then she was in the arms of one of the men she had danced with, who congratulated her as his fingers dug into her bottom, half lifting her into his arms before whirling her around. The music pounded and the lights flashed in the darkness, and eyes devoured her as she moved back in among the crowd of men and women.

And then she was outside in the heat, still gasping, still filled with a trembling sense of sexual electricity. He pushed her back against a wall, his hands up against her breasts, tearing her blouse open, and then his lips were sucking on her nipple as his hands pawed at her naked bottom.

They fell onto a low earthen mound, her blouse open, his hands racing over her body. He tore her thong down her legs and she spread them, gasping as he moved over her, and then he was inside her, thrusting strongly. He was small compared to Emery, but it didn't seem to matter.

She felt wild and hot and sinful and wicked as his hips smashed down into her. She drew her knees back and he grasped the back of her legs and forced them down hard, his face a mask of lust as he jammed her knees down into the dirt on either side of her body, raising her bottom up to meet his powerful thrusts.

There were people walking nearby, voices in casual conversation, and the fear of discovery filled her with a heady excitement as the man thrust himself down into her with relentless force and speed, gasping and panting above her.

She came with a cry of pleasure, her body shuddering from the violence inside, and the pounding outside, her pussy burning up as he continued to pound himself into her. Then he collapsed, all but suffocating her as she lay sprawled in languourous, exhaustion.

He invited her back to his place, but she shook her head, stumbling back to her car. She stood with her back against it, drawing in deep, shuddering breaths, her shirt still open, trying to put her mind back together. Finally, she pulled her shirt together and fished in her purse for her keys, unlocking the car.

"Hey, baby."

She gasped as a hand gripped her arm. It was George, or whatever his name was.

"Come on, baby. How about giving me some of that?" he asked, his face a leer.

She shook her head, pushing him away.

"Come on. You gave some to that other guy."

His hand squeezed her breast and he tried to kiss her, but she pushed him back. "I-I have to g-go," she said, still panting.

"Fifty bucks," he said urgently. "Come on."

"What?" she blinked at him.

"A hundred bucks!"

He had a fistful of twenties and waved it in her face. She stared at him in confusion, then anger, then a strange kind of wonder.

"You want to pay me - ."

He folded the twenties and thrust them into the breast pocket of her shirt, then pulled it open as his head darted forward, his mouth engulfing the centre of her breast.

He was treating her as a prostitute, and Dara realized suddenly, in a flash of blinding intense shock, that if she let him, she would be a prostitute, she would have sold her body for money.

And she groaned as the heat rose up around her with a stunning speed and power, and she felt his hand squeezing and rubbing at her naked sex as he fumbled at his zipper.

His hands were at her buttocks, yanking her up. Her right leg curled up around him, and she half fell back onto the hood of her car, legs spread as he entered her. She moaned in dismay and heat as he bent over her, sucking and chewing on her bare breasts as his hips pounded away.

His hands were on her bottom, jerking her up to meet his thrusts, and his cock sliced powerfully between her swollen labia as he used her with frenzied strength and excitement, cursing and moaning all the while.

And then he was done, gasping, staggering back, giving her a lewd, obscene grin as he fumbled himself back into his pants, and Dara moaned as she slid back onto her feet and fell to her knees. She half fell into her car, gulping in air, and reached down between her legs, rubbing at her bare sex. Her other hand moved up to cup her breast and she felt the bills in the breast pocket of her blouse. She had prostituted herself. The orgasm poured over her, and she arched her back and bucked her hips up at her fingers.

Chapter Six

The money she had made at the contest - and the hundred dollars she had earned by prostitution - made up for most of what she had spent, but she was still broke. And the trip had done nothing to settle the sense of confusion and helpless sexual need within her.

Everywhere she went, at home, driving, shopping, talking with people, everything she did, she did with a deep awareness of her own sexuality and need. Every time she bent forward, with however innocent a motion, she imagined someone, Emery, thrusting himself into her. Whenever she reached up for something she imagined her wrists bound above her. Arching her back, combing her fingers through her hair, washing herself, kneeling for something, it didn't matter. She felt wrapped in an endless wall of sexuality and seductiveness.

They all wanted her. Every man who looked at her. She was so hot, they must smell her, must scent the sexual need within her. She was certain of it, that every male eye turned her way was filled with lust and desire for her.

Her mind was filled with lewd images; Emery, Carla, nameless men in the dark, wild flashing lights and cheering crowds. She masturbated constantly, climaxing with ridiculous ease, it not the intensity she felt with Emery.

It was hard to act "normal", harder still to work, and almost impossible to fight the growing desire to go back to see Emery, no matter what it cost her. Every day that she did made her feel more aroused, more in need, more sexually charged.

She bought leather restraints over the Internet, and fastened them to her wrists and ankles, then tried to tie herself up and use her dildo, pretending it was Emery, or some other powerful man. She bought thigh high boots with stiletto heels, and walked around her living room, wishing she dared wear them anywhere in Kainlen County. She bought revealing lace and leather under things, wearing them beneath her chaste outer clothing. It gave her a sense of smugness when she was around "normal" people, for she had always loved to have a secret, to put something over on others.

Dara drove slowly, which was far from her custom. Despite the time in Jerno her mind seemed to be wrapped in a light haze, and she had little interest in ordinary, common, day to day activities, including her job. She continued to feel as if she were masquerading as someone other than who she was, continued to feel that at any moment her secret would be discovered and she would be cast out amid great howls of outrage and anger.

When the call came she gave the radio an irritated look, ignoring it. One arm was on the door of the car, the other on the steering wheel, and she was slouched lazily in the seat thinking about the bar in Jeno and considering some of the things she could have done, had she only dared, some of the things she might do another night, in another bar.

The radio was insistent, and she sighed wearily, plucking the microphone up from its cradle.

"Car Seven," she said.

"Dara, meet the Sheriff on Route Four at the Grenville Bridge," Nora said.

"Ten Four," she acknowledged.

She felt a quiver of apprehension at the order, though she was reasonably certain that If her uncle had discovered anything he would have called her into his office rather than meeting her out by the Okinawi river. Then again, the meeting place was out near where Emery lived, and that served to tighten her chest a little. Could he possibly know anything? Was he meeting her away from the office so he could give free reign to his rage without being overheard?

As she approached the bridge, however, she saw he was not alone. There were three cars parked nose to tail along the west side of the bridge, and only one of them was a marked patrol car. The other two were a pair of dark vans with tinted windows. Several men in suits were along the edge of the bridge along with the Sheriff, and she recognized one as Hernandez, the DEA man.

She pulled up behind them all and got out slowly, looking over the edge of the bridge at the water rushing by below. She saw there was a man there in a divers suit working beside one of the bridge supports. She wondered if a body had been found, and again, as she often did, she thought of Emery. Emery was quite capable of killing someone, she thought. After all, he had done it before.

She was wearing a lacy, purple, see through bodysuit beneath her khaki uniform. It covered her from ankle to shoulder, and nothing was beneath it but a matching G-string. A small dildo was inside her pussy, and a butt plug inside her anus - for she was trying to work herself open back there in order to accommodate Emery's hard thrusts with less pain.

There were small indentations against the front of her uniform blouse where the rings pierced her almost constantly erect nipples, but they were not obvious, and she had put a pair of folded up tissues in each breast pocket to hide them.

She examined her chest to make sure none of the purple lace was visible above her top button, then opened the door and eased out as carefully as she could. She felt a combination of discomfort and wicked excitement as her body shift around the cylinders inside her lower belly. Once upright she felt a mild nervousness, but the butt plug was not about to go anywhere, and the dildo rested snugly just within the lips of her taut pubic lips. She glanced down to reassure herself, then strolled very slowly forward.

"Dara," the sheriff said in acknowledgement. "You know Agent Hernandez."

She nodded and he nodded coolly back.

"This is Agent Sullivan." He nodded to a pale faced redheaded man in his forties with a thick moustache.

"Deputy." Sullivan smiled.

"What's up?" she asked.

"We had a boat out on the Onigochi watching for suspicious activity the other night," Sullivan said. "We chased a small outboard board moving north without lights around midnight, but lost it around here. We believe it turned in here."

"Waters not more'n a foot n' a half deep. If it came through here it'd have to be a modified swamp boat," she said doubtfully.

"Why modified?" Hernandez demanded.

She shrugged. "Most fast swamp boats, well, all I seen, run about six feet wide. Ain't more'n four feet between those bridge supports.

"It was a small, boat, low in the water, but it moved like hell," Sullivan said.

"Most likely a poachers boat," Dara said.

"What'd they be hunting at midnight?"

'Nothin'. Don't mean the boats disappear off season. Nor the poachers for that matter."

"So what was he doing then?"

"Smugglin', I reckon."

"Yeah, I reckon," Hernandez said sarcastically.

She glared at him.

"This river doesn't go very far," Sullivan said.

"Bout a mile. Then it fades into the swamp."

"Any idea who might live around here might have access to a boat like that?" Sullivan asked.

Emery.

She shrugged. "Anyone in these parts would have access to one. Only a couple of people actually live along this river, both White trash to be honest."

"As opposed to?" Hernandez smirked.

"As opposed to most people, dumbass," she said.

"Would we try an' act as professionals here?" the sheriff demanded.

"Oh come on, Sheriff," Hernandez said with a smirk "You might have to keep your sister happy but the rest of us are under no obligation to pretend this girl is a police officer."

He turned abruptly and walked back to his car, and the Sheriff grabbed Dara's arm and squeezed hard as she started after him. Sullivan gave an embarrassed smile and walked after Hernandez.

"Snotty sonofabitch yankee bastard," Dara hissed.

"That he is but we can do without you getting arrested for attacking him."

'He wouldn't dare!"

"People like that, you never know. Lookit, I asked you out here for a reason. You know the people in this area. I want you to nose around, see if anyone might be spending more time on the river than they ought. That'd draw someone's eye for sure."

"The hell with that. Let him get his shiny shoes dirty an' go talk to people himself."

"You know nobody around here is gonna talk to a yankee in a suit, especially one named Her-nan-dez."

"So why should we help him!?"

"So we can get rid of him," the sheriff growled. "If they stick around here too long they're liable to take an interest in little things like how some of my deputies add to their income every month by fining tourists."

Dara glowered at him sulkily.

"So look around, talk to people. Flash your boobs at the farmers - ."

Dara stared at him in outrage.

"Don't give me that look, girl, we both know to use what works and nature gave you a nice working pair there."

She folded her arms across her chest angrily.

"Even aside from Hernandez causing trouble I don't hold with drugs and neither do you. Find out who might be involved. Then we can get rid of both of them. There's a couple of likelies out this way who're capable of anything" - Including her lover, if that word was not misplaced.

Just thinking the word made her shudder and caused her pussy muscles to contract around the dildo.

What would she do if Emery was smuggling drugs?

She went back to her car and climbed inside, reaching down and giving her pussy a squeeze before starting the engine.

Before going to work the next day she put on a thin leather G-string which had a small, soft bump over her clitoris. She wore a normal bra to the office, but after roll call she drove away, pulled over, and replaced it with a cupless leather halter.

The halter was little more than a wide strap which cupped her breasts from beneath and pushed them upwards. The strap narrowed at either side, curling up around the outer edges of her breasts, then narrowed still further as they curled in again over the tops of her breasts, criss crossing her chest and fastening behind her neck. A smaller strap crossed the top of her bulging breasts to help push them down. The result were that her bared breasts were pushed gently up and together, the ringed nipples burningly erect and sensitive.

Her uniform blouse was barely able to close over them, and she felt a heady sense of excitement as she continued on with her patrol. An hour into it she was able to come merely by squeezing and kneading her breasts through her blouse. But this did little to diffuse her inner heat, and she drove back into town and headed for the wrong side of the tracks.

Dara frowned at what looked like a bundle of rags in the gutter ahead of her. She pulled the patrol car over next to the curb, where she could see the bundle was a man, and the man was beginning to stir. She sighed, looking past him at the narrow entrance to Mika's Bar, then got out of the car and strolled over. Standing over him she could see the man, a Black man, of course, had been beaten up. He reeked of stale beer and cigarette smoke as he slowly raised his head, then brought a hand to a bleeding cut on his chin and muttered dazedly.

"Get off the road," she said in irritation.

"Yesshir, d-deputy," the man grunted, crawling over the curb to lay back on the sidewalk.

She muttered, then hitched up her belt and walked past him. Mika's wasn't one of the County's more stylish establishments. Its one small window had been boarded up years earlier. The door was of unpainted, unvarnished, warped and rotting wood. Even the doorknob was rusting as she turned it and pushed open the door. The hinges squealed and a spring catch overhead fought to keep the door closed. She pushed harder, and the door slammed shut behind her as she let it go.

She stood still, for a moment, letting her eyes grow accustomed to the dim light. The bar was tiny, claustrophobic, the air dank and heavy. The bar was six feet long, of rough wood chipped, cut and scratched, darkened by a thousand spills left too long in place. There were half a dozen small tables with stools around them, all obviously hand made, and not by a craftsman either. There were two men at the little bar, along with the bartender. Three more men sat at one of the tables. All of them were staring at her with sullen, suspicious looks on their faces.

Dara strolled over to the bar, a set expression on her face.

"Customer of yours outside?" she demanded.

The bartender shrugged. He was a small, rat faced man with a bad shave and a scar running down the side of his face.

"You been told before to keep your business inside, ain't you? The good folks don't wanna run into the trash you throw out the door," she snapped.

"People get outa line, gotta be taught their place."

She turned and scowled at one of the men at the bar who'd spoken, then swallowed her words. It was dim in the bar, and it had been even dimmer at Emery's cabin that night he'd given her to his two friends. The man before her grinned mockingly, his teeth showing white against his black face, and her heart began to pound as she recognized him as one of the men.

"Specially women," he said, drawling, leaning casually against the bar. "Women need to be taught what they's here for, what they was put on this Earth for. Ain't that right, honey?"

Damn Emery! What if word got around...

"Ain't that right, little deputy girl?"

He reached over and slid a hand up her side, then onto her swollen breast. Face flushed, Dara gripped his wrist, twisting it up and around, and the man cried out in pain as he was forced down across the bar.

"You like me to break your wrist?" she growled, fighting to keep her voice steady.

If he was Emery's friend would Emery be upset at her treating him this way? Would he punish her?

She felt a fast flutter take her heart as her mind swirled with dark excitement and fear at such a punishment.

And then as if in answer to her wild, fluttering thoughts the door in the rear of the bar opened and a man stepped through, then another. Dara looked up, and froze, recognizing one of them as the second man who'd taken her that night. Then a third man came through, and she forgot to breath. It was Emery. His eyes were cold and hard as they locked onto her, and she felt her chest tighten, her pulse race as he stepped forward.

The three men at the table had risen to their feet, and looked on as Emery crossed the small bar in a few strides. Dara's hands went limp on the man's wrist, and she backed up a step, her body beginning to tremble lightly.

"You done learned no manners," he said, his voice a rumbling whisper.

"I... he - ." Her voice faltered.

He reached out and slipped two fingers into her belt, then tugged her forward until her body was pressed against his.

Dara was acutely aware of the eyes of the other men on her, but could not seem to move, spellbound by the air of menace, of power and masculine heat he radiated. She wanted to say a thousand things. She wanted to snarl at him for the way he treated her. She wanted to sneer at him to pretend she didn't care. She wanted to act superior, cold, formal, as a deputy ought to act around a man like him, around scum like that in the dank little back alley bar.

She did nothing but stare, mouth open, chest rising and falling, and the trembling growing worse.

He leaned in against her, and she felt his hot breath against the nape of her neck, shuddering as his lips and then his teeth made contact with her soft skin. She should have pushed him back. She had to push him back. She could not be seen in a public place allowing - .

His teeth bit into the nape of her neck and she gasped, her hands rising at last, pressing against his powerful chest. She jerked her head aside, staring at the hostile faces surrounding her, and tried to step back.

"We can't - ."

His hands slid around her, then down onto her buttocks.

Blood rushed to her face, and she licked her lips anxiously.

"Emery I - ."

His lips came down on hers, hot, moist, demanding. His fingers dug into her buttocks, pulling her up against him, forcing her onto her toes as his tongue pushed into her mouth. She felt her breasts growing hot as they were pressed against his muscular chest, the nipples sparkling like live wires. He ground his fingers into her buttocks, grinding her up against him as his tongue explored her mouth, pushing her own aside, gliding across the roof of her mouth, then pushing into her cheeks, then dancing along the underside of her own tongue.

She felt breathless, dizzy, her body throbbing with heat and a crackling sexual electricity that made it hard to think. His fingers dug in harder, and he lifted her up. Her legs started to slide around him, then halted, drawing back as she abruptly remembered where they were.

"E-Emery," she gasped.

He turned her smoothly, pushing her back and dropping her bottom on one of the rough, dirty tables. His hands released her, slid along her hips, along her thighs, then closed like steel bands. He lifted her legs up and apart, and she fell back onto her back on the table with a startled gasp. Abruptly, her belt was falling away, then he was tugging down her trousers.

'No!,'' she gasped, trying to sit up.

He shoved her back, yanking them down and off, taking her leather G-string with them. Again she tried to sit up but suddenly his face was over her, his huge hands almost covering her head, his heavy body pressing her back against the table, his lips crushing hers, his tongue driving into her mouth.

She shuddered helplessly, the sexual heat closing in around her, twining itself around her mind and drawing remorselessly tighter. The black faces gathered around, still hostile, watching, staring eagerly. She felt his big, rough hands sliding up under her uniform shirt, pushing it up, forcing it up over her breasts.

Her face flamed as the men whistled and murmured at her bared, squeezed together breasts, and Emery's white teeth showed as he ran a hand over them, tugging at her rings so her nipples stung sharply.

He undid the leather straps, still smirking contemptuously, tearing the whole thing off her and examining it. His arms bulged and he ripped the top strap off, then wrapped it around her right wrists.

"E-Emery..." she panted.

He ripped off the side strap and wrapped it around her left wrist.

"I-I... W-We - ."

He shoved her back hard and she groaned as his lips crushed hers and his big, hard fingers dug into her breasts.

He was grinding into her now, and she could feel his erection against her through his jeans, a hard, warm lump which rubbed eagerly against her sex as his body crushed her against the table. His tongue continued to twist inside her mouth for a long moment, then he drew back, lifting up and back. Her chest heaved, her nipples aching with heat. She was all but nude, sprawled back on the rough table, all those men looking on, sneering, contemptuous, eager.

But they weren't important. She had eyes only for Emery, as he undid his jeans, opened the buttons, and pushed them slowly down over his hips. His erection sprang up like a snake, thick black and angry, the head arching towards her open sex.

His hands gripped her thighs again, bruising the soft flesh as he yanked them up and apart. She felt the head of his cock pushing against her moist entrance and her body bucked involuntarily. She heard the murmur from around her, and shame swept through her.

But she couldn't help herself, couldn't resist him, and as she felt the pressure against her grow she moaned in desperate yearning, then groaned in exultation as he forced her open and began to push inside.

He thrust in suddenly, and she cried out in pain, his thick flesh spearing down into her body. She was driving upwards along the table, her soft white flesh sliding across the rough hewn, scarred wood until hr head hung half over the other side.

So big! So big!

She felt his thick log of a cock grinding deeper into her, ploughing upwards, stretching wide the elastic walls of her pussy, stretching them to the breaking point as he forced himself up against her cervix, then past.

She shuddered, her back arching, a long low moan of sensual elation escaping her, the only sound in the small, quiet room as Emery's cock hit bottom and his hips ground against her thighs and buttocks.

"Slut!" he growled.

His heavy body fell atop her like a wall, blotting out what little light there was. His chest crushed her breasts as his tongue drove into her mouth. He ground his hips against her, one hand pulling on her hair painfully, forcing her head up and back as he tore his lips free of hers, then dove against her exposed jugular, biting, growling like an animal. One of her shoes fell off as her legs jerked spastically, and she shuddered again, her breath catching.

He straightened, looming over her, and pulled his cock back. Her pussy squeezed and clutched at it as it slid free, then collapsed as he rammed himself forward. Her legs flailed up and she cried out, and his hands drove beneath her, hard fingers digging into her buttocks as he began to thrust furiously, using short, savage strokes as his mouth devoured her, biting and chewing and licking up and down her neck and over her face.

The table shook and threatened to collapse under their weight, and Dara grunted helplessly, continuously, buried under his heavy body, groaning and panting for breath as he battered his cock against the back wall of her sex. Her legs rose and tangled around him and she moaned deep in her throat, a curtain of sensual heat squeezing in around her, setting her mind to twisting and tumbling as her body was battered and crushed beneath him.

The heady aroma of his musk was in her mouth, her nose, her throat, and the hard, passionate heat of his body was grinding against her as he pumped savagely, like a raw, bestial creature of lust and animal passion. His thick erection sawed back and forth through her taut opening as her legs clutched helplessly around his pumping hips.

He lifted up her suddenly, his big hands under her buttocks, their tongues twining together as her hands clawed at his back. The men were all around, staring, smirking, leering, aroused, and at the back of her mind was a panicky sense of fear and anxious desire as she wondered if Emery would force her to take them all.

She was lifted up and down, up and down in his arms, riding

his cock, horribly shamed at all the men watching, but intensely, uncontrollably aroused at the same time. And then Emery dropped her back heavily onto the small, rough table, and she groaned as he weight fell atop her.

He thrust wildly, savagely, hurting her, and then straightened, baring her to the other men looking on. He turned and said something she didn't catch to someone she hardly saw other than a dark shadow. Then someone was above her, hands clawing at her uniform blouse, tearing it up over her head and off. Her hands were pulled back over her head, then down beneath the table, and she groaned as her body slid upwards, her head falling back upside down off the far edge.

She felt the leather straps biting into her wrists now, and whimpered, as the heat roared within her. She could no longer see Emery, only feel his hands moving over her naked body. She felt her legs spread, her ankles bound down to the lower legs of the table, and then hard finger pinching at her nipples, plucking at the rings as Emery picked up the pace, thrusting harder and faster, shaking the table as he pounded himself into her.

It was so good! It was glorious! All her inhibitions fled. What else could matter beyond the intense, searing pleasure gripping her mind and body. A fist gripped her hair, and a cock pushed into her mouth. She closed her lips around it, sucking. It began to pump in and out, pushing faster and harder, and then it drove into her throat, half choking her as it pushed in to the balls and her face was mashed up against a sweating, foul smelling groin, testicles plastered against her eyes.

She felt her orgasm arise within her belly, spreading through her body like a flashfire. Her head thrashed from side to side, and the staring Black men were bright eyed shadows The pleasure devoured her, and even Emery's steady pounding paled into a soft, dull shadowy thing.

The orgasm faded, but Emery kept thrusting into her, thrusting and thrusting and thrusting as he used her with violent ease. And her passions rose again even as he grunted and softened and, she thought, came, pulling away. There was a rush of men, and a dozen hands came down on her bared body, slapping, pinching, squeezing and groping. She hardly noticed the scuffle and curses at the other end of the table as the man gripping her head continued to pump up and down in her throat. Then another cock was driven into her body.

Hands fought over her flesh, pinching and groping in rough, eager lust. Crude, cruel words and laughter spilled over her heaving, twisting, bucking body as she came again, feverish with sexual heat, gasping and moaning and choking on the hard male meat forced into her throat, or the spurting wads of semen which issued from them.

Another cock pushed into her mouth, and another into her pussy. Yet she hardly noticed. Her heat soared and dipped, soared and twisted, as the men used her two at a time, and she could only think of Emery looking on, and of the hot cruel lust in the men around her, lust inspired by her, lust fed by the sight of her, the touch of her.

She had no idea how long it went on, yet they were so eager, most of them, and so quick, that it could not have lasted long. And then Emery was undoing her, dragging her along by the arm as, naked, he pulled her out of the bar.

She moaned dazedly, stumbling and staggering, gasping for breath, her body aching all over from the quick, frenzied use. And then she was on the street, on the pavement, naked with the bright sun beating down, and she thought she ought to protest, to draw back.

Emery led her to her car and threw her into the front seat, then slammed the door. He got into the other side, while three of the men from the bar got in the rear.

"Home," he said.

And, hardly capable of thought, she drove them to Emery's cabin, where the four of them continued to use her with savage glee, and her body was bruised, battered and clawed until she could hardly drag herself out to her car to return to the Sheriff's office and sign out.

Chapter Seven

It was getting worse. There was no way of telling herself anything else. Dara was not only letting him use and abuse her now but letting others of his kind do it to her. It wouldn't take long for word to get out at this rate. Already there would be whisperings among the wrong sort, the criminal sort. No one else would believe it was more than slander - at first.

But if the stories kept up they would filter back to the people she worked with and to the Sheriff, and before too very long the truth would be known and she would be in disgrace, and more than disgrace. She would be a pariah; jobless, friendless, abandoned by her family.

But God it had been so good! That sense of sexual exultation, of bliss and sheer maniacal sexual energy, the orgasms which followed more orgasms, until her entire body was one big muscle spasm and she thought she was going out of her mind with the pleasure. How could she give that up?

She did some shopping after "work", and despite the exhaustion and bruises from the rough treatment she'd been given her body thrummed with sexual arousal. Even paying for the most mundane thing reminded her of how she'd earned the money, and sent a jolt of sexual electricity up her spine.

And every bruise brought the reminder of a hard, lust crazed male salivating over her prostrate body and ramming their hungry cocks into her. She was becoming a creature of sex. Nothing else seemed to matter in her life. And it was going to destroy her if she did not gain control of it.

And so instead of going home to bathe in her own sweat and think about what they had done to her she drove back to the area around the Okinawi river, clad in a thin, tight blue halter and short shorts and began talking to some of the people along the river. Salivating at her all the while, the crude rural men denied any knowledge at first, but then, trying to impress her, trying to keep her around, began to tell what they could, what they thought, suspected, or simply could make up.

And it pointed to Emery. It pointed so strongly towards him that if she failed to tell the Sheriff and he looked into it on his own he was going to wonder why.

She should have gone home then, but instead turned down the Breckenridge Mine road and pulled over not far from Emery's cabin.

She licked her lips nervously, wondering whether to ask him, but instead circled wide of his cabin until she found a small trail. It clearly led from his little cabin and shack into the deeper woods, and she nervously followed it.

The vegetation was thick, there, but she could see that it disappeared ahead, and pushed her way through. And then, just ahead, was an open area, the greenery darker and taller. And she recognized a large field of marihuana plants.

"Damn," she whispered.

So Emery was involved in the grass, but was he involved in anything more serious? She didn't much care about grass, having used it on occasion herself (when she could afford it) but if he was involved in smuggling hard drugs she was not at all sure what she would do. Letting it go on was not an option. Yet arresting Emery was even less of one.

She moved closer to the field and something caught roughly at her ankle and pulled. She screamed as she was yanked up and off her feet by a noose trap. It whipped her right leg out from under her and left her hanging upside down, her flailing fingers clawing at the tops of the weeds below.

When she stopped swinging she bent with a grunt, reaching up for her ankle, and trying to undo the rope around it. Then rough fingers gripped her hair and yanked her head back.

"What the fuck you doin' here?" Emery demanded.

"E-Emery!" she gasped breathlessly. "I-I was lookin' for you!"

"You found me, bitch."

"L-Lemmie down!"

"Why you come back here?"

"I-I wanted to be with you," she said piteously.

He snorted, then gripped at her halter and tore it off. She was bare beneath it, and gasped in sudden hunger as she felt his hands on her thighs.

He squeezed her through the shorts, then opened them and tore them open at the crotch, stripping her bare in an instant.

Her left leg hung down, her groin spread wide, and Emery unzipped himself and pushed in. Dara didn't even ask to be let down, knowing and , oddly, accepting without even thinking that he would do to her as he wanted.

And then he was pushing into her and she was groaning and panting and grasping at his legs as he forced himself deep and used her quickly and roughly.

And then he was pulling back, striding away. Dara stared after him, gasping for breath and reaching up to gently stroke and massage her warm, moist sex.

She could not see him through the brush, and wondered if he had decided to simply leave her as she was. But then she felt the rope jerk, and she gasped as she began to lower. But after an instant she halted and went back up, and continued to rise higher and higher, her head coming up out of the brush, the ground five, then ten feet below.

"Emery!' she called, feeling a sudden panic.

The ground continued to recede, and she tried to reach up, to grasp at her ankle and undo the rope. But she felt weak and exhausted, and her arms hung low as the rope drew her higher and higher; now fifty feet, now a hundred. She continued to rise, and then halted in place. She was in among the branches of the willow now, but not close enough to touch any of them.

The rope led higher still, up over the top of a thick branch thirty feet over her feet. She hung in place, slowly circling, moaning, staring downwards, trying to see Emery for long minutes.

She could see the top of his cabin through the trees, and in the other direction a wide field filled with what she first took to be corn. But she quickly realized from the colour and size of the plants it had to be marihuana. That would explain why Emery had put traps around it, too.

She had meant to warn him about Hernandez several times, but every time she got near him her mind seemed to go blank.

The tendons and muscles in her groin ached as gravity pulled her free leg downwards while the rope held the other straight up. Her arms felt heavy, as well, and raising them beyond her shoulders was a struggle. After a while, though, it became clear Emery would not soon return, and so she struggled to sit up, to grasp at her ankle and free herself.

Then she halted, realizing that she was a hundred feet above the ground. She gazed from side to side, but the nearest branches were thirty feet away. That left climbing the rope, and one slip of sweating fingers would drop her straight down.

She leg go of her leg and gasped as she swung back down, her hands dropping below her. She moaned softly, the blood going to her head as she continued to hang. She thought of calling to him but knew it would be futile. Emery would get her when and if he felt in the mood to.

Surely he would feel in the mood soon, she thought, reaching up to finger her nipples, then higher still to run a finger along her sex.

The air grew slowly cooler, the light seeping away with the warmth, and she moaned dizzily. The rope hung still, yet every movement made it sway and twist. Upside down, her view of the world necessarily confused, the blood filling her head, her thoughts grew more confused and disjointed. Her thigh ached, her ankle burned, her foot was numb.

Occasionally she struggled to sit up and grasp her leg. Once she even got ahold of the rope and took some of the weight off her ankle. But she could never hold on for long, and when her fingers slipped she would swung back and down with a startled cry, and the rope would begin to spin her around until she grew dizzy.

The sky darkened. Bugs began to come out, stinging and crawling over her sweating flesh as she slapped and twisted. She began to feel miserable and alone, and wished desperately for Emery to come and release her. She called out for him several times, even knowing he would pay her no heed,

The sky darkened and the sound of the crickets filled the might. Dara hung down from her ankle and groaned dazedly, her skull throbbing with such pain she could hardly stand to open her eyes. Even the dull light of the moon peering through the thick foliage overhead caused her agony.

She had given up trying to fend off the insects. Her mind was too dulled to feel them very well, not even the mosquito which had thirstily driven its needle sharp little beak into the edge of her nipple to feed, and her arms dangled exhaustedly below her, too tired to bat at the cloud of small, fast, buzzing things which swirled around her sweating body.

Mosquitoes lit again and again to crawl slowly across the soft, warm, moist flesh of her body and stab their beaks into her to drink. The heat which radiated out from her exposed groin was an especially enticing scent, and the ticklish feel of tiny feet crawling across her slit caused her to twitch and tremble unconsciously

The moon slid slowly across the sky as Dara hung unmoving, twisting slowly in mid-air, jaw slack, keening softly, half unconscious. Clouds swirled overhead, and it began to rain, softly at first, but growing in strength. Wind buffeted her as the rain spattered against her body, and she groaned miserably, twisting and turning as the water rand own her body in rivulets.

The storm blew over and the insects came out again.

And then, suddenly, she dropped. She fell a dozen or so feet before the rope went taut, jerking her to a sharp stop and setting her to swinging and twisting wildly as she cried out in dazed confusion, fear and pain.

She hard laughter far off, then fell another dozen feet, only to be brought up short once again, the rope yanking hard on her leg, sending the other bouncing and swinging wildly, her body twisting, arms flailing. She fell again, and again, and again, brought up sharp, twisting and spinning and crying out in pain and confusion.

A half dozen more falls brought her scrabbling fingers within a handspan of the ground, until a shadowy figure at her belly, pushing her far to one side, then shoving her back the other way. She swung sharply to one side, and was grasped again on the backturn to be pushed further.

She cried out weakly, spinning and swinging with greater and greater speed as laughter followed her.

She landed suddenly, in a heap, in a bush, the wind knocked out of her as the brush lashed her skin. She flailed about wildly, and one of her wrists was caught as she was dragged from the bush into the open. Then something gripped her hair, forcing her face down into the dirt.

"Crawl, bitch," she heard a familiar voice demand. "Crawl!"

Her hair twisted painfully, pulling her forward, and her hands clawed at the damp earth, her legs, almost useless.

"Crawl, dog!"

She cried out in blurred confusion as her hair was pulled and twisted, and somehow her legs pushed her up and she crawled along, the fist in her hair pulling her forward, yet holding her head low as she moved awkwardly along the path.

"Crawl, slut!"

There was a small pen in the rear of the cabin, a pen once used to cage chickens. She crawled into it, a slap on her upraised bottom sending her scurrying forward, and the cage closed behind her.

Dara didn't care. She was happy to have her hair released, happy to be off the rope, happy not to feel a continuing source of pain, happy not to be swinging and swaying. She dropped exhaustedly to the ground and almost immediately fell asleep.

She slept lightly in the cramped confines of the cage, and so woke to the sound of Emery's feet coming down on the stones and twigs around her cage. She raised her head wearily and peered through the mesh as he looked down at her, her mind filled with confusion as she tried to remember the events of the previous night, and how she had come to be - wherever she was.

She had been hanging from a rope - for a very long time. But that didn't seem to matter as Emery opened the cage and motioned her out. For all she felt was a deep, surging heat in her belly as she pushed herself up to her hands and knees and crawled slowly out through the narrow opening.

He moved suddenly, and she cried out as his heavy foot came down on her upper back, then shifted to the back of her neck to pin her face to the ground.

"You stay away from the swamp. You understand?" he

growled.

"Yes, Emery," she cried. "I'm sorry!"

"What you see in the next field?"

"Nothing!"

"You lying bitch. Well as long as you know - ."

He knelt behind her and she gasped as she felt him pull her arms up behind her back and jam them close together, painfully close together. Her shoulders ached and she whimpered slightly.

"E-Emery? What are you doin'?" she asked, her voice quivering.

His hand slapped across the back of her head and she gasped in pain.

She felt a tight leather strap go around one arm, then the other, and cried out as it tightened and forced her elbows together. He slapped the back of her head again and, dazed, she moaned as he wound another tight strap around her wrists, binding them together.

He yanked her to her feet, then half dragged, half pushed her along before him around the corner of the cabin to the small work shack, where he forced her down onto her knees.

He moved past her, and she knelt in place, panting and watching him. Her body ached everywhere, and was itchy in places she had seldom been itchy before, but none of that seemed to matter as she watched the muscular man move over before a tool chest and fling it open. She licked her thirsty lips and looked around her at the dark, dirty room, wondering where Carla was, hoping Emery would fling her down and use her before the hateful woman showed up.

He drew out a thick mass of leather and metal and carried it over to her, then dropped it heavily to the floor. She looked at it only briefly, for Emery was undoing his zipper, and that took all of her attention as he drew his manhood out and pulled her head forward.

Then it was thrust into her mouth, forcing her lips wide, and she gulped and gagged as Emery began to use her. His big hand cupped her small head and held it in place as he began to slowly pump into her, thrusting deeper and deeper until with a choked gagging sound she felt it forced down into her throat.

Her throat bulged out around the massive log of meat, and she trembled and shook there on her knees. Emery pushed deeper, and pulled her head up and forward, gripping her with both hands now and grinding her face into his groin, burying her nose in his hairy abdomen, crushing her lips up against his pubic bone.

He held her there for long seconds, stroking her hair, knuckles digging into her scalp, then he pulled back just as slowly, pulling his cock free.

Dara choked and gagged and coughed while he looked down

patiently. She gulped in air, then cried out as he jerked back on her hair and pushed his cock forward. It forced her jaw wider and drove straight down her throat. But rather than resting there he began to pump it in and out, using her throat like her sex, pulling her head up to meet his thrusts as she gurgled wetly around his thick slab of meat.

Though it was not the first time, she still had difficulty getting used to it, and even more difficulty drawing breath as he pumped in and out. She began to get light-headed from lack of air, and sagged lower in his grip. He pulled free and she fell back onto her heels, then reeled sideways, falling heavily onto her side with a choked gasp.

Emery knelt and flipped her over as though she weighed nothing. His big hands seized her thigh and side and yanked her up onto her knees, and his knee forced her legs apart as he positioned himself behind her.

Dara moaned as she felt the thickness of his erection pressing against her. It pushed forward as relentlessly as ever, and had soon battered her muscles into submission and driven deep into her body. She grunted and moaned, her cheek pressed against the dirty, grit covered floor as he ground his pelvis against her upraised rear and then began to pump.

Like a steam locomotive he started out slowly and steadily, then began to gradually pick up the pace, his thick cock chuffing in and out of her with ever increasing speed and force until her face was grinding back and forth on the floor and his hips were slapping painfully against her bottom.

His big hands came down on her shoulders, jamming her down into the floor as he rode over her. His hips pounded savagely at her buttocks, and his cock sliced deeply into her aching belly.

Dara's mind floated amid the jerking, aching bursts of pain and rapidly blossoming pleasure which snapped and bit at her consciousness. Her knees scraped against the floor and she grunted dully.

Fucking me. Fucking me. Fucking me.

Her body quivered and trembled under the hard pounding, and her insides turned to jelly, to mush, as Emery's massive pole skewered her deep and hard and fast. She was a sex toy to him, a rag doll he used to masturbate with.

But it didn't matter. Nothing mattered but the dark, savage sexual hunger he showed her, a hunger which was infectious and irresistible. Like a feverish sensual heat it began to inflame her mind and body until nothing else mattered and she came explosively, crying out in wanton, mindless pleasure.

Emery continued to ride her through it, his stiff cock slamming down into her pussy even as she sagged weakly in the afterglow of her come. When he finished he pulled out, gave her a weak kick that had her tumbling weakly onto her sides, and left her alone.

She lay on her side for some time, feeling the ache in her shoulders and arms and trying to work through the confusion and wonder of what was happening to her. Some part of her continued to feel resentment and anger at such crude and thoughtless treatment. Yet the remnants of her outrage only seemed to serve to feed the sexual hunger which gripped her like a fever.

All of her darkest fantasies had come to life, and if they were more painful, more humiliating, more degrading than she had ever imagined that was only because her imagination had been lacking. For the pleasure and heat and ecstasy were far greater, as well.

A pair of big Black feet appeared in front of her face, and her eyes rolled up to see him towering over her. He reached down with a huge fist and grasped her by one arm, yanking her up to her feet.

"Got work to do," he said in a low rumbling voice, hefting the pile of metal and leather in his other hand and pulling her towards the door.

Dara stumbled repeatedly as Emery led her down the rocky, weed infested path which led behind his shack. He took her out to the edge of his field and released her arm briefly. Before them sat an small, rusting metal plough. As she watched, Emery hooked straps to its ends, then turned and motioned her forward, bare feet sinking into the moist earth.

She shuffled forward uncertainly, and he yanked her harder, unfolding the mass of leather and metal into a kind of heavy harness which he slipped across her shoulders.

"What are you doing?" she gasped.

The harness pulled in tight around her chest just below and above her breasts, against her flat belly, and around her hips. She gasped and grunted as the straps dug into her soft flesh, pining her arms even more tightly against her body.

Emery adjusted the plough, then pulled her up in front of it and attached straps to the harness, making his intent clear. She was to pull the plough.

Dara was aware that in the long gone and far away wives had pulled ploughs, but despite that she still felt shocked, for in her experience it was the task of animals, and so she had, in effect, been reduced to the status of an animal.

"Move," he ordered.

Dar stared at him in shock, thn at the plough.

"Move."

He picked up a long buggy whip and she moaned, eyes rolling

as she turned and jerked forward. At first she made some headway, but then Emery angled the plough down and she gasped as the straps dug into her chest and shoulders and hips.

"Pull harder, whore," he demanded.

The buggy whip snapped out and bit at her hip and Dara screamed, lunging forward, bare feet digging into the grass and dirt. She dragged the plough forward, forcing it through the soft earth as Emery followed behind.

This isn't happening. It isn't happening.

And yet her outrage continued to feed her sense of sexual heat. To be forced into such a position, to be degraded into the status of a beast of burden, was a shocking thing, and so the moist heaviness in her loins grew.

"Move."

The buggy whip slashed out and snapped at the underside of one buttock and Dara cried out, bending into the straps, gasping for breath as she forced the plough through the dirt.

They drove a line all the way across the field, then turned and drove another one back. Dara was covered in sweat, exhausted and whimpering, but whenever she slowed the whip cracked against her soft flesh and leant her new strength.

Pain gripped her, and yet a cloud of sexual heat surrounded her mind, and she could feel the lips of her sex almost swelling out, her insides hungry to be penetrated.

They ploughed another row, then another and another. Emery let her rest briefly, threw a pail of cold water over her as she lay gasping in the dirt, then picked her up and ordered her forward once again.

The whip slashed across her shoulders and she sobbed and threw herself forward. The straps cut into her soft flesh as she dragged the plough through the earth.

"Move, whore."

Crack!

The sun beat down on her from above, and sweat ran down her face, between her breasts and along her flanks. The world seemed to reel around her as she struggled foot by foot over the ground.

She was barely conscious when Emery led her, trembling and shaking, back into the shack where his tools and bags of seed lay, threw her down against a corner, and chained her there by the collar.

He closed the door and disappeared, and Dara sat back against the wall, gasping and trembling, every muscle exhausted. Eventually she fell asleep.

She woke to Emery's fingers in her hair. He yanked her out of the corner, dragging her casually along the dirt floor by the hair, then lifted her bottom high, knelt behind her, and jammed his erection against her sex.

Dara groaned dully as his thick prong slowly forced its way into her and he began to rut with growing speed and strength. Every bone and muscle in her body ached but the feel of his big cock inside her overpowered them all. That dark hunger at the back of her mind slid forward and soon the sexual heat was pouring through her body.

She whimpered as she felt the climax roll over her, grunting and jerking there in the dirt as Emery's hips pounded against her bottom. Another followed it, and another, and still another, as she trembled and shook to the power of her hunger and passion.

When he was done he yanked her casually to her feet, half supporting her as he pulled her along behind him into the house. He set her on her knees as he moved to the oven, and a minute later set a bowl of water and another of hot porridge on the floor before her.

He nodded and she sagged lower, sitting back on her heels, then bending until her breasts were crushed against her legs. She began to lick hungrily at the porridge, gulping and swallowing with abandon as Emery pulled out a chair and began to eat his own breakfast.

Dara licked the bowl clean, then slurped at the water, gulping it down quickly to ease the desperate thirst she had not known she possessed.

She sagged then, laying her head on the floor. Emery took the bowls away and washed them, then returned and pulled her to her feet.

"Time to finish the ploughin'," he said.

He led Dara out into the field and once again hooked her to the plough. She sagged wearily, her body aching, but the first snap of the whip sent her staggering forward.

Halfway through the field she dropped exhaustedly to her knees, and even as the whip slashed across her arms, shoulders and buttocks she could not force herself to her feet.

Emery walked up to her and gripped her hair, yanking her face out of the dirt, and looked into her dulled eyes with a grunt. "You stink," he said.

He unfastened the harness, then lifted her up across his shoulder and carried her like a bag of meal back across the field.

He set her down next to his shack, then drew up a pail of water and threw it over her body.

She moaned and rolled weakly from side to side. Another pail had her sputtering and gasping.

He folded her legs back against her body, hands sliding down to grip her behind the knees, then, as his cock forced her pubic muscles to ease their grip, began to pound his hips down against her upraised buttocks with a hungry savagery.

Dara stared up dazedly as she was pounded into the mud and wet earth, grunting and gasping as her knees crushed her breasts, then were jammed down into the dirt alongside her shoulders. Her spine ached as she was bent in two, and she shuddered as he slid his hands along her legs to the ankles and forced them back into the grass beside her head.

All the while his hips slammed down against her bottom, skewering her with brutal lust and hunger which, as always, infected her with the same so that she was soon shuddering to the violence of her own powerful orgasmic storms.

When he was done with her he rose, gripped her by the collar, and dragged her limp body across the ground and into the shack. He unbound her wrists and arms and then she crawled into the cage, fell onto her belly and slept.

Chapter Eight

"You look like somethin' the dog dragged in."

Dara smiled tiredly at her uncle and ran a hand through her hair.

"I been having a hard time sleeping. The heat," she said.

"Stop spending your money on partying and you can buy your own machine," he said with a shrug.

She nodded, too weary to argue.

"You find out anything about who might be running drugs down the Okiwani?"

She shook her head.

"We ain't got forever, girl."

"I asked around. I'll go back this evening and try again."

"See you do. I gotta have these yankees around for another weekend. I want it to be the last."

She nodded.

"I mean it, Dara. I know you like partying on Fridays. Today you go out to the Okinawi and don't come back until you know something. Emery Roosevelt lives out that way. See what he's been doing lately. If anyone's like to be involved it's him."

She nodded, fighting to keep her face expressionless.

She was wearing another of the leather outfits she'd recently bought. Although bought was probably not the best word for things she'd put on her already overloaded credit card. The card was already so high she was going to have to - and a hot shiver ran through her at the thought - find some way of earning extra money to pay it off.

She imagined herself in short shorts and a bikini top out by the Truck stop pushing her chest out at the truckers and a hungry little shudder went through her belly at the humiliation that would be.

She pushed past her uncle and on down the hall, heading for the coffee machine.

Beneath her uniform she wore what would look to casual observers as a latex thong. They would not see the thick, ten inch latex dildos attached to the inside of the crotch, dildos buried in her pussy and rectum.

She wore a bustier made of leather straps which cut horizontally across her breasts, squeezing them in, squeezed in even tighter around her lower chest, and reduced her waist by a good four inches. She had to breath shallowly, and even then the straps cut deeply into her beasts every time she inhaled.

But there was no evidence of it to anyone she passed by as she stopped at the coffee machine. She put in her coins, bent slowly, took out the cup, and continued on, nodding to those she passed and enjoying the secret she was keeping from them all.

The savage open handed blow to her face spun her around and sent her staggering against the cabin wall. Ear ringing, she cried out as Emery caught at her hair and forced her head up and back sharply.

"Why were you asking about me the other day?" he barked.

"I-I wasn't!" she gasped.

She shook her like a rag doll.

"You were asking people about who might have a boat. You were asking them who might be using it on the river. Don't lie to me bitch!"

"I-I was told to!" she cried.

He forced her to her knees, jamming her face against the floor.

"By who? Why?"

And it came pouring out, everything she knew, everything the Sheriff had told her, everything about Hernandez and what they suspected, as Emery growled and muttered and cursed under his breath, tightening his grip on her hair and jamming her face down harder and harder.

"And why didn't you tell me none of this?" he demanded between clenched teeth.

She had no answer and screamed as he yanked her back by the hair.

"Why?! You thinking of arresting me?!"

"NO!"

"That what you were doing out back? Looking for evidence!?"

"No! I wasn't!"

He flung her down and stood up.

"You think I should believe you?" he demanded furiously.

"It's true! I wouldn't!" Dara cried, staring up at him imploringly.

She threw herself at his ankles, clutching at them. "I wouldn't tell them nothing about you, Emery!"

"Why should I believe that?"

"It's true! I'd do anything for you. I love you!"

The word shocked her for some reason, and after a dazed moment she realized why. Because it wasn't true. The thought jarred her, shattering her thinking processes. If she didn't love Emery then why was she letting him do such terrible things to her? Why did her stomach twist and her chest tighten every time she thought of him?

Her head ached trying to understand.

"I should kick your skinny little white ass all the way back to town."

"No!' she cried, feeling a sudden panic. "I'll do anything to prove it to you, Emery!"

"You will, huh?" He glared down at her. "Get naked, bitch."

She scrambled to her feet, fingers tearing at her uniform shirt and yanking it over her shoulders. Emery glowered at the straps clenched tightly around her waist and chest, then at the G-string. She undid the top, breathing deeply in relief, then eased the G-string down. Emery snorted in disdain as he saw the thick, soft leather dildos sliding out of her pussy and anus.

"You fuckin' whore," he said.

Her face burned, but she continued to pull them down, then stepped out of them, standing quivering before him.

But she didn't love him. Why had she even said she had? And why was she so mentally overpowered around him? Why was she so willing to degrade herself?

"You know I gots to punish you."

She nodded jerkily.

He stared down at her a long moment then turned and yanked open the door. She followed him out into the darkening wood, over to the shack. It was dark and hot, smelling of moist wood and oil. He lit a lamp which hung from a hook overhead and turned to look at her, his eyes gleaming with the reflected light.

"Want to ride the horse again?" he taunted.

She looked at the sawhorse and swallowed, her heart beating faster.

"No!" she gulped.

"C'mere."

She moved forward reluctantly and his massive hand caught her behind the neck, yanking her forward. He pushed her against the work bench, against a high backed stool which was tucked in beneath it. She grunted as her soft breasts pillowed out against the rough, chipped surface of the bench and her lower belly pressed down against the top of the stool's back.

He picked up a rough cord and bound her wrists to a hook set in the wall, then bound her ankles apart.

"Carla will punish you."

The words made her gasp, and she pulled against he cords. "No! Emery, you punish me!"

'You don't boss me, girl."

"I-I don't want her - ahh!"

She cried out as he gripped her hair, yanking her head up.

"You do as I say!" he snarled.

"O-Okay," she gulped, eyes wide.

"You gonna heed me, girl?"

She jerked her head up and down.

"You heed Carla too. You got too much starch in you."

He sauntered out of the room and she sagged against the bench wearily, her chest heaving. Carla. That slut! That whore! What did Emery see in her anyway?!

Minutes passed. It was hot in the shack, and she groaned weakly, uncomfortably. The narrow top of the stool was jammed into her lower belly just above her groin. It forced her bottom up so that she was on the balls of her feet, and she hated to think of Carla coming in and seeing her so vulnerably.

She hard a noise at the door and turned, gulping, trying to make her face uncaring as Carla sauntered in, a wide, sneering smile on her face.

"Little white girl needs to be punished," she taunted. "Emery says take the starch out of your pretty little be-hind."

She moved up behind her and despite herself Dara winced at the feel of the woman's hand as it slid over her bottom. "Such a pretty little white ass," she said, marvelling. "What should we do to it?"

Her hand moved up and down the cleft between her taut buttocks, in beneath to caress her soft sex.

Dara clenched her teeth, determined not to show weakness or fear or discomfort as the woman ran her finger up and down her sex and then pushed it slowly inside.

"Think we should find another couple of cucumbers for you, pretty girl?" she taunted, pumping one, then two, then three fingers roughly in and out. "Or maybe you want another fisting, eh? You like my fist up your pussy, bitch?"

Dara said nothing, burning with embarrassment at being given to the black woman to punish, hating her, hating herself, hating Emery. If she just told her to untie her, promised to go away and not return, she was sure Carla would be overjoyed to let her go and wave goodbye. But she couldn't bring herself to do it, couldn't stay away from Emery and couldn't give the bitch the satisfaction.

"Oh, what have we here?" Carla cooed.

She reached past her and plucked a half empty beer can from the bench.

"This ain't no cucumber, but it ought to feel nice and big in your tight little pussy."

"Jealous that I'm tighter than you?" she snarled.

Carla laughed. "It won't be when I'm done with it, bitch."

Dara was about to reply but her words turned into a cry of pain as Carla rammed the base of the can against her sex. She instinctively tried to close her legs, but of course, found the tight cords digging into her ankles as they held her open.

"Fuck!" she gasped.

"Poor baby," Carla sneered.

She twisted the can from side to side, grinding it against Dara's soft mons. Her fingers pushed in between the soft, moist flesh and pulled, and she forced one side of the can into her. Then her fingers moved to the other side of her pussy and tugged to stretch her wide as she twisted the can and pushed forward.

Dara groaned as it went into her, and Carla laughed and slapped her bottom. "There you go, little girl."

She twisted and pushed the can, forcing it deeper and deeper, until it was flush with the base of her sex. Warm beer was spilling out the end, down along her sex and belly and trickling down her thighs to the floor. She could feel the hard, thickness of the can pushing aside the soft flesh within her, filling her pussy sleeve to overflowing as Carla drove it deeper and deeper.

And then she felt the other end pass through her opening, and Carla chuckled again as her pussy lips closed behind it.

"Now about that punishment you're due. What kind of punishment do you think it should be?" Carla asked.

She bent over beside her and leaned on the table, grinning at Dara from up close. "I think the bad little girl needs her bottom strapped. Don't you?"

"Fu-fuck you!" Dara gasped.

Carla smiled and stood, and Dara braced herself as the woman took a thin leather belt from her pants. She had been strapped by Emery, she told herself, and Carla wasn't nearly so strong. It would sting a little, that was all. So what.

Of course, it also stung her that it was Carla at all. She was shamed that the other woman in Emery's life had her at her mercy, that she had no choice but to submit to whatever "punishment" she wanted to give.

She was startled to here a strange, yet familiar sound. She turned to see Carla holding a roll of duct tape, a long piece stretched out from it.

"We don't want the can to fall out," she said with a smile.

Then she pressed the end of the tape up against Dara's lower belly, rubbing it with her hand to smooth it in tight, and pulled the length of the tape up between her legs, up across her pussy and up between her buttocks, her hand rubbing back and forth.

"Don't!" Dara cried, the plea almost instinctive.

"Oh, okay. If you don't want it."

Carla yanked the tape down hard and Dara's eyes bulged as she screamed in pain. Her body jerked violently as the tape ripped the hair from her body.

"Oh darn. Did that hurt?" Carla asked with mock concern. "Maybe I should put it back."

But she tore a fresh strip of tape and quickly pressed it against Dara's burning sex, rubbing her hand up and down.

"Y-Y-You fu-fucking bitch!" Dara sobbed.

"Now that ain't nice, girl."

Carla yanked the tape down again and again Dara screamed. There were far fewer hairs for it to rip free, but her entire groin was red with pain and so the effect was almost as bad.

Carla's laughter tore at her nerved, and Dara screamed and sobbed, cursing her obscenely. The woman only laughed again, then yanked her head back by the hair and stuffed a greasy, balled up rag into her mouth. Her long fingers thrust and prodded at it, forcing Dara's cheeks to bulge out. Then she took a second rag and bound it around her head, the fabric jamming in against the sides of her mouth.

"Now, about that punishment."

The crack of the belt was loud in the small shack, and the sharp, stinging pain ripped through Dara's nervous system.

"Such a pretty bottom," she cooed.

The belt snapped down again, and again, and again, and Dara snarled and twisted and moaned into the dirty rag as the blows cut across her upraised buttocks. Carla paused every few blows to rub her fingers over Dara's bottom, and tell her what a pretty round ass it was. Then she'd lay fresh lines of pain across it as Dara's eyes watered and she furiously tried to blink the tears away.

The belt was thin, and while Carla wasn't as strong as Emery she was no weakling. She laid stripe after strip up and down the blonde girl's bottom and then down along the backs of her thighs.

She paused, her hand rubbing over Dara's now bare sex, fingering and fondling her soft, swollen labia and pressing them back against the beer can nestled within.

"What a pretty pussy," she said. "We'll have to get some more boys in here to gang bang you. You'd like that, wouldn't you, white girl? More nigger cock for you, hmm?"

She rubbed her finger along Dara's clitoris.

"I heard you banged every man at Mika's the other day. You like that, slut? Hhmm? You want me to get them over her to do you again?"

Her fingers rubbed Dara's clitoris back and forth as she spoke, and Dara's fury and outrage at her intimate touch grew even more powerful when she felt the soft, thrumming heat between her legs begin to build.

She was almost grateful when the woman drew back and the belt lashed across her bottom once again.

"You call me slut? I never banged a whole bar of men," Carla sneered. "What kind of a woman would do that? What kind of a sick assed whore would chain fuck a whole bar of men? Especially a place like Mika's full of ratty, scruffy, unwashed welfare bums?"

The belt lashed across her bottom again and Dara moaned into the gag. Her entire backside was a throbbing, burning ache now, yet each new blow sent a sharp crack of pain through her quivering, sweating body.

"Dirty little whore. You really are a bitch in heat, ain't you?"

Dara tossed her head angrily, but a part of her wondered if Carla wasn't right.

"Maybe I got more use for this duct tape," Carla said in amusement.

She knelt behind Dara and Dara felt her hand on her right ankle, undoing the rough cord binding it. Then she lifted the leg up and back and pressed her foot back against her thigh just below her bottom. The woman twisted her heel out and thrust her foot back hard, pressing her ankle against the side of her thigh, now, and then Dara felt the tape pressed against her.

She moaned into the gag, not knowing what Carla was doing but knowing she wouldn't like it. She felt the tape wrap around her ankle, then go around her thigh just below her pussy. Carla rolled the tape around and around and around her ankle and thigh, going downwards, laying tape all the way around her leg, pinning her lower leg to her thigh. She laughed as she did, giggling to herself, and only when she had run the tape back and forth over Dara's knee did she cut it and move to her other leg.

She forced that up and back, too, and Dara grunted as her weight came down on her belly, grinding it into the top of the stool and the rough bench.

As with her right leg, Carla rolled the tape around and around her left from thigh to knee, taping her foot up back against her outer thigh. Then she reached forward and untied Dara's right hand. Dara tried to fight her but was in no position, and had no leverage. Carla forced her hand back flat against the top of her shoulder, then rolled the duct tape around her wrist and upper arm, then ran the tape around and around her arm all the way down to the elbow.

Finally she freed her left hand and pushed it back as well. Dara rolled her eyes furiously, but could do little as that arm too was pushed back and taped in place.

Carla laughed to herself, then put down the tape and slid her arms under Dara's belly, grunting as she lifted her up off the bench and then lowered her to the floor.

"Oh this is so precious!" she squealed. "Now you can really be a bitch in heat!"

Dara was on all fours. More precisely, she was on her knees and elbows, her upper body lower, her bottom high. She glared daggers at the snickering black woman, who merely pointed at her and laughed louder.

Then she turned and hurried to the back of the shack, bending and searching through boxes of junk until she straightened with a cry of success and turned, brandishing a dog collar.

"This was for a doberman Emery had. I don't think he ever called it nothin' but dog, so we'll make that your name."

She wrapped the collar around Dara's neck and buckled it, then ran a piece of rope to the ring in its front to use as a leash and pulled on it.

"Let's go see Emery, bitch dog," she taunted.

Face burning, Dara refused, trying to draw back, but that made her feel even more embarrassed, for the resemblance to a dog resisting the pull of its leash was too great. And then Carla picked up a long thin stick, a switch, and snapped it across Dara's bottom. It stung painfully and she yelped into the gag, lurching forward.

"Move that red little ass of yours," Carla ordered, snapping the switch down a second time.

Miserable, furious, embarrassed, and hoping Emery would order her untied - or untaped - she gave in and let Carla lead her on a leash out of the shack and across the grassy clearing to the cabin.

It was awkward crawling on elbows and knees, harder than hands and knees, and more painful, for all of her weight came down on her knees, without her feet to take some pressure off, and her elbows were even worse, with her elbows grinding against any hard object they pressed down against.

The dirt wasn't too bad, but when she was forced up into the cabin and her elbows came down against the hard wood floor she moaned and winced in pain.

She hated Carla for degrading her like this, hated Emery for allowing it, and hated herself for accepting it. And then Emery looked up from his chair and saw her and laughed out loud, and she moaned in shame, trying not to cry out of her frustration and humiliation.

"A real bitch," he said.

"A bitch in heat, like I said," Carla replied triumphantly.

"Ought to stake her out in the yard like we used to do the other one."

"Come here, dog," he ordered, leaning forward and snapping

his fingers.

He made kissing sounds like he would for a dog, and she blushed angrily, but crawled forward to his hand. He half lifted and turned her so she was kneeling at his feet, and ran a hand over her red bottom, then down between her legs.

"Wha happened to her pussy hair?"

"It all fell out," Carla said with a negligent shrug. "Sick bitch probably caught something."

"You lying whore," Emery said, but in amusement. "That a nice little pussy, all fresh and clean with no hair or nothing in the way."

His fingers stroked along Dara's sex and then two of them pushed inside, where he quickly found the beer can and laughed again.

"She already got somethin' hard and fat in her pussy," Carla said, sitting on the arm of his chair and pressing her breasts against his face. "She don't need you there."

"Quiet woman. I's attending to my dog here."

His big fingers stroked along Dara's pussy, and she felt a moist warmth spreading up through her groin. They pushed into her, wedging in tightly against either side of the can, then slowly drew it up and out. She groaned in relief - yet felt vacant as the can left her.

And then with a gasp, she felt her bottom lifted up as Emery knelt behind her. He gripped her just below her hips and lifted her whole lower body up into the air she was balanced precariously on her elbows, and she felt his tongue against her.

Emery had never licked her before, and she shuddered as his big tongue lapped up and down along her sex.

"Hey!" Carla protested. "You never licked my pussy!"

He paused and looked up at her. "I don't like hair in my mouth."

Then he turned back and began to lick at Dara's sex once again.

"This tastes like beer!" he said in delight, thrusting his tongue in deeper.

His tongue licked up and down her sex like a cat, and he turned to a fuming Carla. "Get me a beer, a fresh one."

"I ain't getting you now - ."

"Get me a beer, bitch!" he growled.

No one says no to Emery, Dara thought smugly.

Emery thrust his fingers into her sex and poured beer into her, then opened his mouth wide and sucked it out again, his tongue thrusting in and out of her as his lips massaged and caressed her sensitive mons. He sucked her lips into his mouth one by one, then lifted her hips higher and licked at her clit.

Dara saw stars flaring before her eyes. She shuddered, her hips writhing and twisting in his hands as he sucked and licked at her clitoris. His fat wet tongue was rolling up and down between the lips of her sex and his hot breath was turning to steam as it struck her quivering nerve endings.

He caught her swollen clitoris between his teeth and gnawed lightly, the pain, strangely, like oil on the fire of her burning lust as she jerked her hips against him. Then he drew his teeth back and let his lips catch her clit, rubbing and massaging, building a firestorm inside her.

When his tongue licked hard and fast against her she came with a scream, twisting and humping and bucking against him, her head thrashing and rolling as the climax tore through her vitals and washed over her already dazed mind.

Emery licked and lapped her through it, then set her down on her knees. She sagged at once, and he slid a fat paw beneath her sex, lifting her up and giving her a slap on the bottom to hold herself steady. Then he entered her, mounted her, thrust into her.

She felt like the bitch in heat Carla had called her, and her body screamed in pleasure as his mammoth cock slid into her and his hands came down around her flanks. He began to ride her, to pump his steely cock in and out of her body as he always did, with raw, furious passion and hunger, the knob of his cock thrusting past her cervix and striking the back wall of her pussy with every deep stroke.

A bitch in heat. That was exactly what she was, she knew. She didn't love Emery. She loved his cock. She loved being ridden like a bitch, like an animal.

Her head rolled up and down, her body shaking to the pounding of his hips as he skewered her, as his big pole of a cock rammed in and out of her oozing flesh.

A part of her felt shamed to be taken like that, especially while someone else was looking on, but a part of her felt like crowing at Carla, who could only watch and fume that what she'd done had made Emery want to use her so strongly.

She grunted with each hard thrust, panting for breath, moaning in a twisted mix of pain and pleasure as his cock pounded into her. Her knees and elbows ached as they ground against the floor, and her insides felt pulped, beaten, like Jell-O.

A climax tore through her body, and her head thrashed and jerked up and down, her hips jerking back and forth in Emery's grasp. Another washed over her, and then a third, as Emery continued to hammer himself against her from behind.

She gasped in disbelief as he picked up the pace, as he thrust in still harder, his cock slamming painfully against the back wall of her pussy until suddenly - he stopped. He exhaled, took in a deep breath, and blew it out again, his fingers loosening against her hips.

"Nice," he gasped. "Nice."

He slapped her bottom lightly as he pulled his softening cock free, and then stood up.

Dara sagged, groaning.

"Did you enjoy yourself?" Carla demanded angrily.

"Yeah," he said, doing up his jeans. "Tie my bitch out in the yard."

Carla stomped her foot angrily, then snatched Dara's "leash" and yanked her towards the door.

"And put her in shade. I don't want my bitch's skin to get all red and burned."

His bitch.

Dara felt a heady sense of almost surreal eroticism as she crawled after Carla. She grunted in relief as her elbows met dirt instead of wood, her bottom wriggling as she crawled along. Her mouth was starting to feel dry with the rags filling it, but she was too tired, too drained to care much over it. She followed Carla out to a tree and watched as the woman tied off her leash, glared at her, called her a bitch, then stomped back into the cabin.

Dara tried to sit, to kneel. She could kneel, but it was more comfortable to just lay back on her back. Of course, with her legs taped together that left her knees up high, and after a few minutes they slowly fell apart, and she let weight pull them farther. Her pussy was sore, bruised, hot, and she let the air wash over it.

Modesty seemed pointless.

She looked down the length of her body and examined her pussy, lifting her head up and staring. It was an interesting sight without hair. It looked girlish, and very very - naked. But if Emery liked it that way then she'd keep it naked. The feel of his tongue on her there had been amazing.

Carla came out of the cabin, glaring at her as she stomped over to the shack. She returned with a longer rope and a bowl. She set the bowl down, exchanged the short leash for a longer one, then undid the rag around Dara's face and tugged the other out of her mouth.

"Bitch," she snarled.

"Whore," Dara replied.

Carla dropped to her knees suddenly, straddling Dara's upper body. With her hands taped to her upper arms there was little Dara could do as the woman looked down at her.

"I like having my pussy licked too," she sneered.

She slid upwards, lifting her short skirt. She was naked beneath, and as her knees pressed Dara's arms down she jammed her sex against her mouth.

"Lick me, bitch dog," she growled.

Dara glared up at her, keeping her mouth tightly closed.

Carla glared back down, then gripped her hair in two fists and started to twist and pull. Tears filled Dara's eyes but she refused to open her mouth, glaring hatefully up at the woman.

"What the fuck you doin', girl?" Emery's voice called. "I told you to water my bitch, not ride her."

"She won't lick me!" Carla complained.

"Bitch, do what Carla says," Emery called.

The words struck at Dara's belly and she wanted to rebel against them, but somehow couldn't bring herself to disobey. She let her mouth open reluctantly and pushed her tongue out and up against Carla's pussy as the woman looked down with triumph in her eyes.

"You ain't his bitch," she hissed. "You're just anyone's bitch, anyone what wants a cheap ride."

She began to grind her sex roughly against Dara's mouth, riding up and down, squeezing her buttocks down against her cheeks, then riding forward over her nose, sneering down at her as Dara's tongue pushed out against her

It only took her a few minutes to come, but by then Dara's face was slick with her juices, and she glared at the smug woman as she rose to her feet and walked away. She returned a minute later with a pale of water, pouring some into the bowl and then with a sniff of contempt, turned and walked away.

Dara rolled onto her side, then pushed herself up on all fours, crawling forward to the bowl. Her mouth was painfully dry, filled with the taste of oil and dirt - and Carla. She pushed her lips into the water and began to suck and slurp at it. Then, something dark and twisted inside her made her pull her lips back. She looked around her, then leaned in and began to lick at the water as a dog would.

A bitch dog. A bitch dog in heat. Emery's bitch.

Her stomach churned and her chest tightened as she licked. She wasn't able to draw much water that way, and wondered idly how dogs did it, but it did help wash the taste of Carla from her tongue.

She turned and looked at the rope attached to her collar, then crawled out to see how far it ran. It wasn't very far at all, but she had no where to go. She crawled back, feeling like a wild, feral slut, a creature of sex and perversion. She licked at the water again and wished she could masturbate.

Her elbows and knees were sore, so she lay down in the shade of the tree, wondering how long Emery would keep her taped up.

Chapter Nine

When she'd been younger Dara had wanted to be a boy. She'd wanted it desperately. She had dressed like boys, acted like boys, and hung around with boys. While other girls were wearing pretty dresses and playing with dolls she was in jeans and t-shirt playing baseball and football and basketball with the boys.

But even when she was dressed like a boy her parents, and other adults, especially women, insisted she maintain a certain level of decorum. And one of the things she was much criticised for was laying or sitting with her knees apart.

She had no idea why that bothered people at the time. She understood why, if she were wearing a short skirt, she ought to keep her legs together so no one would see her panties, but she never wore shorts skirts. She never wore any kind of skirt if she could avoid it.

Boys sat with their legs apart all the time, and she resented not being able to do the same. So whenever they were alone, just her and the boys, she would sit and slouch and act the same way they would.

That became harder as she grew older. When puberty hit it became painfully obvious that she was not going to be able to stay as one of the boys. For one thing, skinny dipping together was going to be impossible. The boys spent too much time ogling her, and they all wanted to wrestle. So soon after adolescence hit she had to give that up.

She continued to hang around with boys, to play sports, to be interested in boyish things, but as her body developed and they became a lot more interested in girls' bodies, she had to start being more careful there, too. Wrestling with them was out since they almost always used it as an excuse to get in some groping. And she had to be careful whenever she bent over in case one of them slapped or grabbed her.

But she had continued to defiantly sit with her legs apart, even as she grew old enough to understand the implications behind why the grownups didn't like it, even as her teenage years gave her the knowledge and understanding of why laying back in the grass, along with the boys, with her knees raised and her legs spread, was more than a little - suggestive.

When she was fifteen, though, Reverend Murdoch's wife had caught her laying around like that and dragged her off by the ear to give her a tongue lashing about the behaviour the church expected of young ladies. Dara had sullenly listened to her and agreed, then ignored her. But the next time Mrs. Murdoch caught her like that she'd bent her over and taken a hairbrush to her bottom until Dara had howled for mercy.

And that was the last time Dara laid or sat around with her legs spread in public, no matter what she was wearing.

And now she was wearing nothing. She was wearing worse than nothing, because her pussy was now so naked and bare that it was almost shameful to even show it to Emery.

And it felt wicked, and exciting.

It was getting on towards evening when she heard the sound of an engine. She whipped her knees up together, her pulse suddenly racing as she rolled onto her side and then tried to wriggle in closer behind the tree trunk.

She heard voices, male voices, and her face reddened as her pulse grew wilder. She was anxious that they not see her, yet another part of her wanted to show off just what she was, just how low and slutty she had become. What would men think of seeing a girl as she was? And would Emery let them use her as he had the other men?

Anticipation made her loins warm even more than her face as she saw three men walking up towards the cabin. Yet she hid behind the tree, keeping low, heart pounding as she sought to avoid the shame of them seeing her.

But it was no use, as one of the men, looking around suspiciously, saw her pale face peering out from behind the trunk and scowled.

"Who the fuck's that?" she heard.

Her pulse racing, she tried to hide more of herself behind the tree, but it wasn't wide enough.

The three men walked over to her, and stared. They were all strangers, and she could not bring herself to meet their eyes, to even look at them. She backed away, keeping her head low.

"Ho-ly she-it!" she heard.

"Ain't that somethin'," another voice remarked.

"Nice titties there."

"Looks like this'un was rode hard and put away wet," the first voice said with a laugh.

"I wouldn't mind ridin' her hard," another voice growled.

Feet crunched in the dirt as Emery crossed from the cabin. "This's my bitch," he said. "You like it?"

He tugged on the rope, forcing Dara's head up, and she stared up at the four men, deeply shamed. Yet even so her loins were throbbing with excitement.

"Looks very nice," one of the strangers said.

"Our business goes well, maybe I let you take her for a ride," Emery said. "C'mon. Inside."

He released the rope and turned away and, staring over their shoulders, the other men followed, whispering to each other as they left her.

Emery's bitch.

Butterflies twirled in her stomach as she lay down - on her side, with her legs together.

What in the hell am I doing here!?

She could go to New York. Sure, it was full of yankees and foreigners, but you probably didn't sweat like a pig every summer as she did here. And she wouldn't have people looking over her shoulders everywhere she went eager to gossip about what she was doing and with who.

She imagined herself as a New York cop, in their dark blue, almost black uniforms. Everyone respected the police in New York. Those were real cops, with training and everything. They had computers in their cars and - and SWAT teams and there were thousands and thousands of them.

She laid her head against the side of the tree and imagined living in New York, where people were sophisticated, where they wouldn't be shocked at the thought of an unmarried girl sleeping with people, even with a Black man. Though even in New York, she conceded, they'd be tsk tsking over a girl letting herself be done by a whole bar of men.

Not to mention being taped up like a bitch dog.

It was humiliating is what it was, and she frowned unhappily as she looked at her taped arms and legs. She was better than them. She was smart, she was pretty, she was a deputy sheriff (even if only on due to her uncle). They were no-account criminals, the people who slunk around in the shadows, wary of the police.

Yet she was letting them use her, beat her, treat her like dirt!

Indignation rose within her, and then memories cascaded before her eyes, hot, steaming memories which tightened her stomach muscles and made her pussy thrum.

She'd had more wild, thrilling excitement in the past few weeks than she'd had her whole entire life. Her mind ran through flickering images of herself being used, being strapped and spanked and fisted and sodomised, being forced to grovel. She saw herself spread back on the table in the bar as the men gathered around, and standing with her wrists tied above her as Emory's two friends came in the night to use her.

When she was old she was gonna have memories like nobody's business!

But how long could this go on? Already word would be

filtering out about what happened in the bar, and as more and more men saw her, as these ones had, that word would grow and spread. In Kainlen, a girl who had sex outside of marriage was pretty trashy. A girl who did it more than once, with someone other than a boyfriend, was a slut.

There just weren't enough nasty words to describe a girl who did the kind of things she'd done. And once word got out she wouldn't be able to walk through town without staring eyes and whispered comments.

Even stopping now and turning chaste probably wouldn't protect her. Too many men knew. Too many men had seen her, had done her. Another few days and someone would mention it to one of the deputies. He likely wouldn't be believed, but as more whispers caught their ears they'd start to think something was going on.

She was done. That realization hit her with a sick feeling in the pit of her stomach. She was done in Kainlen. She could not stay here now. She had a couple of weeks, maybe, and then there'd be hard questions. The Sheriff would find out the truth. Soon as he started hearing the rumours he'd take a few of those men who'd done her into the back room at the jail and get them to tell him exactly what happened.

She remembered Jessica Porter, a girl who'd been a year ahead of her in high school. Just shy of graduation her parents had found out she'd been sleeping with grocery delivery man, a strapping young Black man. She'd been beaten and thrown (literally) out the door naked. None of the neighbours would let her in either. The Sheriff had to come and get her, wrap her in a blanket, and take her away.

Jessica had left the county. Dara had no idea where she'd gone, but everyone knew you didn't mention her name around her family, not ever.

She was done good.

She felt a momentary panic. Where would she go? She had no money. If she took her whole pay check she could probably pay for gas to New York, except her old car probably wouldn't make it that far. She could hitch hike, she supposed, and once there do what? Become a waitress?

She'd talked for years about getting out of Kainlen. Now she was going to have to start doing something about it, and fast.

But that was going to mean losing Emery, going to mean becoming a "good girl" again, being normal, respectable. She'd never find a guy like Emery again, and never be treated like such a - such an animal.

She crawled to the bowl and licked at the water, ignoring a leaf which had fallen in, looking over the rim of the bowl at the distant door and wondering how long it would be before Emery sent the men out and told them to use her body as they wanted.

And then she inhaled sharply as she saw one at the door. He was a young man, possibly even younger than her. He was tall but thin, with short hair. He stared across at her, and her skin seemed to prickle with sexual energy. She looked away from him, flushing red, then turned her body so he could see her profile, could see her breasts hanging below her.

She turned further, crawling away, presenting her bottom and sex to him, ashamed of herself as she did it, but feeling a hot throbbing between her thighs.

Emery's bitch.

The New York police would certainly never hire a girl if they knew she'd done the kinds of things Dara had done. Even if none of it were illegal it wasn't the kind of thing which showed a strong willed, capable person. Only a puny, weak minded little slut would let herself be used like this.

Was that what she was?

She'd always been disgusted by girls who simpered and fawned over boys, sneering at them and shaking her head. But no girl she knew had ever degraded herself as she had the past few weeks.

She came to the end of the rope and felt the pull against her collar.

Her collar! She was collared like a fucking dog!

Shaking a little, she eased back and turned. The man was no longer in the doorway, but she still felt his eyes on her, knew he wanted her, and that Emery would probably give her to him. Would he have a big cock? Would he ride her hard and fast and rough like she needed it? Would he sneer at her and treat her like a whore? Would he use her like a bitch dog?

Her hands pulled at the tape pinning them to her arms, pulled instinctively as she tried to move them between her legs. She wondered what she felt like down there with no hair, how soft and smooth her sex was.

She lay down again, but again on her side. She simply couldn't bring herself to lay on her back with strangers around, to lay on her back and let her knees slowly come apart. She snorted at her own modesty, at the idea that she still had any modesty, any pride.

And yet she did.

This was all just a bizarre, twisted, exciting sexual game to her. She hadn't lost track of who and what she was. She hadn't abandoned it. She hadn't decided to someone's sex toy, someone's belonging. She was just - playing a game. Pretending.

It was exciting and it was dangerous and it was nasty, but it was still just a lewd, sick game.

Even if she was chained up naked like a dog to be used by a gang of nere do wells.

She just wondered if Emery knew that.

She raised her head at a sound and saw them coming for her. Her eyes widened and her mouth got suddenly dry. Her heart began to beat faster, and she rolled onto her belly and then awkwardly pushed herself up on knees and elbows, turning to face them.

But she couldn't, and, face flushed, dropped her eyes as they grew nearer, as she saw the wide grins on their faces. Emery was not with them, and she felt her pulse race as she found herself alone with strangers.

"Hey, lil' bitch," one of them said with a broad grin.

"You don't mind we fuck you, do you?" another taunted.

Two of them were her age or younger, slender, arrogant and smug. The third was older, larger, with broader shoulders and a bit of a belly. The older one put his foot against her and shoved hard so that Dara gasped and was flung up and over to land on her back.

He dropped to his knees and yanked her legs wide, shoving them down hard until they were pressed against the ground on either side.

"Hey, Al, you're supposed to fuck her like a dog," one of the younger ones protested.

"I fuck this bitch any ol' way I want," the other man grumbled.

He unzipped and drew out his cock, which was already semi erect, rubbing the head up and down against her bare sex as he ran a hand up and down her body.

"Nice titties," he said.

He pushed his cock inside her, then lifted her legs up and pushed them back to roll her bottom up. He began to thrust into her slowly, driving his cock fully and deeply into her warm pussy, and then after a few slow thrusts he began to ride her hard, to thrust violently down into her, using the full weight of his lower body.

Dara gasped and grunted at the impact of his hips against her bottom and thighs, but didn't bother to ask him to slow. Nor was she sure she even wanted him to. His pubic bone was grinding against her clitoris as his hardness drove into her soft, wet body, and her breath escaped in short little gasps and pants as she felt, despite her embarrassment, the fires igniting within her.

Slut. Whore. That's what she was. She was a whore for any man who wanted to use her.

She gazed up dull eyed at the man above her, his face a

shadow with the bright sun behind, then dropped her eyes. It didn't matter what he looked like. It didn't matter who he was. All that mattered was that hard cock pounding into her, driving deep into her belly with each hard thrust.

Dara shuddered and groaned aloud, her head falling back as the man drove himself down into her harder and harder. It didn't take long at the speed he was using. He was not, after all, making love to a woman. He was just using a slut, using her body to masturbate.

When he was done he grunted, then stood up and turned away without a word. One of the younger men knelt and rolled her onto her belly, then yanked on her hips to lift her up onto all fours..

"Man this is somethin'," he said excitedly.

"Like a dog you buy at the store or something," the other one said.

Dara felt herself penetrated and gasped in pleasure, feeling the man's stiff erection sliding through the soft folds of her inner sex, pushing deep. His hands caught at her hips and he began to thrust quickly. The other one watched for a moment, then knelt in front of her, gripping her hair in his fist, lifting her head up and back as he unzipped his jeans and drew his cock out.

"Suck me," he ordered.

His cock slid through Dara's open mouth, turning her gasps to muffled moans as it slid over her tongue and jammed against the inside of her cheek. She began to suck as best she could, her tongue sliding back and forth over the moving head whenever she could get at it. But the man was too excited to hold still, his cock twisting and turning and pushing back and forth in her mouth.

Her body was shaking to the thrusts of the man behind her, and she felt herself sinking into a world of sexual hedonism, a world where nothing mattered but the flare of heat sizzling along the surface of her skin. Hands reached down to fondle and knead her breasts and to rub roughly against her clitoris. She winced as her bottom was slapped and her hair pulled, but the stinging pain only added to her sense of dark, wild sexual passion.

The man before her held his cock still for long seconds, letting her suck properly, her lips sliding up and down the shaft, her tongue working on the head as she rolled her eyes up towards him.

But then he started thrusting again, and all she could do was hold her lips tightly around the shaft as it slid back and forth over her tongue. The man behind her ran his work roughened hands up and down her back and sides, roughly caressing her downy flesh, and slid them down beneath to squeeze her breasts flat, then knead them with hard, knobby fingers.

The man in front twisted her hair, pulling on it constantly as he pumped his hips in and out. Dara sucked excitedly, moaning around his shaft as her heat rose and her lower belly began to burn with a deep, spreading fire.

The one behind was gasping, groaning and cursing in pleasure as he rode her, his hips slamming against her buttocks with greater force, his hips working faster as his own passion rose.

Emery walked by in company with the older man, their shoes crunching against the dry earth as they moved past, hardly glancing at the trio, talking about a shipment as they moved back behind the shack and disappeared.

Chapter Ten

Dara could feel the heat in her face and knew she was blushing. She hoped it wouldn't be visible in the low light of the hall as she knocked on Hernandez' door. She reached up and combed her fingers nervously through her hair. She looked around her, feeling a rebellious sense of anger.

Nothing Emery had done to her or made her done so far was as embarrassing as forcing her to give herself to Hernandez. She hoped the man would simply refuse, though that too would be embarrassing. Emery had made it clear, after all, that she wasn't supposed to take no for an answer, that if she had to tear his pants off she was to do it. He'd beat her if she came back with nothing. But she was half inclined to take the beating even now, for it would surely cause less damage to her pride.

She wore her uniform, tight, as always, but with nothing underneath. The hot, humid air had the shirt plastered against her body, and she could feel the seam of the trousers digging up into her labia.

The door opened and Hernandez looked out at her, surprise clear in his face.

"What do you want?" he demanded, looking her up and down scornfully.

Bastard, she thought.

She forced herself to smile. "Why Agent Hernandez, is that any way to treat a fellow law enforcement officer come to call?"

"You're not much of a law enforcement officer," he said cooly.

She ducked under his arm and pushed past him into the room, dodging his hand as he reached for her, and skipping around him to put herself deeper into the room. Then half sat back against a dresser, the smile still on her face.

"But then again I ain't much of a fellow," she said coyly.

He stared at her a moment, then closed the door and turned, arms folded across his chest.

"What do you want?" he asked again.

"Got anything to drink?" she asked, looking around.

"No."

"Not very sociable, are yuh?" she asked. "We southerners always make company at home."

"We northerners wait until we're invited before we call

ourselves company," he said, moving up to stand in front of her.

"A southern man always makes a lady feel at home," she countered.

He smirked and she blushed angrily.

"Lady?"

"What's that supposed to mean?" she demanded angrily.

He leaned in against her and she leaned backwards over the dresser.

"Honey, I might not be intimately familiar with southern culture, but I know a two bit whore when I see one."

Dara felt her blood boil. While it was true the things she had done lately made the accusation more than accurate Hernandez had no way of knowing about those activities.

A more temperate girl would have swallowed her anger at his rude words, especially since she had been sent there for a reason. But Dara had never been much for repressing her emotions, and her fist was swinging up towards his chin before he'd even stopped talking.

His head snapped up and he staggered back with a cry of surprise. Dara lurched forward, her foot coming up fast, aiming for his groin, but he was surprisingly fast, twisting aside, grabbing her ankle as her foot swung up, and yanking hard so she was pulled off her feet. She let out a yell as she landed on her bottom, then kicked at his knee with her other foot. She missed, but he had to let her first leg go to dodge aside.

"Bastard!" she yelled, springing to her feet.

Her fist slammed into his belly, but he was surprisingly well muscled, and though he let out a whoof of pain he didn't go down. Instead he bent, grabbed her around the waist and lifted her up off her feet, then threw her down hard onto the bed.

He jumped on her and she jerked her knee up, hoping to catch him as he landed, but he twisted aside again, and was atop her, their hands twisting grimly together as he fought to pin her and she tried to roll aside. He had the leverage and the muscles and Dara gasped as he slammed her hands down against the mattress above her head.

"You're under arrest!" he growled, panting for breath.

"Fuck you!"

He reached for his belt but found no handcuffs. With a snarl, he forced her wrists together above her head, then pinned them there with one hand while he snatched the handcuffs out of Dara's belt, then, fighting to keep from being flung off, snapped one around her right wrist and closed it. Then forced her other hand beneath the crossbar of the headpost and closed the other one tightly.

He heaved a sigh as he sat back, still straddling her hips, and pushed his hair back.

Dara glowered up at him, but the tight cuffs pinching into her wrists sent a sudden hot thrill through her even as she fought tears of embarrassment and rage.

"Bastard," she hissed.

"Bitch," he replied, glaring.

She looked up at her wrists, then back at him, and then smiled coyly, pushing her chest up a little so her breasts would push more strongly against the thin cotton of her shirt.

"Now that you got me handcuffed to yer bed, what all are you gonna do with me?" she asked in a breathless purr.

He sneered but his eyes looked up and down her body even as he began to shift himself back.

"Maybe you like boys better?" she taunted.

His eyes turned hot and he raised his hand as if to strike her before dropping it again.

"Someone should have taught you how to respect your betters," he snapped.

"Betters? You think you're better'n anyone? Dirty wetback!"

He slapped her face and she gasped, then shook her head to clear the ringing in her ears. He looked hesitant, startled, guilty, and almost apologetic as he lowered his hand.

"That all you kin do, boy?" she breathed. "Aint' there something else you want to do with those hands? Go on. You know what you want to do. Or ain't you man enough?"

"Puta!" he snarled.

"Yeah, an' so's yer mother!"

He slapped her again, then with a snarl of rage gripped the front of her blouse and tore it open. Again, almost instantly, he jerked to a stop, frozen in shock by his own actions. Dara arched her back, leering up at him, heart pounding.

"Too late to arrest me now," she taunted. "How you gonna put this on yer report?"

Glaring, he dropped his hands to her chest just below her breasts, then after a moment's hesitation, slid his hands up and squeezed them together.

"Ooo," she sighed. "Little greaser has his hands on boobies for the first time."

"Shut the fuck up!" he snarled, squeezing her breasts until they hurt and she gasped in pain. "You got a fuckin' mouth on you, bitch!"

Dara ran her tongue across her lower lip and let her eyes narrow into slits. "An' guess what I can do with that mouth?" she taunted.

"I'll bet a lot," he growled, his fingers kneading her breasts roughly.

"Dirty greaser."

He slapped her face, and this time she knew he liked it, knew he was excited by it, knew he had been waiting for another opportunity, another excuse. What shocked her was that she had provoked it deliberately, that it twisted something dark and nasty down deep inside her.

"Gonna do it to me?" she sneered breathlessly. "Think yer man enough, greaser?"

He slapped her again and she saw stars, groaning, blood on her tongue.

She felt him shift backwards off her hips, then grip the front of her trousers and undo them. She blinked dazedly at him, then grunted as he roughly yanked them down, tore them out from under her bottom, and pulled them down her legs and off.

She let her legs fall aside, panting heavily as his eyes raced over her body and his hands followed behind. His fingers were soft, quick, but surprisingly gentle, at least compared to the other men who had used her lately.

His finger pushed inside her and she realized she was sopping wet. It curled in and back and just like that she felt a surge of pleasure roll over her as he touched something inside her that made her shudder.

"Slut," he growled.

"Wetback."

She tried to close her legs, though she had no desire to, and grunted in pain, her mind feeling a surge of excitement as he pinned her thighs down hard with his knees.

"Gonna rape me? Are yuh? Fuckin' greaser. Dirty wetback!"

He let his finger twist and pump inside her, and Dara felt her hips buck up helplessly.

"Bastard!"

He slapped her breasts stingingly. "Puta!"

He undid his trousers and tugged down the zipper, then shoved his underwear down and drew out his cock. He was no Emery, but no man was, and what he had would have once impressed her. She watched as he rubbed it up and down along her glistening sex, his fingers till inside her, her body trembling with lust.

"Get that dirty wetback cock away from me," she panted.

He pulled his finger out and thrust into her hard. Dara cried out, back arching and twisting as he seized her thighs and leaned into her. Then his body wad down atop her and he was thrusting madly into the furnace between her legs.

"Bastard! Bastard!" she groaned, her head rolling from side to side as the hunger rushed through her body and mind.

Her hands pulled against the cold metal of the handcuffs, but her legs rose up and her ankles crossed behind his back as he thrust slowly and deeply into her hot sex.

"M-Muh uncle's gonna k-kill you," she gasped, eyes half closed with the heat burning through her veins.

He was thrusting into her steadily, nothing like Emery's raw animal rutting, yet strong and hard and fast, his hips shifting from side to side, his body sliding up, then down, his cock piercing her from different angles as he twisted her head up and back by the hair and bit gently into the nape of her neck.

Dara groaned in pleasure, rocking her hips up, thrusting her pussy up against his pumping cock as her skin prickled with sexual electricity. She felt an orgasm building rapidly within her trembling body and stiffened, trying to push it back, trying to hide her arousal as Hernandez buried his face against the nape of her neck and chewed at her earlobe.

Her eyes rolled back and she shuddered violently, the sensual heat seeping through her body despite her best efforts so that she knew she couldn't stop the climax. She could only hope he would fail to notice.

Then he rose above her, pulling back to a kneeling position, gripping her thighs and jamming them back, thrusting in hard and fast in short, sharp, deep little thrusts that had her gasping aloud with each stroke. He was glaring at her, sneering at her, his eyes boring into hers. Dara realized he knew how close she was, and her face burned as she saw him waiting and watching.

She clenched her feet, trying to fight off the pleasure, trying to resist its' burgeoning power. She saw his lips curl up in a sneer of contempt and victory, and one of his hands slid over her belly and down between her legs, his thumb finding her clitoris and stroking roughly back and forth against it.

It was too much for her, and Dara cried out as the orgasm rushed over her.

Her body writhed and undulated, legs trembling and jerking on the bed as he thrust into her. Then she exhaled slowly, groaning, going limp, her body still shuddering to his hard thrusts.

"Dirty greaser," she panted.

He pulled out, then roughly rolled her onto her belly and forced her legs apart.

"B-bastard."

She felt him pressing against her anus and moaned, feeling deliciously depraved and abused.

"W-wanna pretend I'm a little boy," she said, deliberately bating him, taunting him, wanting him to –

His hand cracked stingingly across her buttocks and a ripple of heat flared in her belly.

"Bitch!" he snarled, thrusting hard enough that his cock drove several inches deep into her rectum.

She groaned at the pain, but even so soon after her come she was hot again, wild again, her body throbbing with lust.

"Fucking greaser! I'm too good fer you!" she called, her head twisting as she tried to see above and behind her.

Another hard slap to her bottom made her gasp in pain.

"Y-You don't get ta fuck white women, you - ."

He slapped her bottom hard, then again, then again as he drove his thick cock down into her trembling body. She groaned and rolled her hips, angling her entry upwards, easing his path, consciously forcing her muscles to relax as he drove deeper.

He threw his body atop hers and crushed her to the bed, and she gasped as his fist gripped her hair and yanked back cruelly.

"Dirty little racist redneck bitch!" he cursed, twisting her head from side to side by the hair as he ground his heavy body into her buttocks.

Dara shuddered, feeling his thick meat twisting inside her lower belly, her legs spread wide. She felt conquered, used, darkly, hungrily revelling in her own violent abuse.

For long moments she was silent but for her harsh, ragged breaths as he thrust into her deeply, the blood pounding in her head as she screamed upwards towards another climax.

God, God, God! What was wrong with her!? Why did she relish it when men used her so violently? For an instant Dara felt like weeping, like a lost and confused girl. Then a tidal wave of steaming sensory pleasure rolled over her and she cried out in bliss.

"Bitch! Whore! Slut!" he panted, riding her violently, using his cock like a spear and driving it hard into her vulnerable body with every stroke. His fist was embedded in her blonde hair and he eased up off her, pulling on it, forcing her onto her knees.

She groaned in pain, and the sound made something hungry flare with delight inside his mind. He twisted her hair more painfully, pounding his hips into her rounded buttocks, ramming his cock down into her anus. He was showing her, all right. White bitch!

He ran a free hand eagerly along her ribs, then beneath to roughly squeeze her breast. She groaned again and he drew his hand back and slapped her breast, making it wobble and sting. His cock throbbed at her cry of pain and he slapped it again.

He stared down the long length of her beautiful, slender body, down past his fist gripping her hair, down her arms to the silver cuffs binding them together, and came, crying out as her anus swallowed his hot seed, pumping almost frantically as the pleasure burned through his vitals.

He collapsed atop her, bearing her to the mattress, gasping for breath atop her as he strength drained out of him. After long seconds he rolled off slowly, then sat up. He ran his hands over his face and through his hair, trying to think, now that his little head was sated and he could use the bigger one.

"Shit," he groaned.

He had fucked up by the numbers. If word of this ever got out he was dead meat. Then, too, if the stupid little slut did tell her uncle - Christ. The mess that would create! He imagined her outraged uncle calling his boss, screaming over the phone. God, and his boss was a woman and a feminist. Worse, she was a proud Hispanic, and the idea that another Hispanic would so lose control that he couldn't help himself - over a blonde girl - would infuriate her.

The girl was practically a suspect! He knew damn well she took bribes from the local motorists, and probably more than that. She might even be involved with the drug dealers somehow. And he'd just given her enough ammunition to destroy him!

Dumbly, he reached past her and undid the cuffs, feeling another twinge of anxiety at the red marks on her wrists. Oh yeah, she'd even have bruises, and not just there either.

Shit!

He turned away, then tugged at his pants as he stumbled to the bathroom and slammed the door.

Dara sat up, grinning, rubbing at herself a little as she swung her long legs out of bed. She went to the little desk and began to leaf through the papers there, then saw the computer turned on and sat down before it, examining the report he was writing to his boss.

She smirked and looked at the door, then quickly began typing.

She saw that the report was addressed to a Ms. Gomez, and snorted, her eyes scanning the page for opportunities. She halted.

"I know you believe that the drugs are being carried overland, but I believe there is a greater likelihood they are going down the river," Hernandez had written.

She smirked. "So I'm a two bit whore, eh?" she whispered.

She added *"And besides, what would a two-bit whore like you know about drug smuggling? You ought to be home making babies and not getting in the way of mens' business."*

"That ought to make the boss sit up and take notice," she whispered.

She read further down, and bit her lip at mention of Emery as a major suspect. "In conclusion, Hernandez wrote, "Although I realize you are under pressure, I believe our opportunities for exposure of the entire ring are best served by focussing on the individuals listed above."

She licked her lips, then added. *"I am presently engaged in a homosexual affair with one Elwood P Dodd, a young Black teenager who I believe can add considerable information to our investigation. And he can deep throat my entire five inches."*

Unfair, she knew, since he was at least ten, but the hell with him.

She sent the email and then dressed quickly, slipping out the door before he could come out of the bathroom, where, she thought contemptuously, he was probably washing himself over and over again, afraid he'd caught something from her.

Chapter Eleven

"We gotta leave," Emery said.

"That's what I been telling you!" Dara exclaimed.

He glowered at her, then turned to Carla. "Pack up my stuff, woman. We're getting out of here."

He turned and his dark eyes narrowed as he looked at Dara. "And you're gonna drive us, bitch."

Dara blinked up at him in surprise.

"Cops be looking for Black man. Even if they ain't they're less likely to stop a pretty little white girl."

"But I - ."

"You do what you're told, girl," he snarled. "You get a car, one with tinted windows, and bring it here fast as you can."

"But Emery - ."

He gripped her by the scruff of the neck and lifted her so only the tips of her toes touched the floor, then the corners of his lips curved up in an almost cruel smile.

"If that fed catches me I'm going to tell them what a whore you are. I'm going to tell my lawyer and say you fucked me to get information. Your picture will be in every newspaper, bitch, talkin' about how you sucked nigger cock. You want to stick around Kainlen for that?"

He let her go so quickly she stumbled back.

"Now git!" he shouted.

His big hand cracked against her bottom and she yelped and leapt forward, almost hitting the doorframe. His deep laughter followed her as she scrambled out through the door and she ran a few paces down the dirt path towards the car before slowing.

She turned back, scowling a little, but walking quickly down to where she'd left the patrol car. She got in, started the car, and sent dirt spitting out from beneath the tires as she quickly backed up and around, then started forward.

The Georgia sun being what it was there were a number of people in Kainlen who had tinted glass windows on their cars. The closets and easiest to get was the old Lincoln Bobbie Spellman owned. Bobbie worked nights and didn't like the bright sun waking him up on his way home to bed. But Dara didn't think much of the Lincoln, especially if they were going any distance.

Of course, going a distance was itself an odd thought to her.

Dara had never really been far from Kainlen County. Her heart pounded with excitement at the thought, but there was more than a little frantic twist to the beat. If her uncle found out about her and Emery he'd kill Emery for sure. And while he might not kill Dara she might well wish he had after he'd gotten through with her.

She sped down the highway, aware of where the other deputies liked to drive and park, taking back roads whenever she neared a dangerous area. She made it to her place and quickly changed out of her deputy uniform, then, hesitating, packed it with her other things and shoved the case into her own car before taking off.

Bobbie's car was parked in front of his house, like always, and she pulled up behind it, then hurried over to drop to her knees behind it and reach in beneath the bumper. She felt the small, magnetic box and her fingers plucked it free. Bobbie always kept his spares there.

A few seconds later she was heading back for Emery, her stomach filled with butterflies at the thought of leaving Kainlen County. Where would they go? What would they do? Would they become outlaws, riding the highways, one step ahead of the feds?

She pulled to a stop in a cloud of dust and got out of the car. Emery met her before she even reached his old shack, passed her without a word, and went over to examine the Lincoln.

"Get your ass moving, bitch," Carla snapped from the doorway. "We gotta load this shit into the car."

She shoved a box of clothes into Dara's arms, and Dara turned and headed back for the Lincoln. Emery had the front hood up and was looking in at the engine as she dropped the box next to the car and grabbed the keys to unlock the trunk.

For the next half hour she and Carla stuffed things into the Lincoln's big trunk while Emery tinkered with the engine or in the front seat of the car. For some reason he even yanked out the driver's bucket seat and worked on it. Then she saw him stuffing white bags of powder in beneath it and bit her lip worriedly.

He looked up only once. "I don't like what the blonde bitch is wearing," he said.

"You heard him, bitch," Carla growled. "Get that shit off!"

Dara hesitated. She was wearing jeans and a loose T-shirt, figuring on being inconspicious. Carla didn't hesitate, but grabbed at her shirt, yanking it up.

"I'll do it!" Dara snapped.

"Then do it!"

Dara peeled off the shirt, then, hesitating again, undid her jeans and pushed them down and off. "Well what all am I supposed to wear?' she asked.

"Short skirt. Tight top," Emery said. "Show off your legs and titties."

"You heard him, bitch. Move," Carla demanded, slapping her backside.

Dara glared at her, and Carla glared back, daring her to smack her. But knowing Emery wouldn't like it she turned away instead, and went to the trunk, where she'd put her things. She found the little pleated skirt she'd worn to Jerna, and tied the little white blouse together beneath her braless breasts again.

"Lose the thong," Emery said, walking past her. "I want you naked beneath."

Why, she wondered. And the answer made her pussy quiver a little. But she obeyed again, feeling only a little put out as she peeled the thong down and off.

Emery came back with a welding torch, and leaned in through the drivers door. Sparks began to fly from inside, and she wondered what all he was doing. But it didn't take long. Then he was putting the driver's seat back in place while she and Carla packed the last of his junk.

"Okay, Dara drivers," he said. "We'll stay in back, keeping low. All the cops'll see is some white bitch driving, and they won't bother us."

Dara nodded, and let him guide her into the driver's door - then froze.

The seat was back in place, but Emery had cut a little slut in it, and a fat silver bar was sticking up through the slit.

"What - ."

He laughed, his teeth white.

"Want ou to gave a comfortable ride, baby," he said. Carla leaned past him and looked in, then sniffed. "You can sure tell it's a whore's car."

"Get me that french tickler thing!"

"Let the slut sit on it as it is."

"Do what you're fuckin' told!" he snapped.

She glared, but obeyed.

The French tickler was something designed to fit over cocks. It was hollow rubber with all manner of ribs and bumps along its length. Now Emery slid it over the metal tube, shoving it down hard until it was jammed tight.

"Now get in, slut."

"But Emery - ."

"Now!" he snapped.

She climbed into the car, propping herself up high.

"Now slidedown onto the seat," he said, eyes gleaming.

She sighed, then pulled her skirt aside to bare her pussy as she eased lower. She grunted as the rubber pressed against her naked sex, feeling the hardness of the metal bar behind the rubber as her pussy lips were forced in and back, then spread wide around the thing. She slid lower, and the bar slid up into her belly.

A kind of exhilarating hunger swept around her and she forced herself back, gasping as she felt the thing thrusting up into her, as she felt it forcing her sex sleeve wider, as it drove higher into her belly.

"Oh!" she moaned.

It was *hot* out. The metal of the car was hot, and the metal bar within the snug fitting rubber coat was even hotter. She recalled the Emery had only finished welding it in place a few minutes earlier and now she felt the warmth radiating out from the rubber, baking her from the inside. She tried to pull back, but Emery, chuckling, laid an enormous hand on her shoulder, and forced her back down, forced her down deeper, forced her down even as the thick, hard pipe rammed deeper into her belly and brought cramps rippling through her gut.

"Ahh," she groaned.

And at last her bottom was flat on the seat, and she spread her legs and tried to keep her weight from pressing the seat down further, and lowering her even more onto the hard tube now impaling her.

She pulled her hand off the hot door frame, wincing and blowing on it, then jerked the door closed. She gasped in pain as she leaned forward to slide the key into the ignition, quickly leaning back again and extending her arm to its full length. The car rumbled to life, and she gasped again. Emery must have welded the bar to the frame below! She could feel the vibration of the engine through it.

Emery and Carla climbed in at last, closing the doors behind them. The car rocked a little, and Dara exhaled, reaching between her legs to where the rubber coated pipe was driven up through the seat.

"Drive, bitch."

She shifted gears and backed out onto the dirt road, then turned and slowly eased forward, doing her best to avoid the numerous pot holes and ruts as she made her way back towards the highway.

Even so she heaved a sigh of relief when the car finally edged onto the pavement, her insides feeling battered and bruised by the shifting of the heavy metal cylinders within the tight confines of her soft flesh.

As she drove, however, her body began to adjust somewhat, and she found the pain easing, then disappearing entirely. She was even able to ease up into almost a sitting position as the car cruised along.

She wiped a hand across her sweaty forehead, then cursed softly, reaching for some tissues and patting along her face and the sides of her neck. It had been hot earlier, but it hadn't seemed as hot before. Now her entire body seemed sticky and slick. Her numerous cuts and bruises stung, and her groin burned around the thick metal tube.

"Keep on One-Five," Emery called from behind her.

"Kin I turn on the air conditioning?"

"Yeah."

She sighed and closed the windows, then turned the air conditioning on as she headed up the highway. Behind her, Carla and Emery whispered to each other just below her hearing, and she glanced at the rear view mirror suspiciously, jealously.

She knew it made sense to have them in the back out of sight, but it still made her jealous, and she worried what they might be plotting. Occasionally their voices rose, and she realized that at least some of what they were talking about was money. They didn't have much of it, at least at the moment.

She shifted position slightly, gasping softly as her body moved around the hard tube of rubber covered steel. She found that if she sat up especially straight and eased the pressure of her feet on the pedal and floor all her weight pushed down on the seat and made the french tickler grind against the bottom of her sex so that she ached deliciously.

Of course, she had to be careful while doing that, for if she went over one of the numerous potholes the ache would turn into a bruising pain very quickly.

The metal was welded to the body of the car, and transmitted the hum of the engine and the shudder as the tires rolled along the uneven pavement. The trembling vibrations made her clitoris tremble along with it and her pussy flooded with heat and excitement.

She glanced at the rear view mirror, then reached down between her legs, rubbing at her clitoris a little, sending sparks through her lower belly as the sex heat swelled higher.

"Get your fuckin' hand back on the wheel, bitch!" Emery growled.

Dara jerked her hand away quickly.

"You don't touch that pussy unless I tell you to."

Bastard, she thought resentfully. But she obeyed, squirming a little in her seat, trying to raise herself up and down without Emery noticing, to ride the steel pipe and bring herself off.

They turned south on I-90, headed towards the coast. After an hour they crossed the border into Alabama, still headed south. They stopped at a dingy looking little city a hundred miles north of Mobile, and Dara awkwardly slid her bruised, aching, but still sopping wet pussy up off the French tickler and eased out of the car, walking awkwardly as she made her way to a motel office to register.

It was just past dark by then, and Emery and Carla had no difficulty sneaking from the car to the motel room at the end after Dara pulled up in front or it and unlocked the door. She then unloaded the luggage they wanted, and closed the door behind them.

She called a nearby pizza place, and they stayed in the bathroom while she paid the man.

"We need to get more money fast," Emery said around a mouthful of food.

"You gonna sell some of that white stuff?" Carla asked.

Emery grinned and then Carla nickred. Dara didn't understand.

"Yeah. But not the drugs. We save that. We sell some of that other white stuff."

He turned and his eyes settled on Dara, who flushed slowly. "What?" she asked.

"We don't know the local setup," Carla said warningly. "We don't want trouble with the cops."

"Yeah," Emery said thoughtfully. "We don't need that much money, though. She don't gotta sell her pussy on the street. Must be some local joint she could wag her titties and collect enough to pay for rooms and gas and shit."

Dara stared at him dumbly.

"You can show her how to do it," Emery said. "I'll go visit a few places, find one that's right for her."

"You gonna go visit strip clubs?" Carla said dryly. "What hard fuckin' work for you."

"Oh fuck off," Emery said in irritation. "You want I should show the bitch how to dance while you go check them out?"

"I don't understand," Dara said warily.

"You don't have to understand. You just gotta do what you's told," Emery growled.

He went out and Carla got up and stared at her for a moment.

"Pretty little skinny assed white girl," she said. "People pay to see your bony ass."

"What are you talking about?" Dara demanded hotly.

"Talking about you dancing at a local club for a night or two, get us some money."

"Dancing? You mean stripping?!"

Dara's pulse shot up and she felt a surge of alarm and anxiety, but at the same time a rolling wave of liquid heat spread up her spine.

"You shown your bony ass to enough men that it oughto be a natural for you," Carla said dismissively. "Now stand up while I show you a few things so you don't move like a mule."

"I ain't stripping!" Dara said, but there was no force behind it, and Carla smirked.

"You do anything Emery tells you to do."

It angered Dara that she was right, but the anger was directed at herself. She was feeling more and more self loathing at the way she was letting Emery treat her, and could not understand why she got so aroused and wild with sex heat at the man's cruel treatment.

She stood reluctantly, and stripped naked alongside of Carla, then rolled and ground her hips to the music coming off the cheap little radio sitting on the night stand.

"Forget the shit you see in movies. You ain't gonna be in no high class place. The men in any place Emery finds for you will want it down and dirty.

She demonstrated what she meant by bending over and gripping her ankles. "This is what they wanna see," she said with a leer.

Dara made a face.

Showing herself at the wet t-shirt contest was one thing, but this was entirely different.

Besides, that was an amateur hour thing. This was - this was her as a stripper, those girls she'd always thought were so pathetic when she saw them at the road houses.

Even so she felt a hot little thrill as she moved and twisted her body, imagining dozens and dozens of men staring at her naked, wanting her, maybe throwing money at her. And the more she stripped and danced, the more aroused she became.

When Emery returned she grudgingly put on a show for him, even while protesting that she "wasn't no freaking stripper". That got her a cuff to the side of the head and a hard smack to the bare bottom.

Something dirty and nasty and masochistic inside her kept her going.

"I ain't stripping for you, Emery!" she said hotly. "You and Carla can kiss my ass!"

She was mightily afraid she'd gone too far with that one when he grabbed her hair and flung her onto the big double bed. He had Carla tie her right wrist to the top corner of the bed while bound her left to the other corner on her belly.

Inside, her belly twisted and roiled anxiously, but her pussy thrummed with excitement and anticipation, and Dara realized she wanted him to punish her, to hurt her, to use her violently. It was only a fleeting understanding, a confused understanding which was quickly swept away by the turmoil in her mind as Emery shoved a pair of pillows under her belly and her ankles were bound to the lower corners.

He shoved a gag in her mouth and then slipped his long thick leather belt out of the loops of his jeans, doubling it in his fist as he glowered down at her prone body.

"You gonna learn to obey, bitch!" he snarled.

"Don't mark her up," Carla warned.

"Fuck you, bitch!" Emery snapped. "I know how to not mark up my merchandise!"

The heavy belt cracked across Dara's bottom with stinging pain, and she yelped into the gag as her body strained against the leather bonds.

It slashed down again, this time against the soft backs of her thighs, and she screamed and writhed on the bed. Another blow across her lower back, and another across her thighs followed. Then Emery began to rain blows up and down her body from shoulders to knees as Carla looked on and smirked.

The pain rose higher, and her body strained and shook in its bonds as she sobbed and shook. Her buttocks flared red hot as the belt bit into the soft flesh again and again and again, and her back felt raw and torn.

She gnashed her teeth against the gag, her head thrashing from side to side. Tears of pain filled her eyes as she endured the flailing of his heavy belt. Yet through it all a hazy dark cloud of lust and perverse excitement raced through her body and mind. She strained and pulled with all four limbs, screaming into the gag, hammered by the shockwaves of pain each time the belt struck her aching flesh, and yet her pussy was a furnace of need needing only a touch to explode.

He stopped, and she felt a terrible relief and frustrated regret. She was aware of the bed jiggling and shacking with someone else's weight. Then Emery's stiff cock was stabbing at her anus, his fat thumbs forcing her buttocks wider as he jammed himself against her. She was hot and wet but that didn't help as he cursed and battered himself against her sphincter. Dara moaned dazedly as the pain in her rear mounted, and she sobbed and moaned and bit into the gag as he forced more and more of his thick cock down into her aching body.

She groaned low in her throat as his heavy body settled atop her and he began to work his hips, his fat cock forced deeper and deeper with every hard thrust of his hips. He made no effort to please her. His hands stayed well away from her pussy, instead gripping and twisting her hair whenever she went too limp or too quiet.

His heavy weight crushed her down into the cheap mattress, and it was difficult to inflate her lungs with his chest crushing her breasts into the springs. She could only groan into the gag and endure the increasingly savage thrusting of the big man's hips as he forced her anal muscles into submission and began to ram his pelvis against her reddened buttocks.

Her breathing was a series of shallow gasps, grunts and moans as Emery reamed out her back opening, his big cock pistoning back and forth inside her, jamming painfully deep with every stroke so that terrible cramps ripped through her belly.

The bed creaked shrilly, accompanied by the hard wet slap of flesh on flesh as he rode her. He pushed his upper torso up, extending his arms, his bit hands flat against the bed to either side of her head, then he began to thrust even harder, the force of his hips bouncing her on the mattress now as the bed began to shake wildly.

"Shit, Emery," Carla said with a laugh. "I hope there ain't nobody next door."

Emery grunted and growled like an animal, ramming his hips down and forward against Dara's spread bottom, spearing her again and again with his long, thick cock. Her fingers twisted against the bed posts and her body shuddered violently and continuously as she endured his wild, savage sodomy.

And yet despite the pain, that hot shimmering liquid lust continued to bubble away inside her, and she knew that if he only thrust into her pussy instead she would come violently.

Her body was heavy with sweat, her hair tangled and matted, her skin red and swollen as he rammed his thick cock down deep into her anus again and again, like a piledriver jamming its hard steel nose deep into her body, bruising her insides with its force and power.

And through it she hovered and instant away from climax, the hard pounding against her bottom, the painful rutting inside her anus keeping her at the edge of the precipice but not sufficient to roll her over the edge.

He finished with her, giving her a slap to the back of the head that made black spots dance before her glazed eyes, and for long seconds she lay alone, spreadeagled, gasping, moaning into the gag, drenched in sweat and trembling from the need to come. The hot bubbling pressure of sex heat made her feel ready to explode, despite the pain.

The bed jiggled again and she cried out into the gag as Carla yanked her up by the hair. She focussed her blurred eyes and saw that the Black woman was wearing an immensely thick strap-on dildo. The phony cock was like a nightmare vision, all black and bulbous and lumpen, with sharp edged spikes circling it and running all the way up the shaft.

"How you like my new cock, baby?" she demanded with a sneer. "I got it just for you."

Dara groaned as her hair was released and her head hit the mattress. She felt, rather than saw Carla moving around on the bed to kneel between her legs, then felt the woman's fingers on her sore buttocks, spreading them open. She could feel cool air against her anal opening and knew it gaped half open.

Then she felt the woman's sharp fingernails against her inner thighs, and a moment later the bulbous head of the phoney cock was jammed against her soaking pussy opening. Her eyes widened and she gurgled helplessly, fingers opening and closing, the muscles straining up and down the length of her body.

She felt the pressure increase, felt the hard rubber cock forcing its way into her body. Her pussy lips strained wider and wider, aching as they were stretched even wider than they were by Emery's cock. She was on the edge again, gasping, moaning, whimpering with the need to come.

The phoney cock slid forward, ground forward through the clutching sleeve of her soft, wet sex, and stinging pain crackled up her spine as the sharp spikes scratched at her sensitive inner flesh like cats' claws.

But the pain did nothing to ease the pressure inside her. It was like firecrackers within a roaring bonfire, startling and distracting, but offering no surcease from the heat.

"Oh God!" she moaned, her mouth moving around the fat, saliva coated ball stuffed between her jaws. Her pained eyes fluttered as the fat dildo thrust deeper, and she groaned at the straining, aching tightness of her pussy lips as the sharp spikes were forced through.

Carla's hands moved over her buttocks, slapping cruelly, then she gripped Dara's hair in a tight tail and yanked, using the leverage to thrust her hips sharply forward. Dara screamed, her scalp burning, her pussy exploding as the dildo rammed forward. Pain filled her, then was swept aside as the climax finally broke.

Her body strained and arched violently, her head jerking spastically as the shockwave of ecstasy tore through her mind and body. She began to buck and twist, convulsions wracking her. Crackling sexual electricity set her muscles spasming and her nerve endings snapping.

She could feel the cruelly designed sex tool tearing in and out of her pussy now, Carla grunting with the effort of repeatedly stabbing it deep into her belly and then tearing it free. It - hurt - wonderfully.

And the orgasm swelled and swirled inside her, rising and plunging, rising again and again. On it went, too long, exhausting, draining, and she realized, in that small spark of self which was still capable of thought, that it was not a mere orgasm, but multiple orgasms snapping off one after another with barely any hesitation between them.

Her muffled cries grew to screams, dazed, near delirious howls of animal pleasure she did not even realize she was making as the hard rubber tool drove deep into her body again and again and again.

Chapter Twelve

She was surprised how little marks were left by her beating. Emery's thick belt had left her skin feeling as though it had been flayed, but the belt had been too wide and too soft to leave cuts, and he had been careful to not leave welts either. By the next night her skin, while somewhat pink, showed little other sign of his "discipline".

Of course, what was not seen could still be felt. She felt raw and sore and bruised when she moved, and her pussy felt worse still. Her entire abdomen felt bruised and abused by their rough use of both her lower entrances, and she wondered if they had hurt something inside her.

I should leave, she thought for the hundredth time, resentment seeping through the heat into her always independent mind at the way they were abusing her. However arousing it was at times she could still not get used to being treated with such obvious contempt, especially as time passed and she came to understand it was no mere sexual ploy.

Yet she was also alive, wildly alive, with thrills and wonder spilling through her life as they never had before. Returning to her drab, dull, boring, small town life was an option. She had left Mississippi at last! The thought of returning, crawling home, made her cringe. And the thought of getting a low paying job in Alabama, perhaps as a shop clerk, was no more appealing.

So, for now, she would have to obey Emery.

And become a - stripper.

She shuddered, her mind in turmoil at the thought. It was wickedly, hungrily arousing, and terrifying at the same time. Yes, it had been a wild thrill to expose herself at the wet T-shirt contest, but this, this was different, this was - gross, lewd, raw and nasty.

She was to dance that night, and shook and trembled with excitement for hours in advance. A lot of men had seen her naked over the previous few weeks, but it was still a scary prospect, after all, to get up on a stage and strip naked in front of scores of people. Alone.

Emery told her little about the place. He simply ordered her into the car - a dusty Chrysler he had stolen somewhere, and drove her to a seedy looking part of town near the highway, then led her in through the rear door. She didn't even know what the place was called.

The manager was a weasel faced Black man who sweated constantly. He leered at her and groped her whenever he thought Emery wasn't looking - though she doubted Emery would have cared.

Seeing him and the dark, dirty back rooms, her anxiety rose higher. When she opened a door into the bar and glanced inside she felt even worse. The place was a dive. She'd never been in such a cheap, seedy looking dump before. And it was a black bar. She could see no other White face anywhere. The customers were all loud, drunken bores and hurled cat-calls and obscenities at the girls as they danced. She could only imagine what they'd do when she got out on stage.

Still, scary as it was, in an odd way, that just made it more arousing. There was a thread of danger to go with her exposing herself. And she found she craved danger, thrills, wild, adrenalin charged experiences.

Her heart was in her throat all through the previous dancer's routine. As the girl moved through it and approached the end she began to break out in a cold sweat, and her heart pounded louder and louder.

Then the girl was finished to a chorus of derisive boos and scurried off, leaving the stage clear for Dara. Dara had to be pushed forward by one of the girls behind her, but then she walked forward on her own, as if in a trance.

There were immediate shouts and insults. She was dressed in her police uniform, complete with oversized cowboy hat. The sea of black faces stared up at her, some laughing at the numerous shouted insults tossed at the stage.

The music started up and she moved into the lights. There were more whistles and other insulting greetings as she moved to the centre of the stage.

She moved by instinct at first, doing as she'd practised, her mind in a haze.

"Let's see your tits, white whore!"

"I want to see if she's got blonde hair on her cunt!"

"Hey bend over slut, let's see your cunt hair!"

"Lookit that face willya? A face like that should have a cock stickin' out its mouth all the time!

"Take it off, baby!"

"Let's see that white ass, baby!"

She tried to ignore the obscene yelling, doing her routine carefully, rolling her hips, sliding her hands up and down her body, dancing around, arching her back, walking and wigging across the stage. She started to undress the way Carla had shown her, stepping on one heel to pop the shoe off, then doing the same to the other. In white ankle socks she pranced from side to side, rolling her head, shaking her hair.

Then she screwed up a bit. She was suppose to undo her blouse and take it off, then do the pants, but she undid the pants first. There was no way to repair that so she shimmied in place and let the pants slide down to her ankles as the crowd whistled and yelled in approval.

Wearing the tight uniform blouse, she pranced around the stage, moving faster and more gracefully as she began to feel a warm thrumming between her legs. The audience whistled approval at her long, athletic legs, pale in the bright spotlight, and she started winking and grinning, running her tongue across her lips. She swung her hips faster and gave it a little more wiggle as she pranced around in front of them.

She turned her back and slid her blouse up slowly, rolling it from side to side, easing it up over her bare bottom as she leaned forward a little, rolling her bottom at them as they screamed obscenities. She fairly skipped back and forth in front of them, enjoying taunting them now, feeling the wild thrill of excitement in the pit of her belly at that sea of rough male eyes watching her.

They men howled and yelled as she swung her hips from side to side, wriggling them around as they watched her ease the front of her blouse up now, exposing the deep, plunging V of her tiny black thong, teasingly easing the blouse up higher across her belly to just below her breasts as she moved right up to the edge of the low stage. Hands reached for her but she shimmied away laughing.

Her short blonde hair danced around her head as she skipped to the other side of the stage, sliding down to her knees in front of the men there, humping her pelvis out at them as they ogled her and yelled and laughed.

She held her hips forward as one of them reached for her thong. She jerked away, laughing, rising to her feet and prancing back. She grabbed the metal bar and swung herself around it, then began to slowly undo the buttons of her blouse, then held it together with just her hands, teasing them as they watched, exposing the swelling insides of her breasts, then deeper cleavage, flashing them, dancing, taunting them as they demanded she expose herself, yelling insults.

She flung her arms back and let the blouse spill down her shoulders, basking in their naked lust as they howled at the sight of her bare, ringed breasts. Now wearing only her thong, she swung around the pole again, kicking out her long legs.

She backed against the pole, her hands reaching up above her as high as she could grasp, arching her back to shove her breasts out at them. They yelled in approval. She continued her prancing, shaking her upper body to make her breasts jiggle and shake for them. All of them could see as she knelt right at the edge of the stage, that her breasts were swollen and her ringed nipples fully erect.

She fondled them, squeezing and stroking as she pouted down at them. She crawled along the edge of the stage on all fours, her breasts swinging below her. Men reached up and grabbed at her as she passed, some digging fingers into her breasts, others copping feels of her pussy and buttocks. She turned and twisted, gasping, her heat flaring. She held herself still, letting a man get his fingers into the elastic waistband of her thong, then leaning backwards. They began to tear, and she fell back, twisting onto her side, letting him pull the torn thong down her long legs and off.

She was naked at last. Naked. Utterly exposed before a sea of hungry Black eyes. She rolled and rolled again, then got to her knees, her back undulating like a cat as she moved slowly forward. She caught at the pole, spreading her knees wide, letting them see her naked sex and perfect bottom as she rolled her hips at them.

She pulled herself up the pole, leering, turning, twisting, prancing to the other end and sliding down onto her belly. She rolled and spread her legs dangerously close to the crowd.

Hands reached for her, several touching her thighs and pussy before she slid backwards and turned on her belly. She slowly rose to her knees, spreading her legs, humping her bottom out a them as they screamed and shouted.

She was so excited that when one drunk grabbed her thigh and pulled her almost to the edge of the stage, then grabbed her pussy mound and squeezed hard, she saw stars and came furiously. Everyone nearby watched in awed excitement as she grunted and shook and rutted wildly back at the delighted man.

He squeezed her harder, then jumped onto the stage and knelt behind her. He unzipped his cock and started to push into her but one of the bouncers grabbed him and jerked him off the stage. A brawl developed in front of her as she knelt there, her hands going between her legs and fingering her pussy to another orgasm.

Howls and shouts erupted from all around her as men fought to jump onto the stage and plunge their cocks into her moist body. She had a wild image in her mind of the entire bar swarming around her, over her, ramming their cocks into her from every direction. She drove three fingers deep into her sex and pumped frantically, gasping and moaning as she sought to bring herself off yet again.

Mad. I'm mad, she thought dazedly.

She came again.

"What a fucking whore!"

Dara's face burned with shame as Carla laughed at her.

"Man! Repressed little White girls! You just don't know what they're capable of!"

"Leave it be," Emery said from the front seat. "We made good money. Don't fuck her mind up."

Her mind, Dara thought, was already fucked up. She had been as high as a kite through most of her performance and the aftermath. The lap dancing she had done had paid very well indeed, for every grinding, rolling, humiliating minute she had straddled the drunken men and rubbed her naked body against them.

The whole evening was a haze, and she had been pinched, slapped and groped too many times to remember. The place had not exactly had tightly enforced rules, and every man she had straddled had taken the opportunity to squeeze her bottom and breasts, and chew and suckle at her nipples.

Every other minute a new memory would push to the fore in her dazed mind, and with it the thought "I can't believe I did that!".

She gasped as Carla leaned into her and squeezed her pussy. "I bet you're still hot and wet," she sneered.

Her attitude filled Dara with resentment, not the least because it was true.

"Nother minute we'll be back at the motel and maybe we do something about that," Emery said.

Carla ran her wet tongue slowly up Dara's cheek. "You want that big nigger cock, bitch?" she taunted. "You want that black meat inside you?"

It would hurt. She was still sore after what Carla had done to her but - she did want him, badly.

"Get the fuck off me!" she snapped, shoving the Black woman back hard.

A moment later a bullet tore through the front windshield and Emery stood on the brakes. The Chrysler's tires screamed as the car twisted around a half circle, then spun as he stepped on the gas. Dara got a brief glimpse of several men running across the parking lot from their motel room before the Chrysler screamed back up the street, turning corners every block, Emery cursing non stop.

"Fucking Columbian cocksuckers!" he snarled.

The car slowed as all three of them warily checked behind them for signs of pursuit.

"How the fuck they find us?!" Carla demanded.

"One of those fuckers I talked to must have called the wrong people," Emery growled. "We're still too fuckin' close to home."

"The Columbians will be looking for us," Carla said, biting her lip, then staring at Dara. "We need to get rid of this White bitch. Anyone wants to find us just have to look for her."

"There's a lot of blonde whores in 'bama," Emery said.

"Not riding around with a couple of niggers!"

"You want to wag your black ass on stage?" he demanded.

"Fuck you, boy!"

"Then shut up until we unload this shit. Then we can to fuckin' California."

They took the highway further south, arriving in Mobile in the early morning and taking another small motel room on the edge of town. Emery went out looking for contacts to sell the drugs while Dara and Carla slept.

He returned without success, but with a new moneymaking scheme for Dara. This time it involved Carla. The Black woman made a face when he mentioned it, apparently knowing what he was talking about, but neither saw fit to let Dara in on things. She suspected warily that she and Carla would be doing some sort of lesbian thing on stage, though, and her stomach filled with butterflies at going even deeper into degrading public performances.

"I saw how you liked it on that stage, baby," he said. "You and Carla both like to have all the men drooling over you."

Dara looked down at her feet.

"Well this place ain't got so much class as the last one," he said. "But it pays more."

Less class than the last one? Dara raised her eyes in surprise and sudden anxiety.

"Just a little wrestling is all," he said.

"W-Wrestling?" she asked.

"You and Carla. You pretend to do a little wrestling act at this big bar the other side of the border in Mississippi."

"Me and Carla?" she asked in confusion, turning to look at the Black woman.

Carla snorted. "It ain't so hard. I been there before. We just tear each other's clothes off and roll around a little in the ring. The red necks love it."

"I don't know," Dara said.

Emery slapped her face, glaring sternly. "Nobody asked your opinion, bitch. We need money until I can get rid of this stash safely. You rather I put you out on the street? I'll do it if you don't shut the fuck up."

Dara stepped back a pace. She was suddenly breathless at the though of herself parading up and down on a street corner, waiting for a car to drive over so she could offer her body to the driver. It made her mind squirm in heat, but she knew she'd never do it. If Emery tried to insist on that she would put her foot down, and leave. She'd done enough low down, dirty, nasty, disgusting things for him, but she was not about to become a street corner hooker.

Emery drove again, with she and Carla in the back seat. The looks Carla were giving her promised trouble ahead, and she knew that this phony wrestling thing would give the Black woman an opportunity to hurt her without risking Emery's wrath.

Not that Emery seemed to care much what Carla did to her.

Resentment flared within her again. What was she doing with him? She could do a lot better. Even that jerk Hernandez had been nicer to her than Emery. More. He'd started to make her realize that she could get hot, rough, nasty sex from a lot of men, not just Emery.

They entered the place through a steel door in a blank brick wall, and Emery took her arm as if he was afraid she would back out.

Carla had dressed in blue jeans, oversized checked shirt, with a bandana around her head, Dara was actually dressed in her deputy uniform. The manager had said it would be a great gimmick; the cop and the gang banger.

The manager turned out to be a short, fat white man with bald hair and a truly ugly brown beard. He eyed she and Carla with considerable interest as Emery led them into his dirty little office.

"Nice looking girls," he said. "Now remember, we want it to look real nasty."

"No problem," Carla said, smirking, then turning to leave.

Dara swallowed nervously. Well, the hell with Carla. She knew how to fight, and she wasn't afraid of the woman.

"Make sure you tear your clothes off early on, especially your bras. The customers like to see titties rubbing together."

Dara glared at him in disgust.

"I need a drink," she said, her voice higher pitched than normal.

The manager grinned and filled a shot glass with a dark liquid. Dara didn't even ask what it was. She snatched it off the desk and practically threw it into her open mouth. She coughed and choked as it burned her throat going down.

"Fuck!" she gasped.

"Strong stuff, darlin'," the manager said broad grin.

She slammed the glass down on the desk. "Nuther!" she gasped.

He refilled it and she brought the glass to her lips more gingerly, then downed it quickly, gasping again as the burning in her throat moved down to her chest.

"Shiiit!" she croaked.

"That'll burn your belly for ya," he said. "Now get yer ass out there."

She nodded weakly and, breathing deeply with her mouth open, she stumbled from his office and down the narrow back hall behind the stage. Her stomach did burn, but the burning wasn't enough to fry the butterflies spinning around in her belly as she heard the cheering and shouting coming from the bar.

Carla was already standing behind the curtain, waiting impatiently. She glowered as Dara came up to stand next to her. "I'm gonna kick your skinny butt," she said with a nasty smile.

"Bite me," Dara replied.

Carla's grin broadened. "Oh I will, precious. I will!"

Dara ignored her. She could hear the announcer's voice through the curtain, and the butterflies were turning into large, angry squirrels racing around her insides. She'd been excited at the wet T-shirt contest, and even at the strip club, but those had been a whole different kind of thing. Now she was self conscious, anxious, and certain she was going to be humiliated. No matter what money Emery was getting it couldn't be enough.

The manager came up behind them, squeezed Dara's butt, and then pushed them both out through the curtain.

The noise seemed to double as the lights hit them, and Dara cringed at the sea of faces staring eagerly from both sides as Carla took her arm and half dragged her through the crowd towards the – ring.

The ring was inflatable plastic like the kind kids got to bounce around on at country fairs. But this one was sunk into the floor, and instead of having plastic walls there were traditional wresting ropes strung around it. The ring was surrounded on all sides by grandstands – long, cheap wood benches which rose ten high. And they were crowded with men.

Much worse than the wet T-shirt contest. MUCH worse.

The lights shone down from all sides, making the ring bright as daylight, and Dara's eyes blinked rapidly when she made the mistake of looking up at them.

A man standing next to the ring held the ropes apart as Carla ducked in, and a moment late r Dara reluctantly followed, keeping her eyes down as the men howled and shouted insults and obscenities.

The instant she stepped through the ropes Dara's bare foot slipped out from under her and she had to grasp the rope to keep from falling.

The inflatable plastic floor was covered in vegetable oil.

No one had told her about vegetable oil.

Dara stared down at the slick, soaking floor her feet were sinking into, a little dumbfounded as she saw the pools of clear liquid trickling here and there around her feet. Her weight sank the plastic down enough for the vegetable oil to slither slowly down into the depression, forming a slippery pool around her toes.

"What the - ."

"In this round," the announcer shouted. "We have Officer Betty - ."

Boos rained down on her.

"And the evil gang girl, Leona!"

The men shouted, and none of the shouts were pleasant.

"Tear her clothes off!"

"Pull the bitch's hair out!"

The announcer turned and grinned. "Now you girls keep it clean," he said with a broad wink.

Carla lunged for her at once, clearly used to moving on the slippery, uneven floor. Dara, still a little dazed and confused, jerked aside, but lost her feet and started to fall. Carla pounced on her back, riding her down. They bounced on the inflatable floor, but not high enough. Then Carla had her hands in Dara's hair and was jamming her face down into the plastic, rubbing it in the cool vegetable oil. Dara's hands shot to her face, trying to rub the oil out of her eyes, and Carla took immediate advantage, thrusting her arms in beneath Dara's and yanking them – and her – up and back.

Dara found herself kneeling, the big Black woman's body pressed against her, her arms pinned up and back, her chest thrust out. Before she could even consider how to twist away Carla abandoned her hold, her hands dropping immediately onto Dara's chest, where they caught the front of her uniform blouse and ripped it open, sending buttons popping.

Carla knew exactly what the men liked, and always gave it to them.

Dara's hands went instinctively for her chest, which let Carla grab at the sides of her blouse and yank it down over her shoulders. When Dara resisted she only succeeded in pinning her own arms I place at her sides, and Carla gleefully twisted the blouse backwards, yanking her arms with it. Holding it with one hand there she undid the gun belt around Dara's waist, letting the gun (a cap gun now) slide off. Then she undid the catch at the front of her uniform trousers and yanked down the zipper.

Cursing, Dara threw herself to one side, tearing free only by yanking her arms free of the blouse and falling forward onto the slippery plastic.

Her whole front was now soaked in oil, and she'd lost her shirt, but at least she was free to turn and grab at Carla as the woman came after her. Both staggered to their feet, hands gripping each other's hands as they struggled for balance. Dara was taller, but Carla was heavier, and had experience fighting in oil. She twisted one way, then quickly the other, letting go of Dara's hands. The blonde girl slipped and fell to one side, and Carla grabbed at the back of her already opened trousers and yanked. She fell herself, but succeeded in yanking the trousers down Dara's long legs to her ankles.

Again the crowd howled its approval, and Dara fell free of her trousers, scurrying around on her knees and getting to her unsteady feet in just her lacy black bra and thong.

Carla smirked at her, and Dara snarled angrily, legs spread for balance as she warily tried to work her way closer. The Black woman pranced aside, leering, sticking out her tongue. Dara grabbed at her shirt, sank her fingers into the material, and ripped it open, then twisted the shirt to one side and tripped Carla so she could yank it back and off her.

Carla slipped in the oil and Dara jumped on her, hands eagerly grasping at her jeans, yanking them down and off. Too late, she realized Carla wasn't unbalanced, but merely letting her strip her off. As soon as the Black woman was down to her own lacy white bra and thong she went on the attack again.

She charged towards Dara, dropping her head low at the last minute to thrust it through her thighs. She gripped her legs and straightened, lifting Dara up and dropping her forward, then falling over backwards on top of her. She twisted lithely and dropped atop Dara, oily fingers having only a little problem with her bra strap. When Dara grabbed at it a quick punch to the ribs made her cry out and loosen her grip, and Carla triumphantly yanked the bra free, to great cheers, and tossed it from the ring.

It was hardly the first time men had seen her bare breasts, but Dara still burned with embarrassment as she rolled in the oil and twisted free, then climbed to her feet. Slick with oil now from head to toe, and wearing only a tiny black thong, she shifted her position gingerly as Carla did the same. On all sides, the men shouted down at them, hurling obscene suggestions, most of them to Carla.

"Kill the bitch!"

"Tear that thong off!"

"Grab her tits!"

What the hell am I doing here, she thought, marvelling.

And yet, along with the embarrassment came that familiar heat, the heat of sluttish satisfaction at doing the outrageous, the forbidden, the wild and thrilling and shocking. She was wearing nothing but a thong! And all those rows of men were right up next to the stage, staring. It was much worse than the strip club, where the men had been spread out below, most in the darkness, most quiet.

Her breasts wobbled and jiggled on her chest as she dodged from side to side. Slick oil was running down her chest and flanks. Her body glistened under the bright overhead lights. She knew all those men hungered for her, wanted her, would have given anything to put her on her back and plunge their cocks into her. But she couldn't, and she had always loved teasing men.

Carla jumped at her and she twisted aside and tripped the

woman up. Carla hit the floor and slid across it as Dara rushed after her. But the woman was fast, half rising, turning, and aiming a punch at her kidneys Dara barely dodged, falling in the process. Then Carla jumped on top of her and they rolled over and over on the slick, plastic inflatable floor. Carla got behind her, put an arm around her throat, and yanked her head up and back, at the same time squeezing her right breast painfully.

Dara cried out in pain, flipping over on her back and breaking Carla's hold, turned, and drove her knee, almost by accident, into the woman's belly. Carla when "Whoof" and Dara grabbed at her white thong and tore it off triumphantly.

The audience howled in approval as Carla leapt to her feet in just her bra. Her black eyes glared murder at Dara as they turned and circled each other. "Fucking white whore!" she screamed.

The audience laughed, thinking it part of the act, but Dara knew it was mostly real.

They flung themselves forward and grappled wildly, slick bodies sliding together until they lost their balance and went down. Then they rolled across the floor. Dara tore at Carla's bra, tearing it free, but then Carla got a hand in her hair and yanked her head so far back her spine creaked. She used the opportunity to tear her thong off and leave her as naked as she was.

"Whore!" Carla snarled.

"Slut!" Dara screamed.

They rolled and slid and twisted across the ring, legs flailing and flopping as they wrestled together.

Utterly naked, slick with oil, Dara felt her loins thrumming now as her body slid against Carla's own warm, slick flesh. As their legs intertwined and scissored, she felt the other woman's thigh rubbing and grinding heavily against her slick pussy, and barely suppressed a gasp of hot, dirty pleasure. Their slippery breasts rubbed, ground and mashed together as they struggled, and her nipples were painfully erect.

But she hated Carla! And she hated losing! Especially where people could see. She fought grimly, ignoring her arousal, trying to grab at Carla's hair as the Black woman tried to grab at hers. They grabbed each other's breasts instead and twisted viciously, both screaming in pain. Then Carla got a knee in between Dara's thighs and dropped her weight down hard. Dara saw stars, and gurgled in agony, her hands shooting to her groin as Carla slid off.

She felt herself rolled over, and screamed again as Carla grabbed her hair. Her hands shot up and back behind her head to grab Carla's wrist, and were seized and pinned together behind her neck, her own hair mixed in and held tightly.

"Now you're gonna get it, bitch!"

Carla jammed her knees in beneath the struggling blonde's belly and then slapped her hand down hard across her bottom.

Dara yelped in pain as the Black woman's hand met her bottom with a wet crack of noise and a sharp stinging flash of pain.

Carla crowed with laughter and began to rain blows across her bottom as the rows of men looked down and laughed. Dara cringed in shame, twisting and moaning as Carla's hand continued to spank her bottom. She hated it when Carla spanked her, hated it when she was able to treat her like a stupid little girl. And now she was doing it in front of a huge crowd of men!

And yet - and yet that masochistic side of herself revelled in such treatment, in being degraded and abused, and the shame which poured through her at having it happen in front of a huge crowd of people only made her arousal deepen. She was naked, her bottom raised, as the whole room watched her being spanked. And terrible shame and almost unbearable lust twisted around each other inside her mind.

Her bottom was soon hot and aching, but she was no longer seriously trying to escape. She had resigned herself to her helplessness. And - deep inside herself - she didn't really want to escape anyway.

She suddenly felt Carla's slippery fingers moving roughly up and down along her pussy slit as the crowd's cheers rose even louder. Then a hard finger thrust between them, riding a slick layer of oil.

"N-noooo!" Dara moaned, shame and heat deepening.

"Whore slut!"

A second finger and then a third were thrust into her pussy as Dara's bottom squirmed and twisted wildly. She felt her pussy entrance ache as the Black woman began to thrust them in and out, stabbing them into her hard and fast. A fourth finger pushed into her, and she knew with a sudden shock that the woman intended to fist her right there in front of everyone.

She fought harder, but could not wriggle free, and then she felt the thumb against her entrance, felt Carla's hand twisting from side to side as she pushed. She ached, and cried out in pain as the heel of her hand was slowly pushed inside her.

The audience howled.

Carla pushed her hand deeper, letting the blonde girl's pussy lips close around her fist. She opened and closed her fingers in tight confines of Dara's heaving belly, her hand twisting around. She released Dara's hair at last, her free arm going around her waist to pin her against her own body as she drew her fingers into the palm of her hand and then thrust her fist deep.

Dara gave out a shuddering groan of despair and pleasure, her body bucking violently. She felt the fist punching deeper, felt it twisting and turning as Carla forced it to the centre of her lower belly. The pain was intense, but ephemeral, hardly noticed over the clamour of the lust and excitement in her mind. Adrenalin filled her blood as she bucked and rolled, Carla's fist pumping faster and faster as her strength and the oil allowed her to force it back and forth through the tight, slick folds of warm flesh.

"You like that, slut?" she hissed.

"Nooo," Dara groaned.

The fist pumped harder, and Dara gurgled and moaned, her knees twisting, sliding, her feet flailing and bouncing on the plastic floor.

"Shut up!" Carla suddenly screamed, her head raised. "Shut the fuck up!"

The men quieted, almost as much in surprise as obedience.

"This bitch hates my guts!" Carla shouted. "But it don't fuckin' matter cause she's so much of a whore she's gonna come anyway!"

Dara cringed under the words and the silence. She was on the edge of an enormous climax, and had been desperately hoping she could hide it amid the howls and shouts and laughter.

Laughter and cheers sounded again, but only briefly, as Carla yelled once more.

"Shut up!" Carla snarled, quieting them.

She leaned over. "Come, bitch. You know you got to! You know you can't help it!"

"W-won't!" Dara gasped.

The fist pumped hard and fast and deep, while on four sides, the men looked down from their grandstand seats and waited, grinning, leering, filled with eagerness to see the proof of Carla's words.

"Come, bitch!"

Her free hand slid beneath Dara's belly, her finger thrusting down along her abdomen and then rubbing hard against her swollen clitoris.

Dara shuddered and bucked wildly, gritting her teeth, fighting desperately to force back the heat. But it was no use. The orgasm howled down around her and her body began to buck wildly back against Carla's fist as she cried out in wildfire pleasure. She trembled and shook, her bottom thrusting back wildly, the room so quiet she could hear the wet slurping sound of Carla's fist as she rammed her sex back over it again and again.

Cheers filled the room as her head rolled and thrashed, as she grunted and cried out and her hands slapped against the wet plastic floor again and again.

Chapter Thirteen

"What do you think of these guys?"

The man shrugged.

"How long you know them? You sure they ain't cops?"

"They ain't cops, Emery, and they got money to burn. But I wouldn't turn my back on them if I was you."

"I don't turn my back on no one," Emery said darkly.

He took a deep drag of his cigarette and let the smoke out slowly, so it rose around his head, then turned and glanced at Dara.

Dara made a soft, moaning sound, rolling her eyes in appeal, but he looked away.

He had used her savagely when she and Carla had returned to the motel room, and her pussy was still feeling bruised, her insides aching from the hard shaft he had sent pounding up into her belly.

Then Carla had tied her spreadeagled to the bed to play with her using hot wax, cold ice cubes, and her sharp teeth and nails. When Emery had returned he had sat on the chair and watched idly, then stood up after a time, a dark, feral grin on his face.

"Bitch is missing something," he said.

Carla had looked over his shoulder at him. Dara had just lain there moaning softly. Emery rooted around in her things and returned with her badge, tearing it from her oil soaked uniform top. He moved to the bed and pushed Carla aside, then ran his big fingers over her sex and pinched the flesh at the base of her clitoris.

"Shut her up," he said.

Carla hurriedly jammed her hand over Dara's face as he opened the badge and let his lighter burn along the pin. Then, grinning sadistically, he bent and pinched her flesh again, pressing the sharp pin against the centre of her clitoral hood.

At first she felt a mild stinging sensation at her pussy, but the sensation grew rapidly, and Dara's eyes widened, then bulged and she tried to scream. Her body twisted and thrashed against the bonds holding her to the bed. And still the pain mounted, so that she began to roll and buck her hips desperately.

She arched her back violently as Carla grimly held her head and mouth tightly. Tears of pain spilled from her eyes and beads of sweat began to stand out on her body.

"There," he said, easing back.

Carla looked down at Dara's groin and laughed.

She continued to hold Dara's mouth for long seconds, then finally released her.

"Fuck! Fuck! Let me go! It hurts!" Dara cried.

"Keep it down, bitch," Emery said in irritation.

Dara's head jerked up as she tried to see what he had done to her, but she could see little without sitting up.

"He gave you another piercing," Carla said, snickering.

Which was why, as she stood naked on the balls of her feet just across from Emery and the strange man Dara's pussy throbbed with pain. For he had used the pin of her badge to pierce the hood over her clitoris, and the badge now hung in place between her legs, covering much of her bare pussy slit.

The new piercing had drawn his attention to the old ones, as well, and so her nipple rings were held up by thin cords he had tacked to the low ceiling overhead.

Her wrists, of course, were bound together behind her back by thicker cords, bound immovably, as she had learned.

Her mouth was filled with a thick dildo Carla had tied in place, the head almost gagging her.

Her ankles were held apart, the cords around them bound to either end of her own police baton.

And even while she wondered for the thousandth time why she put up with their treatment, why she continued to stay with them, her body felt a throbbing sexual heat as some part of her revelled in her own cruel abuse.

Bastards! Bastards, she thought.

Her nipples ached and burned. Her ankles were shaky, the balls of her feet near screaming with agony. And every small movement made the badge tug at her wounded pussy.

Bastards!

This man was not the first Emery had seen that day. Like the others, his eyes had grown wide and his jaw had dropped when he had entered and seen her standing as she was. Like the others, the crotch of his jeans had immediately begun to bulge as his eyes had feasted on her.

And as he had with the others, Emery had told him she was a deputy sheriff "from some hick county" who was now "his bitch".

And as with the others Dara had felt a deep embarrassment, and yet a fierce hunger, an almost pride in her sexuality and vulnerability.

"You ain't gonna get anyone around here you can trust," the man said. "Every swingin' dick is gonna think about all that powder and how much money they could save if they just popped a cap on your ass and took it."

"They try that, it's gonna cost `em," Emery growled.

"I told `em that."

"All right then."

"They don't trust you for shit neither, man. They don't trust you got as much as you say. They think maybe you're trying to rip them off."

"You told em I showed you the stuff?"

"They don't trust me, man, not with this much money at stake. They know you musta ripped someone off to get that much coke."

Emery glared at him but didn't deny it.

"We gotta get rid of that stuff before the Columbians - ."

"Shut the fuck up!" Emery snarled at Carla.

She drew back, scowling darkly, and he turned his eyes on the man sitting across from him. The man grinned and held his hands up.

"Hey, man, you think I didn't know you took it from them? That's why you said no Latinos, only niggers. You think I didn't guess that?"

"We had a deal, the Columbians and me," Emery said grudgingly, "But someone opened his big mouth and the feds showed up. It sure as shit wasn't me, so I figured they owed me."

"I ain't arguing man. But these guys, for all they know you got nothing to sell but lead."

"So we'll give them a sample. Sell them one bag. Then we can arrange for the rest."

The man nodded, impressed. "Sounds good to me."

"We'll make the exchange at the docks. Pier 9, tonight at midnight."

"I'd still watch my ass, man. Even one bag is enough to kill for."

"They double cross me they'll pay big."

They slapped hands and Emery gestured towards Dara.

'You want a piece of this bitch?"

"That's some piece of ass there," the man said admiringly, staring at her.

Dara scowled back, but dropped the scowl when Emery looked at her.

They got up, and the man moved over to stand next to her. Dara looked away, then winced as his hands began to move over her body, caressing the underside of her breasts, then fingering the badge between her legs.

"She's a real cop, ain't she?"

"Yeah, a real pig cop," Emery said.

"Fuck her in the ass," Carla said in a bored voice. "She likes that anyway."

The man chuckled, his fingers kneading Dara's bottom, then tugging at the butt plug Carla had thrust up her anus.

"Can't believe you got a cop like this," the man said in delight.

"She'll do anything you fuckin' want," Emery said, glaring at her. "She's got a thing for nigger cock."

"I can just do the bitch right here?"

Emery nodded cooly.

The man laughed and glanced at Carla, who sniffed and turned her head away.

Dara felt the butt plug pulling out, felt her anal opening spreading wider as the thicker part of the plug was forced out.

"Man," she heard him say from behind her.

Emery moved away, back to the front part of the motel room, and sat down next to Carla. They ignored her, talking in low voices as the man's finger circled her anus, and his hands moved over her body. Then she felt his cock slide up into her anal opening, pushing in easily due to the long presence of the butt plug.

She moaned and winced in pain as he moved her body, as she was jerked back and forth against the tight cords pulling on her nipple rings.

Bastards!

But Emery had given her to so many men since they had met it was difficult to be angry about it, except for the pain, of course. As his cock slid deep into her belly he began to grind himself against her buttocks, and the pain in her nipples grew much worse.

"You like that, baby?" he whispered into her ear, his hot breath foul against her face.

He began to pump immediately, thrusting up hard into her bottom so that her nipples strained against the rings again and again. Emery and Carla had their heads together, talking about the drop, completely ignoring her as the man used her anus with hard, quick thrusts that rocked her body.

His hands came up beneath her breasts, squeezing and roughly kneading them as he bit on the side of her throat and slapped his hips against her backside.

It was not the pain which decided her. It was not the humiliation of being given to a stranger yet again. After all she had gone through at his hands and on his behalf, it was not his cruelty which caused her mind to shift and twist into sudden understanding. It was the complete lack of interest Emery showed.

Somehow, she could accept it if he got turned on by offering her body to others, if he became aroused at the pain she was being treated to, or even if the pain was the result of some punishment he thought she deserved. But the fact he had offered her so easily, as if offering a glass of water, the fact he showed no interest in what was done her, that made her burn.

She watched his hand slide up and stroke Carla's cheek, and her eyes filled with anger and rage. She suddenly realized just how little she meant to him. She was little more than a thing, a body he could play with now and then when he was bored, an animal who could earn him money. He cared nothing for her, nothing at all. There wasn't even the lust and admiration she saw in the eyes of other men, the eyes of men like Hernandez.

She was shaken by the realization, and her mind tried to fasten on some small touch or word or deed in their relationship which indicated otherwise, scanning back to the first day they had met. And found nothing.

And yet she was stubborn. She had always been stubborn. And refused to admit it, refused to admit she had been wrong, that she was so worthless in his eyes.

Even as her body shuddered to the hard slap of the other man's hips against her bottom, even as her nipples ached and stung and she felt the man's cock thrusting up into her belly again and again.

Emery was examining a suitcase full of white bags and talking with Carla, about weights and rifles and money.

Bastards!

There were other men who could abuse her, other men who could give her the excitement she wanted. She was out of Kainlen County now and - and what would she do to survive? Wait on tables? Become a stripper?

The man finished, and he had Emery slapped hands before he left.

"You gotta be careful," Carla warned.

"I know it, woman," he replied.

"How you gonna make sure they don't just grab the stuff and kill you?"

"I got a plan," Emery said, grinning, at last turning his eyes to Dara.

Dara's wrists remained bound, but her ankles were untied and she was allowed to sit down on the floor in the corner. She remained gagged by the dildo, and the two ignored her.

After a while Emery finally came over to her. Wordlessly, he yanked her to her feet by the arm and examined her nipple rings. Then he tied small cords to them both and pressed a bag of white powder against her belly. He had put a hole in one end, and he slipped the cords through it and tied them in place, then released the bag.

Dara moaned in pain as the weight of the bag tore at her already aching nipples, pulling them downwards.

Carla looked across the room and laughed, but said nothing.

Emery grinned, pleased, then removed the bag and pushed her so she fell back on the bed before going back to Carla.

They did not speak to her the rest of that day, leaving her bound as she was, laying on the bed. They sent out for Chinese food, watched TV, and showered - separately, ignoring Dara completely.

After eleven Carla wrapped a blanket around her and walked her to the door, then outside into the dark parking lot. The Lincoln was gone. In its place was a blue Ford Emery had picked up somewhere, and she was unceremoniously dumped into the trunk, the hood slammed above her head.

They drove through the city for some time, and she grunted and moaned around the dildo every time the car hit a pot hole. The car stopped, and she felt it shift as someone got out. The car started again, driving slowly, turning this way and that before stopping again five minutes later.

The car shifted again, but less strongly, and then the door was closed. A moment later the trunk was opened and she stared up at Carla.

"Get yer skinny ass out of there," she ordered, her voice soft.

She reached in and gripped her hair, yanking and twisting it up and towards her. Dara cried out in pain, throwing her body forward over the hood, tumbling over it and landing heavily on her back on hard packed earth. She scrambled up to her feet as Carla pulled cruelly on her hair, and then stumbled back against the car at a push.

"Stand still, bitch," Carla ordered.

She had the bag of powder in her hand, the two cords attached to one end. She tied the cords to Dara's nipple rings, then led the powder hang there, tugging down heavily on her breasts.

She bent down and removed the badge from Dara's clitoral hood, and Dara winced and shifted her weight from foot to foot at the stinging pain as Carla slid a small stainless steel ring through the pierced hood then began to tie what looked like thread to it.

"This is wire," she whispered without looking up. "It'll pull your fucking clit off if you try to go in the wrong direction."

She fed the wire between her legs and then held it as she straightened and took her arm. "This way," she whispered.

Dara looked around fearfully. The air was cool on her naked body, and the sound of traffic was distant. She could smell sea air as they walked through a weed strewn lot towards a chain link fence. There was a hole in the fence, and Carla pushed her through it, then halted.

"You see that big building across there?" she demanded, pointing.

There was a warehouse of some kind ahead in the darkness, little more than a big shadow against the sky. A string of streetlights ran across the horizon to the right, but there was nothing but darkness and trees to the left.

Carla turned her and drew something in lipstick across her upper chest, then turned her back again.

"You walk straight across the field to it and stop when someone asks you to. You say nothing and do nothing. When they take the bag off they'll give you money. You turn around and walk back here. Make sure you don't trip over the fuckin' wire. I don't want them to see it. It's so you can find your way back."

She slapped at her bottom.

"Move your skinny white ass, bitch!"

Dara stumbled forward, then continued walking, feeling the slight pull of the wire as it trailed out behind her, her head swivelling from side to side, eyes wide as she looked around her.

This was obviously the exchange of money and drugs. And they had arranged for her to do it because - because - because it was dangerous and they didn't care what happened to her.

Her nipples ached from the weight of the bag. It must have been nearly a pound of coke. She moved slowly over the uneven ground at first, wincing as she stubbed her toes on broken bricks and rocks. Then she hit broken pavement and moved faster, but was still slowed by the wire rubbing against her inner thighs.

She approached the large building but saw no one.

Then, suddenly, a bright light flashed at her from nearby. She squinted, turning her eyes away, but sensed someone approaching. She turned her head back, but her eyes were slits and all she could see was a shadowy figure behind the light.

"What the fuck is this?" a male voice asked.

He pointed the flashlight down at her chest, and Dara could read the words Carla had written in lipstick. "Put money in bitch's mouth."

The man laughed again, and another man came up beside him, laughing as well.

"You the delivery boy, bitch?" the first man asked, roughly squeezing her breast as the other unfastened the cords.

They took the bag away and moved to a nearby car she hadn't noticed before. There they examined the powder.

"Looks high quality," she heard.

"Well, at least they sure as shit ain't cops," the other replied to laughter.

They returned to her, and she dropped her eyes before one gripped her hair and yanked it up.

He squeezed her breast painfully, leering at her.

"This is a nice looking bitch," he said.

The other one fondled her buttocks, and then found the wire dangling between her legs and pulled - hard.

She cried out in pain, forced to her knees by the pull against her clitoris, and the two laughed. "That your leash, slut?" one asked.

Black fingers unwound the cord binding the dildo in place then pulled it free of her mouth. Saliva spilled out onto her chest, and she coughed and gasped for breath, her jaw aching from its forced immobility.

"What's your name, bitch?"

"D-D-Dara," she gasped.

"Where you from?" the second voice demanded.

She didn't answer, continuing to breath deeply, and one of them hooked a finger in her right nipple ring and began to twist it.

"Kainlen County!" she cried.

"Where the fuck is that?" the other voice asked.

She was yanked back to her feet, and one of the men took out a thick wad of cash, then twisted it into a tight roll. She felt her hair pulled again and cried out as it was forced back.

"Open wider, bitch," one of the men cursed as they jammed the roll against her mouth.

She forced her mouth wider, and he forced the thick roll of bills between her teeth.

Then the two backed off. A moment later Dara felt a tug at her clitoral ring and stumbled back.

The two men grinned and she turned around, staring into the darkness.

She could not see the wire in the darkness, but felt it pulling on her ring, and lurched forward across the pavement as the car started behind her. The pull grew more intense, and she broke into a weak trot, hurrying along, gasping and moaning as she stepped on broken bits of rock and empty pop cans.

She could not see the fence or Carla, but the pull drew her on, further to the left than she thought she had come from, in amongst some low scrub bushes and trees. Carla was suddenly there in front of her, catching her arm to stop her. She gripped the end of the thick roll of bills and worked it out of her mouth, then unrolled it and began to count.

"All here," she said in satisfaction.

Chapter Fourteen

It had to stop. And, Dara knew, it was going to, whether she worked up the will power or not.

Carla and Emery were smugly content with the thick wad of cash they had been given for the drugs, and chatted eagerly about their future plans, where they would go, what they would do. Dara figured in none of those plans. She did not know if Emery intended to sell her to a pimp, as he had threatened, or simply abandon her.

They showed no hesitation in speaking around her. It was a though they regarded her as less than human, as a dog or other mindless animal, uncaring about what she thought, confident that she would obey them regardless, that her own sluttish nature would keep her devoted to Emery until the last.

In her mind, Dara raged against their contempt, and against her own disgusting weakness. She had always seen herself as a strong woman, and it burned to be thought of as a mindless fuck toy.

Yet her opportunities for simply walking out were much less than they had once been. She was kept bound hand and foot now, whenever they had no use for her, spending hours laying on the floor under one of the motel beds, her wrists bound behind her back, her ankles tied tightly together, a gag stuffed into her mouth.

She could hear them planning for the next sale, the big one. It would be similar to what they had just done, with Dara taking the biggest share of risk by carrying the drugs in to meet them, and carrying the money away. Emery would wait nearby, on a rooftop, his rifle ready to fire if he was betrayed.

But he saw the betrayal coming from only one area - the men he was dealing with. He did not even consider the possibility of Dara betraying him. Again, she burned at being taken for granted. The brutal treatment he gave her, even loaning her to other men, was the stuff of hot, dirty fantasies. But this kind of contempt, not involving sex, was infuriating.

She thought of all that money, and how nice it would be to have it for herself, how she could use it to get away, to go - somewhere, maybe New York, the fabled land of the NYPD.

Her arms ached from her body's weight but there was no room to turn over, She stared out from beneath the bed at the bed across from her. Emery and Carla were on that bed, going at it. She could see the bed shaking and jerking, but no sign of either of them, not from her angle.

How would she do it?

If it was like the last time she would be bound, helpless to do anything but walk where she was ordered. Emery might have made no plans for her betraying him, but there seemed little opportunity for her to do it anyway.

Unless she could get free.

She strained her wrists against the leather laces binding them. They had tied her up so often it was almost routine. They knew she never made any real effort to get free. The laces were tight, but they had been careless in tying them. She could easily feel the edges of the knot with her fingers. If she could get free - .

And then what?

Supposing she took the money and went to New York. What then? She didn't see herself as living in a big penthouse, wearing furs, and going to watch the theatre. In fact, from what she knew of the prices there the money Emery was going to collect wouldn't even buy a place downtown. She needed to work. And the only thing she wanted to be was a police officer.

But they checked those who applied to be police officers in New York. They would call her uncle and he would tell them how she had abandoned him without notice. Then the feds, the DEA would probably say something about her being a suspected drug smuggler, or at least being involved with them. That would kill her chances right there.

She needed to call some people. She needed to make a deal.

"Fuck me! Fuck me!" Carla cried.

Dara's eyes glared at the shaking bed.

Bastards!

Carla's cries rose, and Dara was quite sure that they were rising for her benefit as the woman sneeringly showed her who was in charge, who would be the benefit of Emery's lust and the recipient of his big cock. Well Dara would show her, and she would show Emery too!

The noises eased, and the bed went still. For a while she could hear them talking, mainly about what they would do with all that money and where they would go. Then Emery got hungry and they got up, dressed, and went out to get something to eat. Dara squirmed beneath the bed. It was not easy moving with her arms bound beneath her and her breasts pillowed against the bottom of the bed frame, but inch by inch she worked her way out from under the bed and got awkwardly to her feet.

There was a phone on the table, but first she had to dislodge the gag in her mouth, and that meant getting untied. She backed against the corner of the bed where she had earlier found a loose screw and worked the rope against it, using it to gently and carefully loosen the knot. The ropes came undone quickly then, for they had grown careless.

She pulled the gag from her mouth and then picked up the phone and - hesitated. She bit her lip anxiously, then got up and hopped to the window. There was no sign of the car. She went back to the phone and looked at it, then dialled.

When they got back Dara was beneath the bed once again, the gag in place, her wrists tied behind her back - or at least, loosely tied - as well as she could on her own. They were in a good mood, jovial, and neither spoke a word about the naked girl bound under one of the beds. It wasn't for hours, not until Emery was in the shower, that Carla dragged her out and sat back on the bed, grinning smugly as she pulled no her hair and guided her mouth in between her legs.

"Lick that black pussy, white girl," she sneered. "You ain't gonna get no more black cock after tonight, so you best make do with what you got."

Dara sullenly performed, running her tongue up and down the woman's sex, then sucking and licking at her clitoris. Emery emerged naked from the shower long before she was done but showed little interest, crossing the room to turn on the television. Dara burned in anger and thought of how she would make him pay for scorning her.

She was naked, as she had been the previous night. This time the bags of powder were in a backpack. As before, Emery and Carla were off safe while she made the delivery. Emery was no doubt on a nearby roof with his rifle, waiting to shoot the men if they tried to take the drugs without paying. Bizarrely, he trusted her to look at the money and decide if it was all there. If it wasn't she was to raise her right leg, like a stork, she thought, and he would shoot the men.

Why he believed she would do that and run the risk of getting shot herself was beyond her. Had she really given him that much evidence of what a weakling and idiot she was? She thought over the previous few weeks and gave a mental wince. She supposed she had. Well he would learn better tonight.

Her wrists were bound tightly again, for he had inspected them before leaving the motel. She also had a wire bound to the ring piercing her pussy.

She approached from a different direction this time, eyes casting wary looks around for the other drug dealers, Emery and -

whoever. No one appeared, and she grew increasingly nervous. Then she almost stumbled over the woman in black laying in the grass. She wondered how many there were scattered around, and stopped.

The woman did not speak, but hurriedly moved behind her, on her knees, reached up and slit the knot of the ropes around her wrists, then handed her a small automatic and faded into the shadows. Dara continued on, heart pounding. She checked the gun, then folded her hand around it. It was tiny, and in the dark would be hard to spot as she crossed her wrists behind her back.

She made out the shadows of the car an instant before the lights winked on, making her blink and drop her eyes. The two men walked out from the shadows as she approached, wide leers on their faces as she walked up.

"Our little drug slut again," one said.

The other moved behind her and jerked open the bag, reaching in and pulling out a bag of powder. He tossed it to the first, then tossed a second. A third and fourth man appeared, and they took the bags to the car, laying them on the hood as they performed a test. The first man continued to empty the bag, giving her breast a casual squeeze as he did.

This time there was a longer wait while the drugs in every bag were tested. None of the men was any more trusting than Emery.

"Looks good," a voice said from the shadows by the car.

There were several gunshots just then from over to the right. The men ducked and scattered, and the one next to Dara gripped her hair and yanked her head back with a hiss.

She brought her hands free and slammed the small gun into his temple as she twisted away, diving into the grass as a half dozen dark shapes rose around them, yelling. "DEA! Freeze! Police!"

One of the drug dealers opened fire with an Uzi, but only for a moment before gunfire brought him down. Another jumped into the car and the tires spun and squealed as it started away. Two others ran off into the darkness. There was more gunfire and shouting, and then Dara howled , dropping her little gun at a terrible pain in her pussy.

It was the wire! It was tearing at her pussy, and Dara scrambled frantically to her feet, throwing herself forward as Carla yanked on the wire. She staggered and stumbled into the grass, into the shadows, hands pulling desperately at the wire, trying to ease the pull at her pussy. But the wire was very thin and her fingers could not get a very good grip. She sobbed in pain, stumbling wildly through the grass. She fell again and screamed, crawling forward desperately, then throwing herself to her feet to continue on, half running now, holding onto the wire as Carla reeled her in like a fish on a hook.

Her frantic fingers tried to dislodge the wire from the pussy ring, then to remove the pussy ring, but it was hardly the kind of jewellery most women wore. Emery had squeezed it closed with a pair of pliers. It would take more than her fingers to open it again.

She staggered and stumbled wildly through the dark, brush and grass, the pull on her clit ring relentless, the pain searing her as she ignored the pain to her feet from stones and garbage and the brush clawing at her naked legs and thighs.

And then Carla was there, snarling, and her big fist swung out of the darkness at Dara's face. She didn't know how she ducked in time, but the pain had her in a frenzy, and seeing the wire in the woman's hand made her blood boil. All her anger and frustration combined with the pain to enrage her, and she slammed her knee up into the woman's groin, then hammered her joined fists down on the back of her neck as she collapsed forward, bringing her knee up a second time to meet the woman's face.

Carla collapsed in a heap, and the furious blonde felt little satisfaction as she dropped and punched at her several more times. She slapped her face, trying to get her to wake up so she could hit her again, but strong arms slipped around her and dragged her up and back.

"Enough," the voice said.

It was a large Black woman wearing a blue DEA jacket. Another woman ran up, puffing heavily, and halted, bending to catch her breath.

"Get this off me," Dara demanded furiously.

The woman looked at the ring piercing her clitoral hood and the wire attached to it and shook her head, rolling her eyes. "I seen everything now," she said.

They did not treat her as a police woman since, so far as they knew she was a prostitute turned informant. They did remove the wire, then handcuffed her wrists behind her back and put her, wearing an oversized jacket, in the back of one of their cars.

And she sat there for more than an hour, fuming, no one coming to see her no one speaking to her. Finally the two women got into the car and, still not talking to her, drove off. Dara slumped in the back, sullenly staring out the window as they drove.

At the police station she was unceremoniously pushed into a prison cell in the isolation unit and her hands uncuffed. Then she was left in place for several more hours, the cell locked off from the rest by a heavy metal door at the end of a short hall.

Finally it opened and then closed. She stood up and went to the bars as a man walked up the dark hall and halted before her cell.

"Finally in your element," he said.

"Fuck you, Hernandez!" she snapped.

He grinned and held up an orange prisoners jumpsuit. "Got

something for you to wear."

"When am I getting out of here?" she demanded, reaching for it.

He pulled his hand back. "In time. You want them to know you were a cop? You know what those big mouths would do with a story like that? It'd be all over the state in a week. Hell, they'd be talking about it in Texas and California within a month."

"So you had to tell them I was a prostitute?"

"It seemed - fitting."

"You gonna give me that?"

He grinned lazily. "I need the jacket back. Don't want you passing yourself off as a federal agent. We can stoop pretty low in recruitment but not that low."

"Kiss my ass!"

"The jacket."

He held out his hand and Dara glared at him, shaking her head in anger, then shrugged and unzipped it, yanking it off and throwing it at him. So what if she was naked. He'd seen her naked. Everyone had seen her naked!

He took the jacket and looked at her, and she glared back, refusing to make any effort to cover herself. She straightened her back and stared insolently back. "Like what you see, boy?"

"Nice meat," he said.

She let her eyes drop to his crotch. "And I bet you'd like another taste."

"Now why would I?" he asked, "Seeing as how I'm a gay man and fucking some Black teenager."

She remembered the email she had sent his supervisor then and laughter bubbled out before she could suppress it. "Oh yeah," she said, grinning. "I bet your boss loved that."

"Given he's a fundamentalist Christian he wasn't very impressed."

Dara laughed again and he glared, unlocking the door and striding in. She laughed heartily and he grabbed at her. She tried to fend him off and he gripped her wrists, using his weight to bear her back against the bars.

"What's the matter, Hernandez, did your boss put the make on your cute little butt?" she taunted.

"You little slut!" he snarled. "I ougtho - ."

"What?" she demanded, sneering. "Go ahead! I dare you! I double dare you!"

He glared, then pinned her wrists above her with one hand while reaching back to his belt. Dara smirked at him, making no attempt to pull free.

He pulled his handcuffs out and snapped one quickly around her right wrist, then pushed the other through the bar and pulled it around to grip her other wrist, snapping it closed and standing back.

Dara gasped a little as the cold metal bit into her wrists. She was forced up almost to her toes, and the thick steel bars were cold against her soft flesh. Yet she wasn't ashamed, and truth to tell, began to feel a sudden blossoming heat within her lower belly. That angered her. It showed what a weakling she was, what a slut she was, and she glared at him.

"Gonna rape me, wetback?" she sneered. "Just like last time? Wouldn't your boss like to hear that! At least he wouldn't think you was no faggot!"

He threw himself against her, gripping her hair and yanking her head back, drawing his fist back.

"Go ahead!" she taunted, glaring.

Instead he lowered his fist and let go of her hair. He did not back off, however, but let his eyes wander down her body. A moment later his hands were on her breasts, stroking the underside, his thumbs running up across the nipples, which instantly hardened.

Dara fought to control her breathing, still glaring at him.

"Gonna force yerself on me? Are you?" she hissed.

He ran his right hand down between her legs, his finger stroking her slit, rubbing up across her clit, and she gasped, her right leg drawing up at the pain to her swollen button, but the pleasure was a bonfire igniting within her, and she shuddered as she felt his finger slip inside her rapidly moistening pussy.

"Fucking slut," he hissed.

"Fucking greaser," she panted.

He dropped to his knees and she cried out as his hands roughly spread her thighs, lifting her feet off the floor. His face plunged into her groin and his mouth began to lick and suck and rub against her pussy.

Dara groaned at the pain to her wrists, her feet drawing back, trying to find purchase on one of the crossbars below her, but then Hernandez was standing before her again, his face red, eyes wild, and she let out a long, shuddering gasp as he thrust into her. His hands seized her buttocks and he lifted her legs up, slamming them back against the bars to either side as he began to thrust wildly into her now sopping puss.

"B-Bastard!" she gasped, head lolling back as the sexual heat rolled through her.

"Whore," he moaned, his hips lunging violently forward, his cock pounding up into her trembling body.

They came together, their voices rising in passion as the bars shook against the stone walls.

Chapter Fifteen

"Welcome to the New York Police Department, the largest in the United States."

Dara shook the sergeant's hand, beaming in delight.

There would be more to come, of course. She had to go through training, then probation, but she had no doubt she would succeed at both.

There were hundreds of applicants for every spot with the NYPD, but there was a push on for women, and with her height and experience as a Georgia deputy, not to mention the recommendation she had from the Drug Enforcement Administration for her "dangerous undercover work on a highly sensitive drug probe which had netted more than a million dollars in cocaine" it was a cinch they would accept her.

She'd already found a nice little apartment in the Brooklyn, and was thoroughly enjoying the wonders of big city life.

Her uncle was mightily ticked off, of course, first because she'd left with no word, second for working with the DEA, and third because of the wild rumours which had been running through the county about her involvement with various Black trash. Still, they were just rumours, and as long as she stayed away that's all they would be, so he wasn't about to give her anything but the best recommendation.

Hernandez got the credit for breaking up a drug ring all by himself, and keeping the details of her involvement as secret as possible was as much a necessity to him as to her. He too was happy to recommend her to the NYPD.

Neither Carla nor Emery were doing any talking at all. One of the buyers had been killed by the police during the raid, and with the threat of being charged with that hanging over their heads both were just as happy to plead guilty to drug smuggling and go quietly off to prison without a messy trial.

Dara let herself daydream about both of them winding up as someone's bitch, but realistically, she figured it would be the other way around, and both of them would find weaker prisoners to satisfy their sexual needs.

She walked out onto the busy street, blonde hair streaming in the wind behind her, a broad grin of satisfaction on her pretty face as she moved through the crowds, her long legs carrying her gracefully - even in cowboy boots - over the pavement.

She trotted down the stairs to the subway, made her way through the turnstiles and then onto a ramp to wait. A short distance along were several rough looking young men, grinning and nudging each other, looking at the cute blonde in her tight jeans and leather jacket, but a casual dismissive look from her stopped any thoughts of approach. She appeared far too self confident, too strong, and they moved off, looking for weaker prey.

The subway took her across the river to New Jersey, where few self-respecting New York cops would willingly venture. It was getting dark as she climbed the stairs to the street and her long legs carried her quickly along the empty streets and then in through the rear door of a brick building.

The noise and heat hit her as soon as the door opened, but she was used to it now. She moved up the corridor and pushed open a door marked "dressing room".

"Hey, Jewel," one of the girls said.

'Hey, Crystal."

No one used their real name here, and the customers preferred cutesy pie names anyway.

Dara quickly stripped and put her things into her locker, then donned the college girl outfit, including glasses and the NYU sweatshirt. She was just in time and she hurried backstage for her first set.

The lights hit her as she pranced out onto the stage, the music pounding wildly. The babble of voices included a few shouts, and she paused, bent forward a little and stuck her tongue out at them, drawing jeers in return.

Then she launched into her set, dancing and swaying, swinging around the bar, and gradually dropping pieces of clothes across the stage. Every piece of clothing she removed made her heart pound a little faster, made her pussy throb a little stronger, until she was naked and crawling cat-like across the stage, her tongue sliding along her lower lip as she looked, slit eyed out at the crowd.

She slid into the "bath", which was a wide, round pool like thing at the end of the stage, the walls made of clear plastic. Little fountains of water spit up over her body, and she writhed and twisted to the music, arching her back, her hands caressing her glistening wet body as the crowd looked on. Her insides burned with excitement at how lewd and dirty she was, at daring to act like such a slutty girl before so many men, so many strangers.

She turned and rolled, sliding on her belly, then slowly raising her bottom up, spreading her legs, rolling her bottom at her so they could see her hairless sex. She rolled again, raising her legs high, spreading them wide.

Dirty, dirty dirty!

She slid out of the pool and across the stage, shaking her head from side to side, letting water splash over the front row as she lolled her tongue at them.

The set was over, and she pranced away to applause, gathering her things as she moved. Then it was a quick dance with the towels and a blow dryer before she made her way out into the club. Wearing a light shift she sought out customers for a lap dance, and there was no lack of eager takers.

Soon she was again naked in a small back booth, straddling a man as she rolled and writhed against him, her breasts caressing his chest and moving a bare inch away from his face as she leered at him.

No, the New York Police would not approve, but figured, as she had always figured, that what authority figures didn't know wouldn't hurt them - or her. The money was great, and she would need it until she was finally on the NYPD's payroll. The excitement of doing wicked, wicked things was just too much to pass on, either, and she knew that even after she became a full fledged cop she would have to keep working at places like this, if only now and then.

"A h-hundred bucks," the man panted, his groin bulging.

She smiled sexily, sliding her hands up her body, shaking her head.

"Two hundred!"

She appeared to consider, then playfully shook her head.

"Three!"

She grinned and leaned in, her body still swaying to the music as she pressed her breasts against his face. His hands came up and eagerly squeezed them, his mouth opening to suckle and chew at her nipples. She shuddered as the heat spun up through her body and her hands dropped to his groin undoing his trousers.

The booth was little more than a toilet stall, their legs visible beneath, but the danger only added to Dara's excitement as she rose, guided him into her, and sank back down again. Both of them groaned as his thick cock slid through the soft folds of her pussy.

And then she began to ride.

The music pounded and the heat swirled around her, both within and without. Sweat beaded on her forehead and trickled down her chest as she rode up and down. His hands clawed at her buttocks and his mouth chewed eagerly at her nipples. She moaned softly, the heat overwhelming her.

She came.

End